A Pew[...]g [...]ing
Directly Toward Travis's Head
Made Him Duck Quickly . . .

"What the—?" he began.

Regan grabbed another mug from a wall cabinet. "You enjoyed flirting, didn't you?" she accused. "You liked having all the women fawn over you. 'Oh what a darling man,' they all drooled." The second mug grazed his shoulder . . .

Turning, her chin up, back straight, she started for the door.

It took Travis a moment to realize that she meant to leave him . . . Without thinking what he was doing, he grabbed the back of her dress. With Regan going one way and Travis pulling the other, the thin muslin quickly split from top to bottom, landing in a small heap at Regan's feet.

Instantly, his look changed from anger to desire, his eyes raking her hungrily . . .

"No," she whispered, trying with all her might to pull away from his mesmerizing gaze . . .

Books by Jude Deveraux

The Velvet Promise
Highland Velvet
Velvet Song
Velvet Angel
Sweetbriar
Counterfeit Lady
Lost Lady

Published by POCKET BOOKS

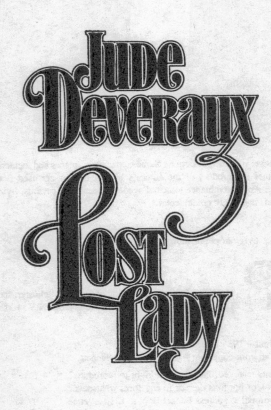

JUDE DEVERAUX

LOST LADY

PUBLISHED BY POCKET BOOKS NEW YORK

This novel is a work of fiction. Names, characters, places and incidents are either the product of the author's imagination or are used fictitiously. Any resemblance to actual events or locales or persons, living or dead, is entirely coincidental.

Another *Original* publication of POCKET BOOKS

POCKET BOOKS, a division of Simon & Schuster, Inc.
1230 Avenue of the Americas, New York, N.Y. 10020

ISBN: 0-671-43556-6

First Pocket Books printing April, 1985

10 9 8 7 6 5 4 3 2 1

POCKET and colophon are registered trademarks
of Simon & Schuster, Inc.

Printed in the U.S.A.

Chapter 1

WESTON MANOR SAT SERENELY AND QUIETLY IN THE MIDST of two acres of garden. It was a small house, unpretentious, looking like what it was—an English gentleman's lodging in 1797. Only the keenest observer would notice that two of the gutters had fallen somewhat or that a corner of one of the chimneys was broken away or even that some of the painted trim was beginning to peel.

Inside, the only room that was fully lit was the dining room, but here, too, could be seen evidence of neglect. In the shadows, the Georgian chairs' upholstery was frayed and faded. Tiny bits of the plaster decorations on the tall ceiling had started to chip, and on one wall there was a lighter space where a painting had once hung.

But the young girl sitting on one side of the table was oblivious to any imperfections in the room, for her eyes were glued to the man across from her.

Farrell Batsford curved his wrist in such a manner that the

1

ruffled silk at his cuff would not be stained by the juices from the roast. Taking only a bit of the meat onto his plate, he gave a thin smile to the girl across from him.

"Stop gawking and eat your dinner," Jonathan Northland commanded his niece, before looking away from her. "Now, Farrell, what were you saying about the shooting at your country place?"

Regan Weston tried to look at her food, even to eat a few bites, but she couldn't manage to swallow any of it. How anyone expected her to be calm and eat at a time like this, when the man she loved was sitting so near her, she couldn't begin to understand. She stole another glance at Farrell, looking up at him through her long, dark lashes. He was aristocratic-looking with his long, thin nose and his almond-shaped blue eyes. The velvet coat he wore with the gold brocaded vest perfectly suited his looks and his slim, elegant body. Blond hair was arranged artfully around his narrow head, waving just a bit at the edge of his pure white cravat.

As Regan uttered a deep sigh, her uncle gave her another quelling look. Farrell wiped the corners of his thin lips delicately.

"Perhaps my bride-to-be would like to take a walk in the moonlight?" Farrell asked quietly, pronouncing each word carefully.

Bride! Regan thought. This time next week she would be his wife, and she'd have him all to herself to love and cherish, to hold, to belong only to her. Overwhelmed by emotion, she could not speak; she could only nod in acceptance. As she tossed her napkin on the table, she was aware of her uncle's disapproval. Once again she wasn't acting as a lady should. From now on, she reminded herself for the thousandth time, she must remember who she was—and who she was to become: Mrs. Farrell Batsford.

As Farrell held out his arm for her, Regan tried not to clutch it. She wanted to dance with delight, laugh with her happiness, throw her arms around the man she loved. But, instead, she followed him sedately from the dining room into the cool spring garden.

"Perhaps you should have worn a shawl," Farrell said once they were a short way from the house.

"Oh no," she said breathlessly, leaning a little closer to him. "I wouldn't have wanted to take a minute away from our time together."

Farrell started to say something but seemed to change his mind as he looked away from her. "The wind is off the sea tonight, and it is cooler than last night."

"Oh Farrell," she sighed. "Only six more days and we'll be married. I'm sure I'm the happiest girl alive."

"Yes, well perhaps," Farrell said quickly as he disengaged her fingers from his arm. "Sit here, Regan." The tone of his voice was much like the one her uncle always used with her, one of impatience and exasperation.

"I would rather walk with you."

"Are you going to start being disobedient before we're even married?" he demanded, gazing down into her wide-set, trusting eyes. Everything she thought and felt showed in those eyes. She was pretty, in a childish sort of way, in her high-necked muslin dress, but she had about as much appeal to him as a puppy begging for affection.

He took a few steps away from her before beginning to talk. "Is everything ready for the wedding?"

"Uncle Jonathan planned it all."

"Of course—he would," Farrell said under his breath. "Then I'll return next week for the ceremony."

"Next week!" Regan jumped to her feet. "Not before? But Farrell . . . we . . . I. . . ."

He ignored her outburst as he held out his arm for her. "I think we should return to the house now, and perhaps you should reconsider the whole idea of marriage if everything I do displeases you."

One look from Farrell stopped her protest. She told herself again to remember her manners and be quiet, that she must never give her beloved any reason to find fault with her.

Once they were back inside the dining room, Farrell and her uncle quickly dismissed her to her upstairs bedchamber. She didn't dare protest; she was too afraid that Farrell would again suggest calling off the wedding.

Inside her bedroom, she could release her pent-up emotions. "Isn't he wonderful, Matta?" she gushed to her maid. "Did you ever see such brocade as he wore? Only a real gentleman could choose such fabric. And his manners! He does everything correctly, everything perfectly. Oh, how I wish I could be like him, to always be so sure of myself, to know even my slightest movement was correct."

Matta's coarse, ugly face frowned. "It seems to me there should be more to a man than just pretty manners," she said in her West Country accent. "Now stand still and get out of that dress. It's past time for you to be in bed."

Regan did as she was told; she always obeyed people. Someday, she thought, she'd be a person of importance. She had money from her father, and she'd have the man she loved for her husband. Together the two of them would keep an elegant house in London where they would give the most fashionable parties, and a house in the country where she could be alone with her perfect husband.

"Stop your dreamin'," Matta commanded, "and get into bed. Someday you're gonna wake up, Regan Weston, and find out the world ain't made of sugarplums and silk brocade."

"Oh Matta," Regan laughed. "I'm not as silly as you think. I had enough sense to get Farrell, didn't I? What other girl could do that?"

"Maybe any of them with her father's money," Matta muttered as she tucked the covers around her charge's slim body. "Now go to sleep and save your dreamin' for the nighttime."

Obediently, Regan closed her eyes until Matta was out of the room. Her father's money! The words echoed through her mind. Of course Matta was wrong, she reasoned. Farrell loved her for herself, because. . . .

When she couldn't remember a single reason that Farrell had given for wanting to marry her, she sat up in bed. On the moonlit night when he'd proposed, he'd kissed her forehead and talked of his home, which had been in his family for generations.

Tossing the covers aside, Regan went to the mirror, looking at herself in moonlight-silvered image. Her wide-set, blue-green eyes looked like they belonged to a child instead of to a young woman who'd been eighteen for a whole week now, and her slim figure was always hidden under loose, concealing clothes—clothes chosen by her uncle. Even now, her heavy cambric nightgown was long-sleeved and high-necked.

What could Farrell see in her? she wondered. How could he know that she could be sophisticated and graceful when she was always dressed as a child? Trying to smile in a seductive way, she pulled her nightgown off one shoulder. Ah yes, if Farrell were to see her like this, he just might do something besides kiss her forehead in a fatherly way. A very immature giggle escaped her as she thought of Farrell's reaction to the coquetry of his sedate, gentle bride-to-be.

Quickly, she looked toward where Matta slept in the little adjoining dressing room and thought it just might be worth any consequences from her uncle to see her beloved's reaction to her in a nightgown. After hastily putting on heelless slippers, she silently eased the door open and tiptoed downstairs.

The door to the drawing room was open, candles blazing. In a golden halo sat Farrell, and Regan could do little more than marvel at him. It was quite a few minutes before she began to listen to what the two men were saying.

"Look at this place!" Jonathan said vehemently. "Yesterday a piece of plaster scrollwork fell on top of my head. There I was, reading my paper, when a damned flower came flying at me."

Farrell concentrated on the brandy in his glass. "It will all be over soon—for you at least. You'll get your money and can repair your house or buy a new one if you want, but I have a lifetime of misery ahead of me."

Snorting, Jonathan refilled his glass. "You make it sound as if you were going to prison. I tell you, you should be grateful for what I've done for you."

"Grateful!" Farrell sneered. "You've saddled me with a brainless, uneducated, clumsy chit of a girl."

"Come now, some men would be happy to have her. She's pretty, and her simple-mindedness would be liked by a great many men."

"I am not like any other man," Farrell said warningly.

Unlike many people, Jonathan did not find Farrell Batsford intimidating. "True," he said evenly. "Not many men would make a bargain such as you have."

As Jonathan finished his third brandy, he turned back to Farrell. "Come now, let's not argue. We should be celebrating our good fortune, not going for each other's throat." He raised his full glass in salute. "Here's to my dear sister, with many thanks for marrying her rich young man."

"And dying and leaving it all within your reach—isn't that the rest of the toast?" After drinking deeply, Farrell turned serious. "Are you sure about your brother-in-law's will? I don't want to marry your niece and then find out it was all a big mistake."

"I've memorized the document!" Jonathan said angrily. "I've lived in barristers' offices for the last six years. The girl cannot touch the money before she's twenty-three, unless she marries before then, and even at that she couldn't be married before she was eighteen."

"If that hadn't been the case, would you have found someone to marry her when she was twelve perhaps?"

Chuckling, Jonathan set his glass down. "Perhaps. Who knows? As far as I can tell, she hasn't changed much since she was twelve."

"If you hadn't kept her prisoner in this crumbling house, perhaps she wouldn't be such an immature, uninteresting child. Lord! When I think of the wedding night! No doubt she'll cry and pout like a two-year-old."

"Stop complaining!" snarled Jonathan. "You'll have money enough to repair that great monstrosity of a house of yours, and all I get for years of taking care of her is a measly pittance."

"Caring for her! Since when have you left your club long enough to even know what she looks like?" Sighing heavily, he continued, "I'll leave her at my house and then go to London. At least now I'll have money enough to enjoy myself. Of course, it won't be pleasant not being able to have my friends to my house. Perhaps I can hire someone to take care of a wife's duties. I cannot imagine your niece managing an estate the size of mine." Glancing up, he saw that Jonathan's face had grown pale; his hands clutching the glass were white-knuckled.

Turning quickly, Farrell saw Regan standing in the light by the doorway. Acting as if nothing had happened, he set his glass down. "Regan," he said gently, warmly. "You shouldn't be up so late."

Her big eyes were magnified by the tears sparkling in them. "Do not touch me," she whispered, her hands clenched at her side, her back rigid. She looked so small, with her thick dark hair hanging down her back, swathed in a little girl's nightgown.

"Regan, you are to obey me at once."

She whirled on him. "Don't use that tone with me! How dare you think you can tell me what to do after the things you said!" She looked at her uncle. "You will never get any of my money. Do you understand me? Neither of you will ever get a farthing of my money!"

Jonathan was beginning to recover himself. "And how do *you* expect to get any of it?" he smiled. "If you don't marry Farrell, you won't be able to touch the money for five years. Until now you've been living on my income, but I'll tell you now that if you refuse to marry him I'll throw you into the streets, since you'd no longer be of use to me."

Putting her palms to her forehead, Regan tried to think clearly.

"Be sensible, Regan," Farrell said, his hand on her shoulder.

She backed away from him. "I'm not like you said," she whispered. "I'm not simple-minded. I can do things. I don't have to take anyone's charity."

"Of course you don't," Farrell began patronizingly.

"Leave her alone!" Jonathan snapped. "It's no use trying to reason with her. She lives in a dream world just like her mother did." His fingers bit into her skin as he grabbed her arm. "Do you know what it's been like the past sixteen years since your parents died? I've watched you eat my food and wear the clothes I paid for, yet all the while you were sitting on millions, *millions,* that I would never be able to touch. Even after you were old enough to inherit, what reason did I have to think you'd give me a pound?"

"I would have. You're my uncle!"

"Ha!" He pushed her back toward the wall. "You would have fallen for some worthless, dressed-up dandy, and he'd have run through everything in five years. I just decided to give you what you wanted and at the same time make sure I got what *I* wanted."

"Now see here!" Farrell half choked. "Are you calling me—? Because if you are—."

Ignoring him, Jonathan continued, "What's it to be? Him, or you walk out right now?"

"You can't—," Farrell began.

"I damn well can, and I am going to. You're crazy if you think I'm going to support her another five years just for the pleasure of it."

Dazed, Regan looked from one man to the other. Farrell,

her heart cried. How could she have been so wrong about him? He didn't love her but only wanted her money; he'd talked of the horrors of being married to her.

"What's your answer?" Jonathan demanded.

"I'll pack," Regan whispered.

"Not the clothes I paid for," Jonathan sneered.

In spite of what the two men seemed to believe about her, there was a great deal of pride in Regan Weston. Her mother had run away from her family and married a penniless clerk, yet because she'd worked with him and believed in him they'd made a fortune. Her mother had been forty when Regan was born, and two years later she'd died with her husband in a boating accident. Regan had been left in the care of her only relative, her mother's brother. Over the years she'd had no reason to show any of the spirit she'd inherited from her mother.

"I'm leaving," she said quietly.

"Regan, be reasonable," Farrell said. "Where will you go? You don't know anyone."

"Should I perhaps stay here and marry you? Won't you be embarrassed at having such an ignorant wife?"

"Let her go! She'll come back," Jonathan snapped. "Let her get a taste of the world, and she'll come back."

Regan's spirit was leaving her quickly as she saw the hate in her uncle's eyes and the contempt in Farrell's. Before she could change her mind, before she fell to her knees before Farrell, she turned and fled the house.

It was dark outside, and the wind from the sea moved the tree branches overhead. As she paused on the doorstep, she lifted her chin high. She would make it; no matter what it took from her, she'd show them that she wasn't an ineffectual person, as they seemed to believe. The stones were cold under her feet as she walked away from the house, refusing to think about the fact that she was in public—however dark—wearing only her nightgown. Someday, she thought, she'd return to this house wearing a satin gown and tall feathers in her hair, and Farrell would go down on his knees to her, saying that she was the most beautiful woman in the world. Of course, by then she'd be renowned for her brilliant house parties, a favorite of the king and queen; she'd be celebrated for her wit and intelligence as well as her beauty.

The cold was becoming so intense that it was overriding her dreams. Stopping by an iron fence, she began to rub her arms. Where was she? She remembered Farrell saying she'd been kept a prisoner, and it was true. Since she was two years old she had rarely ever left Weston Manor. A succession of maids and frightened governesses had been her only companions, the garden her only place of amusement. In spite of being alone, she rarely felt lonely. That feeling didn't come until she met Farrell.

Leaning against the cold iron, she put her face in her hands. Whom was she trying to fool? What could she do alone in the night wearing only her nightgown?

She lifted her head when she heard footsteps coming toward her. A brilliant smile lit her face; Farrell was coming after her! As she moved away from the fence, her sleeve caught in the iron and tore at the shoulder. Ignoring the tear, she began to run toward the footsteps.

"Here, girly," said a poorly dressed young man. "So, you came to greet me, all ready for bed."

Backing away from him, Regan tripped over the edge of her long gown.

"There's no need to be afraid of Charlie," the man said. "I don't want nothin' that you don't want."

Regan began to run in earnest, her heart pounding wildly, her sleeve tearing a bit more with each movement. She had no idea where she was going, whether she was running toward something or away from it. Even when she fell the first time, she hardly slowed her pace.

It seemed like hours before she slipped into an alleyway and allowed her heart to calm enough to listen for the man's footsteps. When everything seemed to be quiet, she leaned her head back against the damp brick wall and smelled the salty, fishy odor from the sea. She could hear laughter from somewhere to her right, a door slammed, there was some metal clanking, and she could hear the call of the seagulls.

As she looked down at her nightgown, she saw it was torn and muddy; there was mud in her hair and, she guessed, on her cheek. Trying not to think about how she looked, she wanted only to control her fear. She had to get away from this bad-smelling place and find shelter before morning—a place where she could rest and find safety.

Trying as best she could to smooth her hair, pulling the torn pieces of her gown together, she left the alleyway and started walking toward the place where she'd heard the laughter. Perhaps there she would find the help she needed.

Within minutes, a man tried to grab her arm. As she jerked away from him, two more clutched at her skirt; the fabric tore in three places.

"No," she whispered, backing away from them. The smell of the fish seemed to be overpowering, and the darkness was as heavy as velvet. Again she started to run, the men following her closely.

As she looked back, she saw that there were several men

behind her—just following her, not really hurrying, seeming to tease her with their pursuit.

One moment she was running, and the next she felt as if she'd slammed into a stone wall. She hit the ground, landing on her seat as if she'd been dropped from a window.

"Travis," a man above her said. "I think you've knocked the wind out of her sails."

An enormous shadow bent over Regan, and a rich, deep voice asked, "Are you hurt?"

Before she could think, she was swept from the ground and held in strong, safe-feeling arms. She was too exhausted, too terrified to consider proprieties but hid her face in the deep shoulder of the man who held her.

"I think you got just what you wanted for the night," another man chuckled. "Shall we see you in the morning?"

"Perhaps," said the deep voice against Regan's cheek. "But I may not come out until the ship sails."

The men laughed again before continuing on their way.

Chapter 2

REGAN HAD NO IDEA WHERE SHE WAS OR WHOM SHE WAS
with; all she knew was that she felt safe, as if she'd awakened from a terrible nightmare. As she closed her eyes and
let her body sink against the man who held her so easily, she
felt as if everything was going to be all right. A burst of light
made her close her eyes more tightly, and bury her face
more deeply into the hard shoulder.

"Whatcha got there, Mr. Travis?" came a woman's
voice.

Regan felt a deep chuckle run through the man. "Bring
some brandy and hot water to my room—and some soap."

The man seemed to have no trouble climbing the stairs
with the extra weight of Regan in his arms. By the time he lit
a candle, she was nearly asleep.

Gently he set her on the bed, her back propped against pillows. "All right, let's have a look at you."

While he seemed to inspect her, Regan got her first look

at her rescuer. An extraordinarily thick crop of soft, dark hair topped a handsome face with deep brown eyes and a finely shaped mouth. There were little sparks of laughter in his eyes, tiny lines at the corners.

"Satisfied?" he asked as he went to answer the knock at the door.

He had to be the largest man she'd ever seen—a totally unfashionable figure, of course, but at the same time fascinating. The depth of his chest was probably twice the circumference of any part of her body. No doubt his arms were as big as her waist, and she could see that his snug buckskin trousers clung to massive muscles in his thighs. Tall boots reached to his knees, and she wondered at them because she'd only seen men in silk hose and little kid slippers.

"Here, I want you to drink this; it'll make you feel better."

When the brandy was too hot in her throat, the man urged her to sip it slowly.

"You're cold as ice, and the brandy will warm you."

The brandy did warm her, and the golden candlelit room, and the man's quiet power all reinforced her feeling of security. Her uncle and Farrell seemed far away. "Why do you talk so strangely?" she asked softly.

His eyes crinkled further. "I might ask you the same thing. I'm an American."

Her eyes widened in a mixture of interest and some fear. She'd heard many stories about the Americans—men who declared war on their mother country, men who were little more than savages.

As if he had read her thoughts, the man dipped a cloth into the hot water, rubbed it on the soap, and began to wash Regan's face. Somehow it seemed so natural that this man, whose palm was as big as her face, should gently and tenderly wash her. When he'd finished her face, he began on her feet and legs. She looked down at his hair, cut just above his collar, curling a bit, and she couldn't resist touching it. It was firm and clean, and she thought that even the hairs on his head were strong.

As he rose, he took her hand and kissed her fingertips. "Put this on," he said, tossing her one of his clean shirts. "I'll go downstairs and see if I can find us something to eat. You look like you could use a good meal."

The room seemed cavernous when he was gone. When Regan stood, she weaved a bit and realized the brandy had gone to her head. Her Uncle Jonathan had never allowed her to drink spirits. The thought of that name brought back all the ugly memories. As she pulled off what was left of the torn and soiled nightgown, she began to imagine how Farrell and her uncle would feel when she returned with a big, handsome American on her arm. The Colonial was big enough to enforce anything he wanted. As she climbed into bed, wrapped in his clean shirt, the tails past her knees, she imagined how she'd be reinstated in Weston Manor, this time in glory. And the American would always be her friend, would even attend her wedding to Farrell. Of course, he would have to learn some manners, but perhaps Farrell could teach him.

She drifted off to sleep, a smile on her lips.

Travis returned to the room with a tray heavily laden with food. When his efforts to wake Regan only made her snuggle deeper under the covers, he dug into the food alone. He'd been drinking with his friends from America since early afternoon, celebrating their safe voyage and the completion of Travis's business in England. In a week he'd be sailing for Virginia.

All four of the men had been saying they'd like a sweet girl in their bed when this one ran into Travis. She was pretty, young, and clean, in spite of the pound of dirt he'd washed from her. He wondered what she was doing alone at night, running through the streets in her torn nightgown. Perhaps she'd been kicked out of the house where she usually worked, or maybe she wanted to try it on her own and found that working the streets frightened her.

Having finished most of the food, Travis stood and stretched. Whatever the girl's problem, at least she was his tonight. Tomorrow he could return her to the streets.

He undressed slowly, his hands clumsy with the buttons. The way the girl had clung to him had excited him, and he wondered where she'd learned such a trick; no other whore he'd met had used that technique.

When he was naked, he slipped between the sheets and pulled the girl to him. Her body was limp, but as he slipped his hands beneath the shirt she began to awaken.

Regan felt the warm, masculine hands on her body, and it seemed to be part of her delicious dream. No one had offered her affection before; even as a child, when she'd longed to be held by someone, there was no one there to offer her love. In the back of her mind was the memory of some recent, horrible hurt, and she wanted someone to cling to, someone to take away the pain.

In a half-daze between sleep and wakefulness, she felt her shirt being removed. When her breasts touched his chest and felt the hardness of it, the coating of hair, she gasped with delight. Lips kissed her cheek, her eyes, her hair, and finally her mouth. She'd never kissed a man before, but she knew instantly that she liked it very much. His firm-soft lips moved over hers, parting them just a bit, savoring the sweetness of them.

As he pulled her closer to him, her arms went around his neck, glorying in the size of him, and she moved closer, pushing her body next to his, wanting to touch all of him.

But as Travis's movements grew quicker, she opened her eyes in surprise. Her senses began to return rapidly, and she started to pull away from him. Yet Travis's strength was such that he didn't notice her weak efforts to push him away. His head was none too clear from the whiskey he'd consumed, and the girl's eager response had inflamed him.

Regan pushed harder, but Travis's arms only tightened as his lips swept down on hers, sealing off any negative response she might make. In spite of her growing awareness that what she was doing was wrong, she couldn't resist for long, and so she started to respond to him fully, arching against him, wanting from him she knew not what.

Travis's hand held her head, cradling it, caressing it, his thumb running along the back of her ear. His teeth nipped her earlobe. "Sweet," he whispered. "As sweet as a violet."

Smiling, Regan moved languorously as Travis's thigh came across hers. She moved her head to one side, allowing him access to all her throat and shoulder. She felt she might dissolve into a pool of liquid when he began to make love to her collarbone. Running her hands through his hair, losing them in the thick mass, she held his head down, didn't want him to move. When his hand first touched her breast, her body went rigid with surprise. Then, as the exquisite feeling flowed through every pore and vessel of her body, she pulled his head back to hers. Eagerly, passionately, thirstily, she sought his lips.

When he moved on top of her, her first thought was that for a man so big he was extraordinarily light. The next instant she felt pain, and her eyes flew open, her body lost its feeling of pleasure, and she pushed at him with all her might.

But Travis was past hearing her. His desire for this ardent, willing bit of heaven was raging, towering, and he could not listen to her protests.

Fuzzy from drink or not, he knew what he felt when he hit the tiny membrane. Somewhere in the back of his mind a bit of sanity told him that he was making an error, but he could not stop. He thrust into her quickly, much of his original zeal gone.

When he was finished he lay still on top of her, feeling her small, delicately boned body begin to shake with sobs. Her hot tears wet his neck, mingling with the sweat on his body.

As he rolled away from her, he didn't look at her. The sun was beginning to come in through the window, and Travis had never felt so sober in his life. When he had put on his pants and boots, and then his shirt, which he didn't bother to button, he turned back to her. Only the top of her head showed above the cover.

As gently as he could, he eased himself down onto the bed to sit beside her. "Who are you?" he asked quietly. A shake of her head and a loud sob were all the answer he got. Taking a deep breath, he pulled her upright, keeping the sheet around her bare breasts.

"Don't touch me!" she hissed. "You hurt me!"

Wincing once, Travis frowned. "I know I did, and I'm sorry, but. . . ." His voice got louder. "Damn it! How

was I to know you were a virgin? I thought you were. . . ."
He stopped because he could see the innocence in her eyes.
How could he have thought she was a prostitute? Maybe it
had been the mud or the poorly lit room last night, or more
likely the whiskey he'd drunk, but today he could see that he
should have known her for what she obviously was. Even
sitting naked in his bed, her hair a tangle about her shoulders, she exuded an air of refinement and gentility that only
the upperclass English could keep in times of stress. As it
began to dawn on him what he'd done—taken some lord's
virgin daughter to his bed—he started to realize the seriousness of his actions.

"I don't guess I can apologize for what's happened," he
began, "but perhaps I can explain myself to your father. I'm
sure that he'll. . . ." Understand? Travis thought.

"My father is dead," Regan said.

"Then I'll take you to your guardian."

"No!" Regan blurted. How could she return to her uncle
like this, with this great American confessing what they'd
done together? "If you would get me something to wear, I
will leave you. You needn't bother about taking me anywhere."

Travis seemed to consider this for a moment. "Why were
you running around the docks in the middle of the night?
Unless I miss my guess, a child like you"—he smiled at her
look—"pardon me, a young lady like you has probably
never even seen the docks before."

Regan tilted her chin upward. "What I have or have not
seen is no concern of yours. All I ask of you is a dress,
something simple if you can afford it, and I will leave immediately."

Again Travis smiled. "I can probably manage a dress.

21

But I'll not release you into that pack of animals out there. You know what happened to you last night.''

She narrowed her eyes at him. ''And what worse could happen to me than what you did last night?'' She buried her face in her hands. ''Who would want me now? You've ruined me.''

Sitting beside her, Travis pulled her hands away. ''Any man would want you, sweetheart. You're the most delightful bit—.'' He cut himself off.

Regan wasn't sure she knew what he meant, but she had an idea. ''Why, you vulgar Colonial! You are as savage as I've heard. You pull ladies off the street and drag them to your room where you do''—she sputtered—''horrible things to them.''

''Now wait just a minute! If I remember correctly, you came flying at me from out of the dark last night, and when I tried to help you up, you practically leaped into my arms. That's not the action of anyone I'd consider a lady. And as for last night, you didn't think what I did was so horrible when you were pulling my hair and running your feet up and down my legs.''

Dropping her jaw in sheer horror at his words, Regan could only blink at him.

''Look, I'm sorry. I didn't mean to say anything to shock you, but I want you to get your facts straight. Had I known you were a virgin and not a street girl, I wouldn't have touched you. But we can't change the facts. I did touch you, and now you're my responsibility.''

''I . . . most certainly am not your responsibility. I assure you I can take care of myself.''

''Like you did last night?'' he asked, lifting one eyebrow.

"It's a good thing you ran into me, or there's no telling what could have happened to you."

Moments passed before Regan could speak. "Is there no end to your arrogance or your insufferability? There was nothing good in meeting you, and I now know I was better off on the streets than locked away with a mad, despicable ravisher of women such as you are, sir!"

The corners of Travis's eyes crinkled as he broke into a dazzling smile. Running his hand through his dark hair, he chuckled, "My, my. I believe I've been cursed by an English lady." As his eyes roamed over her bare shoulders, he smiled at her. "You know, I rather think I like you."

"But *I* do not care for *you*," Regan said, exasperated at his ignorance and lack of understanding.

"Let me introduce myself. I am Travis Stanford from Virginia, and I am pleased to make your acquaintance." He held out his hand to her.

Crossing her arms over her chest, Regan looked away. Perhaps if she ignored him and was rude to him, he would allow her to go.

"All right," Travis said, rising. "Have it your way, but we will get something straight between us. I am not going to release you onto the Liverpool docks by yourself. Either you tell me where you live and who takes care of you, or you remain locked in this room."

"You can't do that! You have no right!"

He towered over her, his face serious. "Last night I earned the right. We Americans take our responsibilities seriously, and last night you became my charge—at least until I find out who your true guardian is."

As he finished dressing, he watched her in the mirror, trying to puzzle out her reasons for not telling him who she was. When he had his coat on, he leaned over her. "I'm trying to do what's right for you," he said softly.

"And who gave you the right to decide what was good or bad for people you don't even know?"

Chuckling deep in his throat, Travis replied, "You're beginning to sound like my little brother. How about a kiss before I go? If I find your guardian, it may be our last moment alone together."

"I hope I never see you again!" she spat. "I hope you fall into the sea and no one ever sees you again. I hope—."

He cut her off as he lifted her out of the bed, one arm behind her back, and the other pushing the sheet from between them. As his hand caressed the soft, peachy flesh of her hip and thigh, his mouth touched hers. Gently, ever so gently, he kissed her, careful not to frighten her or to be too harsh with her.

For a moment Regan pushed at him with her hands, but his big hands on her body, and the sheer power of him as he pulled her to him were overwhelmingly exciting. It surprised her that such an arrogant bully of a man could be so gentle.

Putting her arms around his neck, she turned her head to one side as her hands lost themselves in his hair.

Travis was the first to pull away. "I'm beginning to hope I don't find your guardian. You make an awful nice armful."

As her arm went back to strike him, he laughed and held it, kissing her knuckles one by one. "It was only a wish. Now, you stay here and be a good girl, and I'll bring you a pretty dress when I get back."

She heard him laugh when the pillow she threw hit the

door as he closed it behind him. The key turning in the lock sounded as if chains had been clamped to her ankles.

The awesome silence was nearly deafening as Regan sat, stunned, and gazed sightlessly at the big room. For a while she couldn't believe that she wasn't at home in her own blue bedroom, that Matta wasn't going to bring her chocolate at any moment. Instead, in the last few hours her world had crumbled about her ears. She'd heard the man she loved say that he didn't want to marry her and her only relative admit that he cared nothing for her. And now, worst of all, her virtue was gone and she was held prisoner by some savage American. Prisoner, she thought. She hadn't known it, but she'd been a prisoner all her life, held in a gilded cage of a pretty garden and a rundown house.

As these thoughts went through her mind, she began to look about the room. There was a large window along one wall, and it occurred to her that perhaps she could do something about her imprisonment this time. If she could escape, then surely she could find help, perhaps someone to take her in or to employ her. At that thought, she stopped. What could she do? How in the world could she earn her keep for five years until she came into her inheritance? The only thing she was really good at was growing flowers. Perhaps. . . .

No, Regan, she cautioned herself. Now is not the time to run off on a tangent. First she must escape and show this boorish Colonial that he could not kidnap an Englishwoman and have her remain docilely in custody.

Once out of bed, she realized that her first problem was clothes. A trunk stood in one corner of the room, but a quick examination showed it to be locked.

At a knock on the door, she jumped and had only time to

slip into Travis's shirt before a rosy-cheeked, plump girl entered bearing a heavy tray of food.

"Mr. Travis said I was to bring you food and a bath if you want it," the girl said nervously, her eyes searching the room, her back firmly against the closed door.

"Can you get me some clothes?" Regan asked. "Please. I could return them later, but I have to have more than that man's shirt."

"I'm sorry, miss, but Mr. Travis said I was not to give you clothes or anything else besides food and hot water and that I was to tell you he'd hired a man to stand below the window all day, in case you tried to escape that way."

Running to the window, Regan saw that what the girl had said was true. "You have to help me," she pleaded. "This man is keeping me prisoner here. Please, please, help me escape."

The girl hastily set the tray down, her eyes wide with fear. "Mr. Travis threatened me life if I let you go. I'm sorry, miss, but I've got meself to think of." Without another word, the girl was gone from the room, and the heavy lock was securely refastened.

Regan wasn't sure at first of the feeling that ran through her. All her life had been pleasant, uneventful, almost bland, with few problems to cope with and fewer people to know, but now everything was piling on top of her, weighing her down. She hadn't wanted to leave her uncle's house, nor did she want to remain the prisoner of some horrible man.

Picking the tray up with both hands, she threw it against the wall and then stood watching as eggs and jam went sliding down the smooth plaster surface. Her outburst did not help her mood but instead made it worse. Flinging herself onto the bed, she screamed into a pillow, kicked her feet, and slammed her fists into the feather mattress.

In spite of her anger and her complete frustration at her helplessness, her exhaustion was stronger. As her muscles began to relax, she fell into a heavy, lifeless sleep. She didn't even wake up when the maid cleaned the food off the wall, nor did she awaken when Travis entered the room, his arms full of bright boxes, and leaned over her, smiling at her sweet, innocent face.

Chapter 3

"YOU'RE A SWEET TIDBIT TO COME BACK TO," TRAVIS whispered, nibbling at her earlobe. As she began to awaken, he stepped away, wanting to watch her as she stretched, her curvy little body molding the shirt she wore into enticing hills and valleys. As she stretched, her eyes still closed, her breasts strained against the buttons, pulling the fabric apart and letting him glimpse an exquisite diamond of flesh. A little smile touched her lips before she opened her eyes and saw him.

"You!" she gasped. With an agile leap, she flew out of the bed and dove for him, fists clenched, shirttail riding up.

Travis caught both her fists in one of his. "Now that's what I call a greeting," he practically purred, pulling her into his arms. "It's not easy for me to remember I'm supposed to treat you like a lady when you fling yourself into my arms like that."

"I did not fling myself at you," she said, gritting her

teeth. "Why do you always twist everything so? You couldn't possibly believe I want anything from you except to be released. You have no right—."

A quick kiss cut her off. "You know I'll release you just as soon as you tell me where to take you. Surely a young lady like you has relatives. Give me a name, and I'll take you there."

"And have you brag about what you've done to me? No, I couldn't possibly agree to such a thing. Release me, and I'll find my own way home."

"You are not a good liar," he smiled. "Those eyes of yours are as clear as a doll's. Every thought you have is written across them. I've told you several times the conditions under which I'll release you, and that's the end of it. I'm not going to give in, so you might as well resign yourself to the fact that you will have to."

Jerking away from him, she set her jaw. "I can be as stubborn as you." She smiled wickedly. "And besides, I know you're leaving for America soon. You'll *have* to release me then."

Travis seemed to consider this idea for a moment. "I'll have to do something with you then, won't I?" he replied, rubbing his chin. "I'd certainly hate to sail for America and leave those legs of yours without a proper protector."

Gasping, Regan grabbed an edge of the bed sheet and tried to pull it off, but a far corner was caught. As Travis moved toward her and leaned across the bed to release the corner, he slipped a hand up under her shirt and gave her buttocks a firm caress.

Regan squealed once before she stood up and snatched the sheet from him, wrapping it tightly around her lower body.

"How can you treat me this way? What have I ever done to you to deserve this? I've never hurt anyone in my life."

Her words were so heartfelt that Travis lowered his eyes. "I've never done anything like this before. Maybe I should just release you, but somehow I can't. It would be like throwing a wildflower into a snowstorm or, considering the life on these docks, more like a fireplace." When he looked back at her, his eyes were soft and tender. "I don't have much of a choice about what I do. I can't let you go, yet I don't want to keep you prisoner. Lord! I don't even own slaves, much less lock up innocent little girls."

When he'd finished his speech, he sank heavily into a chair in a corner of the room, and Regan had the oddest feeling that she wanted to comfort him. During the awkward silence she noticed the boxes on top of the big trunk. "Did you bring me a dress?" she asked quietly.

"Did I bring you a dress," he grinned, seemingly over his momentary distress. Pulling string from one box, he began to unfold a piece of velvet of a color that Regan had never seen before: almost brown, almost red, but with an overall gold sheen to the fabric. As he handed it to her, draping it across her arms, he said, "It's the color of your hair, not red, not brown, not blonde, but all of them."

She looked up at him in surprise. "How . . . how romantic. I didn't know you'd—."

Laughing, he took the dress from her. "You don't know anything about me and I know even less about you. You haven't even told me your name."

Hesitating, she ran her hands across the velvet in his arms. All her clothes had always been of the cheapest cloth available. The velvet was the most beautiful fabric she'd ever seen, yet as badly as she wanted to feel it next to her skin, she was cautious. "I'm Regan," she answered quietly.

"No last name? Just Regan?"

"That's all the name I'll tell you and if you think you can bribe me with a pretty new dress, you're wrong," she said haughtily.

"I don't use bribes," he said flatly. "I've told you the conditions for your release, and the dress has nothing to do with them." Tossing the velvet garment onto the bed, he went to the other packages, tearing them open one by one and dumping them on the bed. There was a dress of pale blue silk crepe trimmed with peacock blue ribbons and a nightgown of cotton lawn embroidered with hundreds of tiny pink rosebuds. Two pairs of thin leather slippers, dyed to match the velvet and the blue, tumbled from the last package.

"They are beautiful, absolutely beautiful," Regan gasped, holding the silk to her cheek.

Watching her, Travis was enchanted. She was such a mixture of child and woman—raging one moment, looking like an angry kitten, then changing to a girl of innocence and great charm. As he watched her smile lighting her turquoise eyes, he felt as if he'd been bewitched by her, as if a spell had been put on him so that he could think of nothing but her. He'd spent hours today in dress shops, feeling damnedly out of place but wanting to make her happy.

He sat down by her on the bed. "You like them? I didn't know what kind of dresses or colors you liked, but the woman said these were the latest fashion."

As she turned her smile toward him, he felt a flash of possessiveness tear through him such as he'd felt only for his land in Virginia. Before he could think of what he was doing, he leaned across the clothes and dragged her to him. Giving her no time to protest, he kissed her hungrily, trying to make up for every moment he'd thought of her during the day.

"My clothes," Regan gasped. "You'll crush them."

With one movement, Travis swept all the clothes up and tossed them toward the chair. "All day I've thought about you," he whispered. "What have you done to me?"

She tried to sound uncaring, in spite of the fact that Travis's nearness caused her heart to race. "Nothing I *want* to do to you. Please release me."

"Do you really want me to?" he asked throatily, running his lips along her throat.

Why, she thought, does this disgusting, vile man do these horrible things to me? But even as she was thinking this, she didn't push him away—so badly did she want to be held in his arms, so much did she like the way he kissed her, the way his breath smelled, and how his hair caressed her face. The bigness of him made her feel small and safe, taken care of, protected.

Her thoughts were interrupted as Travis's lips found her bare breasts. No more thoughts were possible as she groaned and ran her hands across his shoulders.

Slowly, Travis left her, and when she opened her eyes in bewilderment she saw him standing over her, removing his jacket. Unable to take her eyes off him, she watched as he leisurely removed his clothes.

The light of the setting sun came through the window and filled the room with a red-gold glow, transforming the ordinary room into a place of magic and jewels. Speechless, Regan could not take her eyes off the sight of Travis's body as bit by large bit was exposed. She'd never seen a naked man before, and her curiosity was acute.

Nothing could have prepared her for the sight of a nude Travis. His body was heavily muscled from years of work, his arms sculpted, his chest like an ancient Roman breastplate that she'd seen once in a book. Yet his waist was slim, the stomach etched with rivulets of muscle. When his pants were removed, massive thighs were revealed, each muscle outstanding, separate.

"Oh my," she gasped, her voice betraying her awe. Only when her eyes reached his manhood did she blink.

Travis laughed at her and stretched out beside her. "For all your protesting, I wager you'll be a lusty wench when you've been taught properly."

"No, don't," she said in one last feeble attempt to push him away, but Travis paid no attention to her. Deftly, he removed the last bit of her clothes and began to stroke her stomach, kneading it lightly, his fingertips playing with the sensitive area, his palm exciting her skin. All the while he kissed her, using his teeth on the curve of her ear, his tongue just grazing the warm, pulsing spot beneath her earlobe.

She ran her hands over his shoulders and down his arms, her fingers tracing each long indentation where one muscle joined another. His hard body was so different from her soft one, so strong to her weakness. Moving under him, she slipped her arms down to caress his ribs, to feel the muscles in his back as they rippled under his hot, dark skin, and then to touch the sides of his tight buttocks. Wonder was mixed with the pleasure she found in touching him, and with each fondle her heart seemed to beat harder, her breath coming deeper and faster.

"Regan, sweet Regan," Travis said in a voice she felt as much as heard in the place where their chests joined.

When he seemed to pull away from her, her fingers dug into his arms painfully. "Yes, my eager kitten, yes."

Travis entered her slowly, easily, and although she would have thought it impossible, her heart rate increased. There was no pain, just something she wanted very, very much. As she arched against him clumsily, erratically, Travis held himself away from her. "Slow, kitten, slow," he murmured, his hand on her hip, his thumb making love to her navel.

Although she had no idea what he meant, she had no choice but to obey him. As new as she was to lovemaking, she could still feel that he was holding back, taking the time to be a teacher instead of a blind participant. By slow, careful tutoring, he showed her how to enjoy herself, how to lead as well as to follow.

Regan thought her body would burst, that it was getting larger and larger, and that when it did explode she would perhaps die. Suddenly Travis increased his pace, and his excitement flowed through to her. She arched against him, and it was as if fireworks exploded inside her—brilliant, hot, dazzling fireworks.

Travis collapsed on top of her, his body limp and sweaty, and Regan felt drained and weak, but oh so very good, as if a great burden had been taken from her.

She wasn't sure, but she believed she dozed for a while, and when she awoke, the intimate time with this man who was still virtually a stranger seemed like one of her dreams. As she lay there, one of Travis's arms sprawled across her; she imagined what it would be like to see Farrell again. Of course, he'd have heard about her time with this American, and he would be ashamed of her, perhaps wouldn't even speak to her. She imagined trying to explain, saying she'd resisted, but he'd know the truth. The American said that all her thoughts showed in her eyes. Would this new experience of hers show also? Would everyone in the world see her as a woman of no virtue?

Beside her, Travis stirred, lifted himself up on one elbow, and smiled down at her. "I was right," he murmured. "With a little training. . . ."

Regan pushed his hand away from a curl of her hair. "Don't touch me!" she hissed. "You have forced me to do too many things against my will."

Travis gave an exasperated little laugh. "Are we back to that again? I thought perhaps you'd see the truth this time."

"The truth! I see the truth! I know you are holding me against my will, that you are a criminal of the lowest order."

Sighing, Travis rolled from the bed and began to dress. "I've told you why I'm holding you." He turned back to her quickly. "Do you have any idea what those men on the docks want from you? They want a violent version of what we just did."

"And what's the difference between them and you?"

"Even with your innocence you should realize that I make love to you, but they'd just throw your skirts over your head and do whatever they wanted—one after another."

"I have no skirts!" Regan gasped. "All I have is one very torn nightgown."

All Travis could do was throw up his hands in despair. "You are only going to see what you want to see, aren't you? Therefore I feel it is my duty to protect you from yourself and your rosy dreams, as well as from men who'd do you harm."

"You have no right! Please, please let me out of here."

Acting as if she hadn't spoken, Travis went to the door and bellowed down the stairs for supper to be brought up. "You'll feel better once you've eaten," he said, closing the door again.

"I am not hungry," she said, her nose in the air.

Travis clasped her chin in his hand and twisted her head to look at him. "You are going to eat if I have to force it down your throat." His eyes were hard, unlike the softness she'd always seen.

All she could do was nod in answer.

"Now," he said, cheerful once again. "Why don't you put on one of the dresses I brought you? That will make you feel better."

"You'll have to leave the room," she said weakly, still somewhat frightened by his threat. She hadn't felt the least fear of him until now.

Lifting one eyebrow at her request, he picked her up out of the bed, and stood her naked on the floor. "You don't have anything I haven't seen before, and if you don't want the landlord to see you like that you'd better get dressed."

As she looked at the clothes Travis tossed to her, she realized there was no underwear. But rather than ask for it, she slipped the velvet gown over her head and had just finished the last button when the landlord knocked. The dress was high-waisted, the deeply cut bodice front filled with sheer silk gauze. Catching a glimpse of herself in the mirror opposite the bed, she was pleased that it wasn't a child's dress. Her hair hanging down her back in a mass of unruly curls, her flushed cheeks, her bright eyes, all went together to present a picture of a woman who had just been made love to—and had enjoyed it.

The landlord's appreciative looks made Travis almost push him out the door.

"Why did you do that?" Regan asked in awe, wondering if Travis was jealous.

"I don't want him to get the wrong idea," Travis answered, lifting the cover off a piece of roast beef. "I have to leave you alone again tomorrow, and if he thought I wouldn't mind, he just might send someone else up here. The last thing I want is a fight or any other trouble so close to sailing time. Nothing is going to stop me from going home. I've been in this cursed country too long."

Deflated, Regan took the seat he offered her. After one whiff of the food, she realized how long it had been since she'd eaten. Her last meal—her eyes widened when she remembered—had been with Farrell and her uncle.

"What's wrong?" he asked, filling a plate for her.

"Nothing. I just—." She put her chin up. "I don't like being held prisoner, that's all."

"You don't have to tell me if you don't want to. Eat your supper before it gets cold."

All through the meal, Travis tried to get her to talk, but she wouldn't since she was afraid she would inadvertently give him some clues about where she lived. There was no possibility now that she could go back to the life she once knew; after what had happened this evening, she probably no longer qualified as a lady.

Putting his hand over hers, Travis leaned close to her. "It's a shame Englishwomen are taught that they shouldn't like lovemaking," he said sympathetically, correctly reading her thoughts. "In America the women are earthier; they like their men and aren't afraid to show it."

She gave him her sweetest, most insincere smile. "Then why don't you go back to America and the women there?"

Travis's laugh made the dishes rattle, and he planted a hearty kiss on her cheek. "Now, little one, I have some paperwork to do, so you can snuggle up in bed and wait for me or—."

"Or leave perhaps."

"You are persistent, if nothing else."

And you are stubborn, she thought, watching him stack the dishes on the tray and put it outside the door. Later, when she was in her nightgown and in the big bed, she watched the back of him, saw how he ran his hands through his hair as his quill pen flew across the papers before him. She was curious about what he was doing but refused to ask, refused to make their relationship more personal than it was.

As she stretched out in the bed, she began a dream in which Farrell came to rescue her, beating the American in a sword fight. Her Uncle Jonathan would be there begging her forgiveness, saying he was quite lonely without her. The thought of Travis cringing in fear made her smile. In her vision she imagined pulling away from Farrell's arms and going to Travis, giving him her hand and forgiving him, telling him to go back to America and forget her—if he could.

When Travis slipped into bed beside her, she pretended to be asleep, but he just pulled her to him, nuzzled her ear, put his hand on her stomach, and eased into sleep. It was odd, but she felt that now she too could go to sleep.

In the morning, she was alone in the big room, but no sooner had she awakened than the maid let herself in. "Oh, beg pardon, miss. I thought you were still asleep. Mr. Travis said I was to bring you a bath if you'd like one."

Regan wouldn't humiliate herself by a repeat performance of begging the maid to release her. She told the girl to bring the tub and hot water, and in spite of herself she enjoyed the bath. It was almost a comfort to be able to do something for herself. Always before, a maid had dressed her, and washed her hair, and her uncle had chosen cheap, childish clothes for her. Clean once again, she toweled her hair, ate a big breakfast, and put on the blue silk dress. A delicate scarf embroidered with flowers in several shades of blue filled the deep neckline.

The day was long, and since she had nothing to do, she was bored. It was cool in the room, yet there was no fireplace, so she walked about, rubbing her arms. The early spring sun was weak through the window, but it was still the warmest place in the room. She pulled up a chair, gazed absently out the window, and made up her dreams, ranging from a garden plan to how she would never forgive Travis and would let Farrell run him through.

When the sun was setting and she heard what could only be Travis's voice—deep, golden-toned, filled with humor—she found her heart pounding. Of course it was only because of the sheer loneliness of the long day, but still she had to force herself not to smile when he entered.

His big brown eyes raked her as he smiled in greeting. "The dress looks good on you," he said, removing his hat and then his jacket. Practically collapsing in a chair, he gave a big sigh. "Working the fields all day would have been less work," he said. "Your countrymen are a bunch of close-minded snobs. I could hardly get anyone to listen to my questions, much less answer them."

Running her finger along the edge of the table in a nonchalant way, Regan tried to hide her curiosity. "Perhaps they didn't like your questions."

Travis wasn't fooled for a moment. "All I wanted to know was if someone had lost a pretty but unreasonable young female."

Opening her mouth to retort, she closed it, realizing he was baiting her. "And had they?"

Frowning before he answered, Travis seemed to be puzzled by what he'd discovered. "Not only couldn't I find out about a missing girl of your description, but I couldn't find anyone who'd even met a girl looking like you."

There was no reply Regan could make. There had never been visitors at Weston Manor. All she knew of life was what she'd learned from the stories of her maids and governesses, with their talk of love and gallant gentlemen, of the world outside the grounds of the house. Of course there was no one who knew of her.

Watching her, Travis tried to read what was in her face. All day the question had been haunting him: What was he to do with her when he sailed for America? He didn't tell her, but he'd hired three other men to help make inquiries about her. The night he'd found her she couldn't have run from very far, so she lived in either Liverpool or the surrounding area—or she'd been traveling through. After checking every lodging house in the area, he knew she must live there, but he could find no trace of her. She seemed to have materialized on that dark night near the docks.

"You're a runaway," he said quietly, watching when her expression confirmed his thoughts. "Only I can't figure out who you're running from and why no one is moving heaven and earth to find you."

Turning away, Regan tried not to think that it was because the people she thought loved her didn't care where she was.

"The only thing I can figure," he continued slowly, "is that you did something to make your people pretty damned angry at you. I know for a fact you weren't caught in bed with the gardener's boy, so maybe you refused to do something they wanted you to do. Did you refuse to marry some rich old duffer?"

"Not even close," she said smugly.

Travis only laughed because her eyes told him he wasn't too far wrong. But his laughter covered his true feelings. It made him very angry to think that anyone could just toss out a pure young girl into the streets, wearing only her nightgown. Perhaps in the heat of passion it could have happened, but how could they have let days go by and not searched for her?

"I was thinking that, since there doesn't seem to be any reason for you to stay in England, maybe you should go with me to America."

Chapter 4

"WHAT!" REGAN GASPED, ALMOST STAGGERED BY HIS words. "America is full of boorish, illiterate people who live in log cabins. What is there besides wild Indians and terrible animals, not to mention great, savage people? No, I will not under any circumstances go to that backward place."

The humor quickly left Travis's eyes as he rose to come toward her. "You damned Englishwoman! I get this all day from your 'gentlemanly' countrymen. I get snubbed because they don't like the way I talk or dress, or they had a relative killed in a war that happened when I was a boy. I'm getting damned tired of being looked at like something unclean, and I'll sure as hell not take it from you."

Backing away from him, Regan lifted her hand to her throat as if to protect herself.

"I've tiptoed around you enough, and from now on you're going to do what I say. If I left a child like you alone here, when it's quite clear you haven't a friend in the world, I'd never sleep again. I won't bore you with what America is when you have such clear ideas of your own, but at least in my country we don't toss young girls out just because they're disobedient. When we get to Virginia you'll have choices of what you can do—something more suitable for an English 'lady' ''—he sneered the word—''than walking the streets as would be your only alternative if I left you here.''

Narrowing his eyes, he glared down at her, pressed against the wall. "Is that clear?" He didn't give her a chance to answer before he slammed from the room, locking the door after him.

"Yes, Travis," she whispered to the still echoing emptiness.

She was glad when he was gone, since it was quite impossible to think when Travis was around. At least, perhaps, if she made him angry enough, he wouldn't force her to do those horrible things in bed, and he just might possibly release her if she provoked him. Smiling, she sat down and began to imagine her escape, how good it would be to get away from this boorish American. Imagine! she thought. The very idea of her going to America!

Snuggling in the chair, a quilt around her, she fantasized about what a dreadful place America must be, remembered every tale that had been told to her by a maid whose brother had traveled there and returned with horrible, treacherous stories, all of which the maid had told Regan in gory detail. As the candle sputtered and the room grew dark, she began to glance at the door, wondering when Travis was going to return. Sometime deep in the night, she left the chair and climbed into the big, cold bed, placing the pillows so that she could snuggle against them. They weren't as good as a large, warm body, but at least they helped.

In the morning, her head ached, and she was in a foul mood. That the American would leave her alone all night, unprotected, and at the mercy of anyone who could get the key to her room made her furious. One moment he made speeches about how much he was going to care for her, and the next he abandoned her to the mercies of any outside element.

Her sulks were interrupted when the door was given a quick tap and then unlocked. Folding her arms across her chest, she tilted her chin up, preparing to let Travis know she was unaffected by his abandonment of her. But instead of Travis's deep voice came the light laughter of women. Turning, Regan gasped in astonishment at the sight of three women who entered her room carrying great books and several baskets.

"You are Mademoiselle Regan?" asked a pretty little dark woman. "I am Madame Rosa, and these are my assistants. We have come to begin your wardrobe for your journey to America."

It took Regan several minutes to piece the story together, but it seemed Travis had engaged Madame Rosa, a French emigree and former dressmaker to one of Queen Marie Antoinette's ladies, to create an entire wardrobe for his captive. Too angry at his presumption to speak at first, Regan just sat in the bed and gave a vacant stare to the women. But as she saw the puzzled looks on their faces she knew she could not let them be on the receiving end of her anger. Her quarrel was with Travis Stanford and not these women who were merely doing their jobs.

"Perhaps I will look at your wares," she said tiredly,

thinking of all the other times she'd been allowed to choose clothes. Her uncle had allowed her to wear pink or blue or white, and the only trim was what she and her maids embroidered.

Smiling delightedly, the designer and her assistants began to spread fabric samples out on the bed. There seemed to be an endless array of colors and textures, most of which Regan had never seen before. There were a dozen colors of velvet, more of satin, linen, at least six types of silk, and dozens of colors in each type. Wools took up one corner of the bed, and Regan marveled at the variety: cashmere, tartans, a long-haired softness she was told was mohair. And the muslins! There seemed to be hundreds of colors, stripes, painted, printed, embroidered, pleated.

Eyes wide in wonder, Regan looked up from the beauty of the fabrics to Madame Rosa.

"Of course, there are the trims," the woman said, signaling for those samples to be brought.

Feathers joined the fabrics, then satin and velvet ribbons, topped by hand-drawn laces mixed with strings of tiny seed pearls, silver cord, jet beads, silk flowers, gold net, and intricately knotted frog fastenings.

Bewildered, Regan didn't move but just looked at the glorious colors.

"Perhaps it is too early for Mademoiselle," Madame Rosa said gently. "Monsieur Travis said we were to get everything done in one day so the clothes can be cut before you are to sail. He has hired a woman to sail with you to do the sewing so everything will be ready when you reach America."

As her head began to clear, Regan wondered if Travis knew what he was getting himself into; she doubted if a

Colonial had any idea of the cost of women's clothes. Uncle Jonathan had certainly made Regan aware of the exorbitant fees dressmakers charged. "Did Travis ask after the cost of the clothes?"

"No, miss," the dressmaker said, surprised. "He came to my house late last night, saying he'd heard I was the best in Liverpool and he wanted a complete wardrobe for a young lady. There was no mention of price, but then I got the impression Monsieur Travis didn't need to ask."

Opening her mouth and then closing it, Regan smiled. So! The big, brawling Colonial thought he was still in the forests of America! It might be fun to play with fabrics and trims for the day, to pretend to order an extensive wardrobe, and then watch Travis's face when he received a bill higher than any sum he'd ever imagined. Of course, she'd have the bill presented before the women began to cut the clothes; she wouldn't want them to lose out when Travis couldn't pay.

"Where shall we start?" Regan asked sweetly, her eyes dancing as she thought of defeating the braggart.

"Perhaps with day dresses," Madame Rosa suggested, lifting the samples of muslin.

Hours later, Regan was quite wistful about the whole plan. Too bad she wasn't going to get the clothes, because she'd planned a wardrobe a princess would love. There were muslin dresses of every color and trim, ballgowns of satin and velvet, walking dresses, a riding habit which made Regan laugh since she had no idea how to ride a horse, capes, cloaks, redingotes, spencers, as well as many nightgowns, camisoles, and lace-edged petticoats. When she finished, there wasn't a single fabric she hadn't used and very few colors.

The noon meal was brought to them, and Regan was glad the session was over because she was getting tired.

"But we have only started," Madame Rosa said. "The furrier is coming this afternoon with the milliner, the cobbler, and the glovemaker. And Mademoiselle must be measured for everything."

"Of course," Regan whispered. "How could I have forgotten?"

As the afternoon wore on, she ceased to be astonished at anything. The furrier brought pelts of sable, ermine, chinchilla, beaver, lynx, wolf, and angora goat, and she chose linings, collars, and cuffs for the coats she'd already selected. The cobbler took samples of cloth, planning to dye a pair of soft, heelless slippers to match every outfit, and he described the walking boots he would make. The milliner and Madame Rosa coordinated hats and clothes with the glovemaker.

At dark, everyone's energy began to fade, especially Regan's. She felt bad at the thought that the day's work would come to nothing because no American could possibly pay for all the clothes she'd ordered. She told Madame Rosa she was to submit everyone's bills to Travis before a pair of scissors was raised, that she should see the money in her hands before she started filling the order. The dressmaker smiled politely and said she'd have it ready first thing in the morning.

When she was finally alone, Regan slumped into a chair, weary from the long day and the constant feeling of guilt. All day she'd known she was playing a game, but the tradespeople were going to be very angry when they learned that their day's work would go unpaid.

By the time she heard Travis's heavy footsteps on the

stairs, she was feeling quite low—and it was all his fault. The moment he opened the door, she threw her shoe at him, hitting him on the shoulder.

"What's this?" he grinned. "I thought tonight you'd at least be a little glad to see me. You're always complaining because you have no clothes."

"I did not ask you to do anything about my clothes! You have no rights over me whatsoever and especially not to take me to your barbaric country. I will not go, do you hear me? I am English, and I will stay in England."

"Where all your family and friends are?" he asked sarcastically. "I've just spent another day trying to find where you've spent your life, and I can find nothing. Damn them!" he said, running his hands through his hair. "What kind of people could discard a child like you?"

Perhaps it was the tiredness from not sleeping well and the exhausting day, but her eyes filled with great, crystal tears. She'd been so angry for the last few days that she'd had no time to think about her feelings at hearing Farrell's disgust at the idea of marrying her and her uncle's declaration that he detested her. For days she'd lived in a dreamworld of hoping they would rescue her, but no doubt Travis had gone to their door. Had Farrell and her uncle told him they didn't know her?

Before she could speak, Travis pulled her into his arms. Pushing him away, she tried to protest. "Leave me alone," she whispered feebly, but even as she attempted to pull away from him, he held her tightly until she buried her face in his chest, and the sobs began tearing through her body.

Travis wasted no time before he lifted her into his arms and then sat in a chair with her, cradling her like a child.

"Go ahead and cry, kitten," he said softly. "I guess if any-one deserves to, it's you."

His holding of her, this stranger who made love to her and saw that she was cared for, when the people who should care for her denied her existence, made her cry harder. Worse than anything was the end of her dreams of being rescued by Farrell, of once again seeing the man she loved. Now she'd never even have a chance to prove to him that she could be a good wife; now she was going to be dragged off to America, and they'd never even know she'd gone.

As her sobs finally began to quiet, Travis stroked her damp hair. "Want to tell me what you're so unhappy about?"

She couldn't possibly tell him about Farrell. "Because I'm a prisoner!" she said as firmly as possible, pulling away from his shoulder.

Travis continued stroking her hair, and when he spoke his voice was full of patience and understanding. "I think you were a prisoner before I ever met you. If you hadn't been, you wouldn't have been discarded like so much rubbish."

"Rubbish!" she gasped. "How dare you call me that!"

Bewildered, Travis smiled at her. "I didn't say you were rubbish, only that someone had treated you as such. What I can't understand is why you seem to want to return to some-one who treats you like that."

"I . . . I . . . no one. . . ." she sputtered, tears begin-ning again. He had such a crude way of stating everything.

"It's not so bad being an orphan," he continued. "I've been one a long time. Maybe we belong together."

Regan looked up at him, thinking that she couldn't imag-ine this man belonging to anyone. No doubt, in spite of what he had said, he often kidnapped young girls and held them prisoner.

"I don't think I like what you're thinking," he warned. "If you're getting any ideas, let me warn you that I take care of what belongs to me."

"Belongs to you!" she exclaimed. "I hardly know you!"

He smiled just before he brought his lips down on hers and kissed her with such tenderness, such longing, that Regan found her arms going about his neck. "You know me well enough," he said huskily. "And get it through your head that you are mine."

"I'm not yours! I'm. . . ." she trailed off as he began to kiss her neck with little nibbling bites, and Regan sighed as she bent her head to one side.

"You are a temptress," he laughed, "and you're playing havoc with my work schedule." Firmly, he pushed her out of his lap. "As much as I'd like to stay with you, I have business to attend to, and I'm afraid it will take me most of the night. Did you know we sail day after tomorrow?"

Head lowered, she didn't answer him. She felt like such a fool because she'd reacted to him so quickly and so totally. Day after tomorrow! she thought. If she was ever to escape his hold over her, she must do it very soon.

"No goodbye kiss?" Travis joked, standing by the door. "Nothing to keep me warm out there all alone?"

Grabbing her other shoe, she threw it at him, but this time he ducked before it hit him. He was laughing as he locked the door behind him and went down the stairs.

At least tonight she was too tired to stay awake, but the bed did seem to get larger each night.

She woke to the quiet thunder of what could only be Travis attempting to tiptoe about the room. Keeping her eyes closed, she pretended to be asleep, even when he leaned over her and kissed her cheek. When he seemed to have left the room, she drowsily listened for the now familiar turn of the lock, and when it didn't come she sat bolt upright in bed. After rubbing her eyes twice, she was sure that what she saw was real—the door was wide open.

Not another second was lost as she jumped out of bed, slid the velvet dress over her head, and grabbed her shoes. Ever so quietly, she hugged the door with her back as she left the room and went onto the stair landing. Never having seen the inn except for the inside of one room, she was startled to see how isolated the room was—alone at the head of narrow, steep stairs, and, from the smells, at the bottom seemed to be the kitchen. Craning her neck until it threatened to break, she saw what was unmistakably Travis's leg and high boot near the foot of the stairs. But even as she began to lose hope, a clatter of horses and carriages sounded outside, and a man's voice cried for help. With great happiness, she saw Travis run for the door.

Within an instant she was down the stairs, through the nearly empty kitchen, where the few employees were intent on the activity outside, and finally out into the bright sunlight of the street.

There was no time to spend on the fact that her feet were bare, because she knew Travis would discover her escape very soon. For now she had to put time and distance between them if she was ever to manage her escape.

In spite of her good intentions, her feet began to hurt too badly to ignore them much longer, and people were begin-

ning to notice her. Slowing down for a moment, she saw a
dark alleyway between two buildings, and she made her way
there, crouching down between several horrible-smelling
wooden fish crates. I must think! she commanded herself,
because she knew that without a plan she could never gain
her freedom.

Sitting on one of the crates, she slipped on her shoes, tying the laces about her ankles. As she did so, she calmed her
racing heart and began to consider her alternatives. She
needed somewhere to go, a place to hide until she could get
a job, and especially a place to hide until that insane American left the country.

Lost in thought, she wasn't aware of the shouts in the
street until she was practically looking at Travis, his legs
spread wide, hands on hips, his profile to her. It was minutes before she realized that he didn't see her, that he was
only shouting orders to the people in the streets. The idea
that he'd give orders to strangers renewed her determination
to escape this man. Making herself as small as possible, she
crouched down among the boxes, praying he wouldn't see
her.

Even when he turned and ran down the street, she didn't
relax or move, because she felt he wasn't one to give up.
No, Travis Stanford was too sure he was right to ever give a
thought to anyone else's opinions. If he'd hold someone
prisoner, he'd certainly not let that prisoner escape without a
fight.

Remaining in her stiff, uncomfortable position, she tried
to come up with a plan. First she'd have to get away from
the docks, and the way to do that was always to keep the sea
at her back. Smiling, she thought that shouldn't be difficult
to do and was sure she had half her problem solved. The

other problem was where to go when she was away from the docks. If she could find her way back to Weston Manor, maybe Matta, her old maid, would know of some place Regan could go.

Hours and hours seemed to pass, yet the sun was still bright, the noise of the docks still loud. Using all her powers of concentration, she tried to ignore the cramps in her legs, and the ache in her back. Twice she saw Travis go by, and the second time she was close to calling out to him. Perhaps it was the pain in her aching body, but she seemed to remember all too clearly the last time she'd been alone on the docks. Of course, then she'd been wearing only her nightgown, and how could she expect to be treated as a lady when she was dressed as a woman of low morals? Now, wearing the elegant velvet dress, everyone would recognize her as a lady, and they wouldn't dare touch her.

Smiling, her confidence somewhat restored, she tried to twist her hair into some semblance of order. Yesterday the French dressmaker and her assistants had worn their hair short, à la greque, and Regan wondered if possibly she should cut hers. Maybe it would give her an added air of sophistication in her new life—whatever that was to be.

Her musings made the time pass, and when she saw that the sun was setting she felt as if she were about to embark on a great adventure. She had escaped the awful American, and she was free to go wherever she wanted.

Slowly, painfully, she left her crouch, shaking her tired legs, and letting the blood return to them as she put her weight on them. As she stood erect, she realized that her feet were cut and the sores inside her shoes were covered with dried blood, which broke apart when she took her first step.

Pulling her courage together, she stepped toward the darkening street. A lady, she reminded herself. She must carry herself like a lady and not let a little thing like lacerated, swollen feet make her limp. If she kept her shoulders back, her spine straight, her chin high, no one would bother her—no one would dare molest a lady.

Chapter 5

NEWS OF A PRETTY YOUNG BIT OF FLUFF WALKING ABOUT the docks unescorted spread like fire through a dry forest. Men who were too drunk to walk somehow managed to drag themselves out of a stupor and stagger in the direction of the young woman. An entire shipload of sailors just in from a three-year voyage grabbed bottles of rum and ran toward where someone said there was a whole passel of women just waiting for them.

Bewildered, trying very hard not to let her fear show, Regan did her best to ignore the ever-increasing crowd of men gathering around her. Some of them, grinning toothlessly and stinking of fish and worse, stuck out filthy, trembling hands to touch the velvet of her dress.

"Ain't never felt nothin' so soft," they whispered.

"Ain't never had me no lady before."

"Think ladies do it the same way as whores?"

Faster and faster she began to walk, weaving away from

57

the hands and the bodies placed in her way. No longer did she think of keeping the sea to her back; all she thought of was escape.

The men of the docks seemed to toy with her just as they had the night she'd been wearing her nightgown, but it was when the young, virile, hungry sailors from the ship found her that the relatively gentle games ceased. When the sailors realized there was only one woman and not fifty as they'd been told, they grew angry, and their anger was directed at this one frightened-looking female.

"Here, let me at her. I need more than a feel of her pretty dress," leered one vigorous young man, reaching out and grabbing the shoulder of Regan's dress.

The fabric tore all the way to the top of her breast, exposing one fat, soft mound that made the men laugh delightedly. "Please stop," Regan whispered, backing away from the sailors, only to have three pairs of hands lift her skirt and slip up the back side of her legs.

"She may be little, but there's a lot of her in the right places."

"Stop larkin' about. Let's have at her."

Before Regan was aware of what was about to happen to her, just as she seemed to hear Travis's words about men forcing her to do what they had done together, one of the sailors gave her a firm push, and she fell backward over the men behind her. With one futile effort at a scream, she tried to right herself, but the men under her, scrambling away, held her under an ocean of grabbing, exploring hands. Over her, grinning wildly, were the sailors.

"Now, let's see what's under those pretty skirts."

The man put his hand on her skirt, and Regan kicked him in the face, sending him sprawling. Her arms were pinned above her head by the men behind her, and the second after she kicked her ankles were grabbed, legs pulled wide apart.

"You won't kick me, missy," laughed another sailor, grabbing the edge of her skirt.

One second he was above her, smiling at her terror, enjoying her struggles against the hands that held her, and the next he was flying through the air, and grabbing his shoulder, which was quickly reddening. The sound of the shot seemed to come after the sailor flew away.

Two more shots rang across the tops of the men's heads before they began to react to something besides their vicious sport.

Regan, still held by the men, was first aware of their silence, and when she felt their grip loosening she kicked out, freeing one leg. The next moment an angry, violent Travis stepped over her, and before the men could comprehend what was happening, Travis grabbed arms, necks, belts, whatever was available, and sent sailors and waterfront riff-raff flying through the air.

Shaking with fear, Regan lay still as, one by one, every hand was taken from her body. Travis straddled her hips, his back to her, a pistol in each hand. "Anyone else like to try for the lady?" he challenged.

Backing away, looking like the untamed, cowardly scum they were, they muttered at Travis for spoiling their fun, but no one openly opposed the dangerous-looking American.

Sticking the pistols into his belt, Travis turned and looked down at Regan, watched her panting with fear, and quickly noted that most of her clothes were intact. With one swift gesture he bent and threw her over one shoulder like a sack of flour.

The breath nearly leaving her, Regan slammed against the back of him. "Put me down!" she demanded.

Travis gave her buttocks one hard smack, which was fortunately padded by the thick velvet, before nodding to the two other men who still held pistols on the cowering crowd, and started back toward the inn.

One of the sailors, the one Regan had kicked in the eye, yelled after Travis that Yanks certainly knew how to treat women, and the others laughed, glad they'd had no fight with the angry man. The sailor Travis had shot limped away, back toward the inner structures of the waterfront.

Regan didn't say another word to Travis as she bounced along in the awkward, embarrassing position, and she was glad her long hair hid her face from passersby, especially people at the inn. By the time he'd climbed the stairs and reached the room they'd shared, she was ready to tell him what she thought of his treatment of her, that he was little better than the ruffians on the street.

But her courage left her when Travis slammed her into the bed so hard she dove through a foot of down-filled mattress, striking the rope lacing below. Gasping for air, she surfaced, pushed her hair out of her face, and looked up into Travis's livid, raging temper.

He didn't give her a chance to speak. "Do you know how I found you?" he said through clenched teeth, the muscles of his jaw working vigorously, hands on hips. "I hired men to walk the waterfront and to report to me when there was a commotion. I knew if I waited you'd show up, and when you did they'd be all over you." Leaning forward, he snarled at her, "You lasted longer than I expected. What did you do, hide somewhere?"

Watching her face, he saw that his guess had been correct. He threw up his hands in frustration while taking heavy steps across the room. "What the hell am I going to do with you? I have to keep you locked up to protect you from yourself. Don't you have any idea at all what the world's like? I told you what would happen if you left here, but you didn't believe me. No, instead you had to get yourself nearly raped and possibly killed. The first time I found you, you were being chased by men, and now, through your own fault, it's happened again. Did you think it would be different the second time?"

Holding the torn top of her dress together, she toyed with the luscious velvet of the skirt. Her mind was working hard to block out what had just happened to her, to make it seem like one of her dreams. "I thought because I was dressed like a lady, they wouldn't. . . ." she whispered.

"What!" Travis bellowed, then sank into a chair. "I cannot believe anyone could truly, actually think—." He cut himself off to look at her, so small, probably unaware that she was shivering, a long scrape down the side of her face, and once again he felt possessive about her. "There's no question about it now. Tomorrow you leave with me for America."

"No!" she gasped, her head coming up. "I can't possibly. I must stay in England. This is my home."

"You want a home where you're attacked every time you step out the door? You want a repeat of what happened to you today?"

"This isn't the real England," she pleaded. "There are beautiful people and places full of love and friendship and. . . ."

"And what?" he asked, hard. "Money? Money is the difference between the filth just outside here and the gentility you seem to adore, the gentility that seems to have kicked out an innocent little thing like you. It looks to me like the lovely people you know are about even with the ones tearing your clothes off a while ago.''

Slowly, great tears began to form in Regan's eyes, and as she looked up at Travis he saw her sadness. She needed her dreams, she thought, needed to believe in love and beauty, had to have something to make up for all the emptiness in her life.

Not exactly understanding the thoughts going through Regan's mind, Travis did see her hurt, and her tears made him weak. Instantly, he was beside her on the bed, folding her into his arms, trying his best to shelter her from whatever painful memories haunted her.

"You'll like America," he said gently, stroking her hair. "The people are good and honest, and they'll like you. I'll introduce you to half of Virginia, and before you know it you'll have more friends than you know what to do with."

"Friends?" she whispered, clinging to him, only now beginning to realize how the experience on the waterfront had upset her. There still seemed to be clutching, greedy hands on her body.

"You can't imagine all the wonderful people in America. I have a little brother, Wesley, who will love you, and of course there's Clay and Nicole. Nicole is from France and can talk French as fast as lightning."

"Is she pretty?" Regan sniffed.

"Almost as pretty as you," he smiled, caressing her hair. "And when I left she was just about to have a baby. It's probably months old by now. Of course, she's already got the twins."

"Twins?"

Travis laughed and held her away from him, wiping away her tears with his fingertips. "Don't you understand yet that I'm taking you to America, not to punish you or because I like kidnapping little girls, but because I have no choice? There's nothing else I can do with you."

His words, meant to calm her and said in Travis's own special blunt way of calling a problem by its true name, had the opposite effect on Regan. Her uncle and Farrell had said similar things about having to put up with her. She was tired of being a burden to everyone. "Let me up!" she demanded, pushing against him.

"Now what the hell's the matter?"

Twisting her head, she tried to bite his hand on her shoulder.

Travis pushed her back into the mattress and rubbed his hand. "I don't understand you at all. I save your life not more than an hour ago, and now I tell you, as kindly as you please, how I have your own best interests at heart, and you get madder'n hell at me. I don't understand you at all."

"Understand me!" she gasped, eyes spitting fire. "I wouldn't have had to run away if you hadn't been holding me prisoner, and I wouldn't have needed rescuing if it hadn't been for you in the first place. In a sense, you saved me *from* yourself *for* yourself."

Bewildered, his mouth falling open, Travis could only gape at her. "Does your mind always work that way? Do you always go down ten different twisted paths before you get to where you want to go?"

"I assume that is an American colloquialism, meant to cover your lack of logic. The fact is that you are holding me prisoner, and I demand to be released," she said smugly, arms folded, chin tilted away from him.

Travis's anger faded quickly to laughter, which he tried very hard to suppress. Whatever her understanding of logic was, it was far away from the true meaning of the word. He considered explaining again what would happen if he released her, but since she'd been assaulted twice and it seemed to have made no impression on her, he had no desire to try to explain again. Nor would he try painting a glorious picture of America for her. All he could do was to let her see for herself. He also considered throwing open the door and giving her another chance to try to make it out of the docks, or he could pay for a cab to take her wherever she wanted to go.

At this last thought, something inside him tightened. If he sent her away, he might never see her again, this starry-eyed little vixen who seemed to look at the world through her own special pink haze. The thought of the long sea voyage without her to entertain and delight him made him feel very sad.

"You're going to America with me," he said firmly as he ran his hand along her bare shoulder. He'd felt so guilty about seducing her when she was so innocent that he'd forced himself to stay away from her for two nights, but now the near panic he'd felt all day when he couldn't find her, combined with the seductive image she presented now with her bare shoulder and partially exposed breast, made him forget about logic.

"Do not touch me," she said haughtily.

"We may disagree about . . . logic"—he smiled at the word—"but there's one area where we seem to be in complete agreement."

Regan really tried to keep herself aloof from Travis's touch, but the feel of his hand—that wide, warm, sensual palm running along her neck—was impossible to ignore.

She wanted to appear unaffected by what had happened to her, wanted him to think she was courageous and brave, but truthfully she wanted to climb into his lap and hide, perhaps crawl into his pocket. When he had stood over her this evening, pistols drawn, she'd never in her life been so glad to see anyone.

Turning her head to one side, his fingers stroked her neck, and she closed her eyes as his other hand went to the opposite side of her neck.

"You're tired, aren't you, love?" Travis whispered, the pressure of his hands increasing. "Muscles stiff?"

Her nod was barely perceptible as she felt her body relaxing. She had no idea what he was doing, only that by some magic he seemed to be making her body melt. She closed her eyes, giving herself over to Travis, hardly aware when he slipped off her dress and laid her naked body face down on the bed. The gentle, deep sound of his voice added to this new pleasure she was experiencing.

"When I was a boy," he said, "I shipped out on a whaler for three years. Terrible experience, but at least there were some interesting stops, such as China, where I learned to do this."

Wherever he'd learned it, she was grateful. His hands dug into her and sometimes even hurt her, but she soon found that when she relaxed the pain stopped. Fingers massaged along her spine, kneading out the soreness from crouching in the alleyway for hours. Cramps in her legs and calves relaxed, and when he started on her feet new areas of her body sank deeper into the soft mattress. It amazed her that even her arms could be tense, but Travis's hands loosened knots of tight muscle and made them limp.

Since Regan was too relaxed to move, he turned her over

as if she were a heap of rags and began on her front. From the feet up, he rubbed, pummeled, stroked, gouged, caressed every pore of her body. When he reached her face, his thumbs gently touching the muscles in her cheeks, and around her nose, she was near senseless.

Feeling so relaxed, she wasn't aware of the sensuality of the massage, that the feel of Travis's strong hands, his eyes on her nude body, had awakened her passion. She felt like a big cat stretching in the sun, every muscle quiet, awaiting the adventures that lay ahead.

When Travis's hands returned to her thighs, it seemed the most natural thing in the world. A sweet, knowing smile curved her lips as she kept her eyes closed, preferring only to feel, to give her mind over to her senses. The change of pressure in Travis's hands, perhaps his own lust coming through his fingertips, was subtle, but she understood it.

"Yes, love," he growled throatily, his breath extraordinarily deep.

He didn't use his lips or any other part of his body except his hands—those marvelous, big, hard hands that she'd seen used to toss grown men about as if they were weightless. Wide, callused fingers were artfully agile, deliciously provocative as they reexplored the skin they'd just touched.

Regan felt a deep hum inside her, some primitive piece of machinery beginning to work. Arching slightly, rhythmically, she gave herself over to him. "Please," she whispered, her hands rising up his arms, fingers tracing the muscles. "Please."

Travis lost no time in obeying her, as he was close to the breaking point. The sheer sensuality of their lovemaking and the beauty of her slim young body had fascinated him, and when he entered her it was slowly, very slowly, never once relinquishing the gentle, ethereal quality of their pleasure.

Regan had learned enough about lovemaking to know to prolong their movement, and she followed his lead as if they were two heavenly bodies joined in a union that would last through eternity. Yet she could not hold off long, and soon she began to breathe quicker and to dig her hands into Travis's flesh. Within seconds their gentleness turned into ferocity, their hunger equal, greedy, starving.

When at last their passion peaked, Regan cried out and felt tears coming to her eyes at the violence of her release.

For some minutes she lay still, afloat in a sea of nothingness, sated and happy, relaxed and deeply quiet.

Slowly, Travis rolled off her, propped his head on one elbow, and looked down at her. His brown eyes were dark, and she noticed the thickness of his short lashes.

Who is this man? she wondered. Who is this man who makes my body sing to some heavenly music? He didn't say a word, and she felt she was seeing him for the first time. He held her prisoner, yet he took care of her, acted as if he valued her, and even a few times seemed remorseful about enslaving her. What sort of man could be so gentle and so strong at the same time?

Studying him, she thought how little she knew of him. What thoughts went through his mind, who were the people he loved, and, yes, who loved him? She put her hand to the side of his face, running her fingertips along his cheek. Could this man, who seemed to think the world was his for the taking, ever be made to love? Could a mere woman ever make a slave of this man, hold his strong, pounding heart in her small hands?

She moved her hand to his bare chest, felt his heart under

her palm, twined her fingers in the hair on his chest, and then on impulse gave it a sharp pull.

"Stop that, you little imp," he growled, then kissed her fingers. "I'd think you'd be more grateful after the way I just made you squeal."

"Grateful!" she gasped, but concealing a smile. "Since when does a slave thank her master?"

Travis refused to take the bait but merely grunted and gathered her to him. He seemed to give no thought to the fact that he twisted her body into an impossible position.

Regan started to protest that she could not possibly sleep entwined about him in such a way, but even as she formed the words they disappeared. Feeling rather like a vine twirled about the trunk of a great oak, her body relaxed, and she drifted into a deep sleep.

Chapter 6

REGAN'S LANGUOROUS, CATLIKE MOOD DISAPPEARED AStoundingly quickly the next morning when Travis roughly pulled her out of bed and then dashed a handful of cold water in her face. Gasping for air, she finally managed to open her sleepy eyes just in time to see a towel flying at her.

"Get dressed," Travis tossed over his shoulder as he jammed clothes, hers included, into the too-full trunk.

Seeing her torn velvet dress further mutilated as he wadded it into a tight little ball, Regan flung herself at him. "Stop that! I will not have you treat my beautiful dress like that," she said, taking it from him and smoothing it lovingly.

Pulling back, Travis eyed her with interest. "It's torn anyway. What good is it except for a dust rag?"

"It can be patched," she said, folding the dress carefully. "I'm very good at mending my own clothes, and, besides, the nap of the velvet will hide the repair work."

"Since when have rich young English ladies had to patch their own clothes?"

She whirled on him. "I never said I was rich," she smiled smugly.

"There must be money involved somewhere, or you wouldn't have been thrown out on your ear." Eyes twinkling, he caressed her bare buttock. "Or should I say thrown out on your pretty little rear?" Before she could give him the scathing reply he deserved, he smacked her smartly. "Now get dressed before we end up back in bed and the ship leaves without us."

Thoughtfully, she began to dress; then on impulse she turned back to him. "Do you think I really could tempt you to . . . to do something?"

Travis had no idea what she was talking about, but the sight of her, half-dressed, the silk making her eyes brilliantly blue, her skin still glowing from last night's lovemaking and his head still dazzled by it, he felt that she could persuade him to do anything. "Stop tempting me and get dressed. You'll have months on board ship to play the seductress, but for now there's work to do."

Blushing because he'd misunderstood her, Regan concentrated on dressing. Perhaps, she thought dreamily, perhaps this American could be. . . . Glancing at Travis, tossing boots into the trunk on top of clean white shirts, she smiled. Maybe he could never be a gentleman, but he did have possibilities. Her eyes widened as he locked the trunk, bent, grabbed the leather handle, and rose with it hanging down his back.

"Ready?" he asked, seeming not to notice his enormous burden.

She nodded and preceded him out of the door.

Downstairs, a breakfast the size of which she'd never seen before was hot and waiting for them. "You've made me miss more meals than I ever have before in my life," Travis informed her.

She coolly glanced up at his great height, then pointedly at the thickness of his chest. "Perhaps you could stand to miss a few meals."

Travis laughed, but a few minutes later she saw him glancing at a mirror as if he were inspecting himself. His reaction made her smile, feeling a touch triumphant.

The food was delicious, and Regan was ravenous. She was pleased to see that Travis's table manners were quite good, perhaps without the delicacy of Farrell or another gentleman of his quality, but he would pass in decent society.

"Have I grown horns?" Travis asked, teasing.

Ignoring him, she looked back down at her food and wondered at her own lack of spirit. Perhaps it was yesterday's terrible experience on the docks and Travis's rescuing of her, but, truthfully, she was beginning to feel some excitement about the idea of going to America. People said that, since the people of America were free, you could get rich there. Maybe she could make her fortune in the primitive country and return to England—and Farrell—in triumph.

Travis's hand under her chin brought her out of her dream. "Were you leaving me again?" he asked quietly. "Or perhaps planning to murder me in my sleep?"

"Neither. I wouldn't waste my time."

Chuckling, Travis stood, offered her his hand, and helped her up. "I think you're going to do quite well in America. We need more women with your spirit."

"I thought you considered all American women the epitome of grace and courage."

"There's always room for improvement," he laughed, taking her arm. "Now, stay close to me and you'll be all right," he said seriously, his eyes warning her.

She didn't need a second warning, and as soon as they left the inn she found herself clinging to Travis's arm. The fishy smell and the noises peculiar to the waterfront hit her hard, and for a moment she was transported back to the time when the men's hands had clawed at her.

Travis was watching her thoughtfully, aware of the fear in her eyes. He threw the heavy trunk onto the waiting wagon and told the driver which ship to take it to. When it was gone, he turned back to Regan. "There's only one way to lick a fear, and that is to face it straight on. If you fall off a horse, you have to get right back on immediately."

Regan barely listened to this confusing bit of advice but instead moved even closer to Travis, her fingers digging into his arm. "Will the carriage be here soon?" she whispered.

"We're not getting a carriage," Travis said heartily. "You and I are going to walk to the ship. By the time we get there, you won't be so afraid. I don't want you cowering every time we get near a wharf or you smell rotten fish."

It took several moments for his words to reach her brain. Pulling away from him, she looked up in astonishment. "Is this some sort of American logic? I do not want to walk through this . . . this place. I demand you get me a carriage."

"Demand, is it?" Travis smiled. "From what I've learned in life, people shouldn't make demands unless they can carry them through. Are you prepared to walk to the ship by yourself?"

"You wouldn't do that, would you?" she whispered.

"No, love," he said quietly, grasping her hand. "I won't even leave you in this country alone, much less in this slimy place. Now, come on and smile at me. We'll walk to the ship, and you'll see how safe you are with me."

In spite of her misgivings, Regan soon began to enjoy the walk. Travis pointed to buildings, warehouses, and taverns, and told her a humorous story about a fight he'd seen in one tavern. Before long, she was laughing and had stopped clutching so desperately at his arm. Several sailors lounged against a brick wall and made remarks about her that she couldn't quite hear but certainly understood the essence of. Calmly, Travis excused himself and went to say a few words to the men. Within seconds they doffed their caps and came to murmur good mornings to Regan and to wish her a pleasant trip.

Bewildered, then as pleased as a cat with cream, she looked up at Travis as she took his arm again.

His eyes bright, he bent and kissed her nose. "Keep looking at me like that, sweetheart, and we'll never make it to the ship. We'll have to stop at one of these inns."

She looked away from him, but her shoulders went back, her chin up, and she walked as if her feet could hardly touch the ground. And best of all, her fear left her. Her fingertips never left Travis's arm, but now she knew that even this slight touch was enough to keep her safe. Perhaps it wasn't so bad being with this great American and having these men, as low as they were, nodding their heads respectfully at her.

Sooner than she wanted to be, they were at the ship, and

Regan was awed by the size of it. Weston Manor could have been set on the open deck.

"How do you feel?" Travis asked. "Not scared, are you?"

"No," she answered honestly, taking a deep breath of the cleansing sea air.

"I didn't think you would be," Travis said proudly as he led her up the gangplank.

She didn't have a chance to see much before he pulled her toward the pointed front end of the ship. There were tangles of rope as big around as her leg, and overhead was a spider web of cables. "Rigging," Travis murmured as he maneuvered her between sailors and boxes of supplies.

Quickly, he pulled her down narrow, steep stairs and into a little cabin that was neat and tidy. The walls were raised, arched panels, painted in two shades of blue. Against one wall was a large bed, a table was anchored to the middle of the floor, and two chests were on the opposite wall. A skylight and a window gave the room ample light.

"Nothing to say?" Travis asked quietly.

She was surprised at the almost wistful quality in his voice. "It's very pretty," she smiled, sitting down on the seat in front of the window. "Is your room as nice?"

Travis grinned. "I'd say it's exactly as pretty as this one. Now, I want you to stay here while I see to the loading of my supplies." Pausing at the door, he turned back. "And I'll go through the passengers and find that seamstress I hired and send her to you. You might want to look through those trunks and decide what you want to make first." His eyes twinkled. "And I told her to forget the nightgowns, that I had my own way of keeping you warm."

With that he was gone, and Regan was left to gape in

puzzlement at the closed door. Passengers! He'd told the passengers she was to be sleeping with him? Were these passengers American friends of his, people she hoped would someday respect her?

Before she could even contemplate the horror of this new situation, the door opened, and a tall, thin woman entered.

"I knocked, but no one answered," she said, eyeing Regan with interest. "If you'd rather, I could come back later. It's just that Travis said there was so much sewing to do, it would take the whole voyage. There's another woman on the boat—oh, no, Travis said it was a ship. Anyway, I think I can get her to help out. I don't know if she can do fancy work or not, but she can probably at least do the straight seams."

The woman was quiet for a moment as she seemed to be contemplating Regan. "Are you all right, Mrs. Stanford? Are you getting seasick, or maybe you're homesick already?"

"What?" Regan asked blankly. "What did you call me?"

The woman laughed as she moved to sit by Regan. She had lovely eyes, a full, pretty mouth, but in between was a sharp, long nose. "Neither you nor Travis seems used to being married yet. When I asked him if you'd been married long, he looked at me like he didn't think I was talkin' to him. That's a man for you! It takes them ten years before they admit they've given up their freedom." Glancing about the room, she didn't stop talking. "But if you ask me, marriage was made for men; they just get another slave when they get a wife. Now!" she said abruptly. "Where are your new clothes? I reckon we'd best get started."

There were about a hundred thoughts whirling together in

Regan's head, all of them confusing. In the turmoil of the last few days she'd completely forgotten about the clothes.

The woman patted Regan's hand sympathetically. "I guess with you being a new bride with a husband like Travis and all, and going to a new country, it's just too much for you. Maybe I should come back later."

New bride, Regan thought. She was a bride in a way. At least it was pleasant to imagine that she was a bride rather than facing up to the reality of the situation.

The woman was already at the door before Regan recovered herself. "Wait! Don't leave. I don't know where the clothes are. No, Travis said they were in the trunks."

Grinning broadly, the woman held out her hand. "I'm Sarah Trumbull, and I'm happy to meet you, Mrs. Stanford."

"Oh yes!" Regan sighed, liking this woman very much in spite of her extraordinary manipulation of the English language.

Sarah was on her knees in seconds as she threw open the lid to the first trunk. Perhaps the best indication of her admiration was her complete silence as she gazed down at the riot of colors and soft, silken, finely woven fabrics. "These must have set Travis back a bit of gold," she finally managed to whisper.

A sharp wave of guilt passed over Regan as she remembered how she'd purposely chosen many more clothes than she needed just to embarrass Travis when he found he could not pay the bill. Yet, obviously, he had paid the bill, and she wondered how much it had cost him—mortgages perhaps, selling what he owned?

"You're looking a little green again. Are you sure the ship's rolling isn't bothering you?"

"No, I'm all right."

"Good," Sarah said, looking back at the trunk. "Travis wasn't exaggerating when he said this was going to take months. You think that other trunk is as full as this one?"

Swallowing hard, Regan glanced at the closed lid. "I'm afraid so."

"Afraid!" Sarah laughed, pulling a leather portfolio from the trunk. "Look at this!" she said, emptying it onto her lap. Several pieces of heavy paper fell out, and on each one were four delicate watercolors of women's gowns. "These the dresses you picked out?"

Taking them, Regan smiled. They were beautiful dresses, and the sketches themselves were works of art. As Sarah and Regan began exploring, they found that each dress and coat had been carefully cut, and the trims for the particular garments were wrapped inside.

"It looks like I have my work cut out for me," Sarah said, then laughed at her own pun. Gathering drawings and fabrics, she said she'd like to get started, and as abruptly as she had appeared she left the cabin.

For a few moments, Regan sat alone on the window seat, looking at the cabin and wondering what adventures were ahead of her. She thought of Farrell and wished he knew she was on a ship bound for America and that a wardrobe fit for a princess was being sewn for her.

She had no idea how long she sat immobile on the seat, but gradually she became aware of the sounds outside her door. For all of her life she'd been forced to stay in a very small area, and the only living she could do was inside her head. Now she realized that she was free to see and do things, that the door to her cabin was not locked, and all she had to do was walk up some stairs and she'd be on the deck of an actual ship.

Taking a deep breath, feeling like a bird let out of a cage, she left the cabin, standing for a moment at the bottom of the dark stairwell. When a door next to her opened, she jumped in surprise.

"I beg your pardon," came a polite male voice. "I had no idea anyone was here." When Regan didn't answer, he continued, "Perhaps I should introduce myself since it looks as though we're to be neighbors. Or am I being too presumptuous? Maybe the captain could do the honors."

The young man's formal manners were a welcome relief after the last few days' complete suspension of anything resembling courtesy. "We will be neighbors," she smiled, "so perhaps just this once we can suspend formalities."

"Then allow me to present myself. I am David Wainwright."

"And I am Regan Alena . . . Stanford," she said as an afterthought, not wanting to reveal her true identity or let this man know the truth about her relationship with Travis.

Gently, he shook her hand, then asked if she'd accompany him up to the upper deck. "I believe they're still loading. It may afford us some amusement to see these Americans among themselves, though I confess I sometimes have difficulty understanding their dialect."

The sun was warm and bright on the deck, and Regan caught the feeling of excitement as people rushed around her everywhere. They emerged at the base of the quarterdeck, a partial additional deck at the fore end of the ship. Soon realizing they were in the way, she and David climbed the stairs to the top of the quarterdeck. Here they had a good, high view of the activities on the rest of the ship as well as on the wharf. And here, too, she had a view of David Wainwright. He was a small man with a plain face topped with straw-colored hair. His clothes were of good wool, his cravat perfectly white, and his slim feet were encased in soft kid slippers. He was the type of gentleman she'd always known —his hands made for the keys of a piano or to idly twirl a snifter of brandy. Looking at his long, slim fingers, she thought with disgust that an uncouth man such as Travis would probably hit two keys at once with his big fingers. Of course, she had to admit that those wide fingers sometimes hit the right chords.

As her lips curved in a secret smile, she looked away from David, who was explaining why he was going to such a heathen place as America, and searched for Travis.

"I can't tell you how glad I am to be traveling with an English lady," David was saying. "When my father suggested I go and see to his holdings in that wilderness, I dreaded the journey. I've heard more than my share of stories about the place, and as if that weren't enough, just meeting a single American can turn one against the country. Look at that!" he gasped. "That is just what I was speaking of."

Below them, two sailors dropped the burdens they were carrying to the center of the deck, where another man carried them downstairs, and began shoving each other. Within seconds, one swung his fist at the other's jaw and missed, but before he could strike again the second man slammed his fist into the first's nose. Blood seemed to gush forth instantly, and the hurt, angry man began to swing wildly.

Out of nowhere, Travis appeared, grabbed the much smaller men by the backs of their shirt collars, and lifted them from the deck. There was no difficulty in hearing Travis as he told the sailors what he thought of their behavior and what he promised to do if they gave him any more trouble. Shaking them like puppies, he tossed them aside, told them to get cleaned up and return to work, as he carried both their bundles to the waiting sailor.

"That is an example of what I mean," David said. "Those Americans have no discipline. This is an English ship with an English captain, yet that . . . that American lout thinks he has every right to enforce his will over the crew. And besides, the men should not have been let off so lightly. Their bad conduct should be made an example of. Every captain knows that the only way to stop insubordination is at the very outset of it."

Regan agreed with him, of course. She'd heard her uncle say the same sort of thing many times, but the way Travis had handled the angry men seemed to her efficient and sensible. Frowning, she was puzzled by her thoughts, wondering who was actually right.

Her mind on other things, she did not at first see Travis waving at her.

"I believe that man is trying to get your attention," David said, half in disgust, half in disbelief.

Trying to be sophisticated, Regan gave Travis a polite return wave before looking away from him. She had no desire to make a spectacle of herself as he had just done.

"I don't think he was satisfied," David said wonderingly. "He now seems to be coming this way. Perhaps I should get the captain."

"No!" Regan gasped, her eyes turning to Travis and smiling in spite of herself.

"Did you miss me?" Travis laughed, sweeping her into his arms and swirling her around once.

"Let me down!" she said angrily, but her voice did not agree with the pleasure on her face. "You smell like a gardener."

"And what would you know of the smell of a gardener?" he teased.

From behind her, David cleared his throat noisily.

Blushing, Regan managed to push Travis's hands away from her. "Mr. Wainwright, this is Travis Stanford." Her eyes looked up pleadingly at him. "My . . . husband," she whispered.

Travis's eyes didn't flicker. Actually, his smile seemed to grow warmer as he thrust out his hand, enveloping David's slim, smooth one. "I am glad to meet you, Mr. Wainwright. Did you know my wife in England?"

How smoothly he said the lie! she thought. Yet how kind of him to save her honor this way. She would have thought he'd laugh at her, as he did so often.

"No, we just met," David said quietly, looking from one to the other, seeing Travis's possessive arm about Regan's small shoulders, seeing a refined, elegant English lady in the grasp of a half-savage, mannerless, working-class man. He very much wanted to wipe his palm where Travis had touched him.

If Travis saw the delicate curl of the small man's upper lip, he did not show it, and Regan was too busy trying to regain some of her dignity by pushing Travis's hand away.

"I was hoping you'd known her before," Travis said, and ignored Regan's look because his words had an odd ring to them, almost as if he wasn't telling the truth. "I have to get back to work, love," he smiled. "You stay up here and away from the lower deck, you understand?" He didn't wait for her to answer but turned to appraise Wainwright. "I trust

I may leave her with you?'' he said politely, formally, but at the same time he gave the impression that he was laughing. Regan very much wanted to kick him.

Swiftly, he turned and bounded down the stairs, leaving Regan to wonder if he were jealous. Perhaps Travis was worried that he couldn't compete with a gentleman of Mr. Wainwright's quality.

Chapter 7

THE SHIP SAILED WITH THE TIDE. REGAN, TOO EXCITED TO eat, too curious to leave the quarterdeck even for a moment, was unaware of the way David's face whitened or of his constant swallowing. When he excused himself, she smiled and stayed where she was. Noisy seagulls flew overhead as the men ran the sails up. The rolling of the ship reminded her that they were about to set out on a journey, that with the moving of the ship she was starting a new life.

"You look happy," Travis said quietly from beside her.

She hadn't been aware of him coming up the stairs. "Oh yes, I am. What are those men doing? Where do those stairs lead to? Where are the other passengers? Do their rooms look like ours, or is everyone's a different color?"

Travis gave her a grin and fell to telling her what he could about the ship. It was a twenty-four-gun brig, the guns needed to keep away pirates. The other passengers lived in the lower deck, amidships. He didn't tell her about the close airlessness of their quarters or the strict rules governing the passengers' infrequent exercise. Only the two of them and Wainwright were allowed to come and go freely.

He explained why nearly all ships were now painted a shade of ochre. Before America's revolution, all ships had been swabbed with linseed oil, which made the wood darken with each coating. The older the ship, the darker it was. During the war, the English made a point of attacking the darker ships, until someone decided to paint all the ships the color of a newly built one.

Travis pointed to several patches of red paint and said that almost all the interiors, especially around the cannons, had been painted red so that the crew would be used to the color and not panic when, during a battle, they were surrounded by the red of blood.

"Where did you learn all this?" Regan asked eagerly.

"Someday I'll have to tell you about my time on the whaler, but for now let's get something to eat. Unless, of course, you don't feel like eating."

"Why shouldn't I want to eat? It's been a long time since breakfast."

"I was afraid you might have a touch of what your little friend had—seasickness. It's my guess that half the passengers below are spilling their guts into chamber pots."

"Really? Oh, Travis, I must see if I can help."

He caught her arm before she could reach the stairs. "There'll be plenty of sick people later, but for now you're going to eat and rest. You've had a long day."

Maybe she was tired, but also she was sick to death of his orders. "I am not hungry, and I can rest later. I will go to help the other passengers."

"And I say you will obey me, so you'd better make up your mind."

She glared up at him, refusing to move.

Leaning down, his face close to hers, he said quietly, "Either you do what I say or I carry you downstairs in front of the entire crew."

A feeling of helplessness came over her. How could she reason with this man? What could she do to make him understand that it was important to her to feel useful?

As he moved his hand toward her shoulder, she pivoted on one foot and sped down the stairs, through the door, and into the cabin. Sitting down on the window seat, she tried hard not to cry. It wasn't easy to keep to her dreams of someday being a respected lady when she was ordered about like a child.

It was some time before Travis came back to the room bearing a tray laden with food. Quietly, he set the table before going to sit by her. "Supper's ready." He tried to take her hand, but she drew it away.

"Damn it!" he exploded, jumping up. "Why do you sit there looking like I've just beaten you? All I said was I didn't think you should miss your supper and do without sleep to help a bunch of people you don't even know."

"I know Sarah!" she gasped. "And you did not say I *should* rest; you said I *had* to rest. You never suggest anything; you always demand everything. Did it ever occur to you that I have a mind of my own? You held me prisoner in England, wouldn't so much as allow me out the door, and now you hold me prisoner in this little room. Why don't you tie me to the bed or chain me to the table? Why not be honest about what I am to you?"

Several emotions flickered across Travis's handsome

face, but the predominant one was confusion. "I told you why you couldn't stay in England. I even asked that boy you were with if he'd known you. The ship hadn't set sail then, and if he'd told me, I could have taken you to your family."

More tears came to Regan's eyes. To think she'd thought Travis was jealous, and all he'd actually wanted was another chance to get rid of her. "Excuse me for being such a burden to you," she said haughtily. "Perhaps you should throw me overboard and save yourself so much trouble."

Astonished, Travis could only look at her in bewilderment. "If I live to be a thousand, I don't believe I'll be able to understand your reasoning. Why don't you eat something, and then if you want I'll take you below, and you can hold sick heads over pots all night."

He looked so sweet, his big eyes so liquid, pleading with her, trying his best to please her. How could she explain to him that what she wanted was the freedom to choose, the right to make her own decisions? She wanted to prove to herself and to her uncle that she was worth something.

Accepting his hand, she let herself be led to the table, but she couldn't seem to pull herself out of her dark mood. She pushed her food around, barely tasting it. She tried to listen to what Travis was telling her but couldn't seem to keep her mind on it. She kept thinking of her whole life as someone's prisoner, never allowed to make even a single decision.

"Drink your wine," Travis said gently.

Obediently, she drained the glass and felt her body relaxing. It seemed natural when Travis swept her into his arms, held her so securely, and carried her to the bed. While he was undressing her, she was awake only in a haze. Even when she was naked and he was kissing her neck, she only smiled and fell into a deeper sleep.

Seeing that she needed sleep more than anything else, Travis snuggled her under the covers before taking a cigar and going up to the top of the quarterdeck to smoke it.

"All settled in?"

Travis turned to the captain behind him. "We'll make it, I guess."

The captain watched Travis as he leaned on the railing, a long cigar hanging out of his mouth. "What's wrong, boy?" he asked seriously.

Travis smiled. The captain and Travis's father had been friends for years, until cholera took the older man. "What do you know about women?"

"No man knows much," the captain said, trying not to smile, glad there was nothing seriously wrong. "I'm sorry I didn't get to meet your bride. I hear she's a beauty."

Studying his cigar, Travis took a moment before answering. "My bride, yes. I'm just having some trouble understanding her." He wasn't a man to share confidences, and this was as much as he could say. Straightening, he changed the subject. "You think that furniture will be safe in the hold?"

"It should be," the captain said. "But what do you need more furniture for? You haven't added a wing to that mansion of yours, have you?"

Travis chuckled. "No, at least not until I have about fifty kids to fill all the rooms I already have. The furniture's for a friend. I did buy some land, though. I'll put in more cotton this year."

"More!" the captain gasped before gesturing toward the deck in front of them. "This is all the space I need. I couldn't keep up with—how many acres of land do you own now?"

"About four thousand, give or take a few."

The captain gave a snort of disbelief. "I hope that little bride of yours is a good housewife. The place took all your mother's talents, and you've nearly doubled it in size since your father died."

"She can handle it," Travis said confidently. "Good night, sir."

In their cabin again, he undressed thoughtfully before climbing into bed and drawing Regan to him. "The question is, can I handle her?" he murmured just before he fell asleep.

It took Regan exactly twenty-four hours to learn that Travis was completely correct about what an awful job it was dealing with seasick people. From early morning until late at night she did little more than wash vomit from people and belongings. The passengers were too sick to hold their heads over the porcelain basins she held toward them and too ill to care what happened to the contents of their stomachs. Mothers lay in their narrow bunks, their babies crying beside them, while Regan and two other women cleaned, tried to comfort, and worked long, hard hours.

As if the seasickness weren't enough, the condition of the passengers' accommodations appalled Regan. There were three dormitories, one for married couples, and two for single men and women, and the discipline enforced by the crew to keep unmarried men and women apart was strict. Sisters were not allowed to speak to brothers, or fathers to daughters, and each worried about the other in these first few days of illness and misery.

In each dormitory were many narrow rows of hard, small bunkbeds. In the close aisles were the passengers' belongings: trunks, boxes, parcels, baskets, containing not only clothes and what goods they needed for the New World but also the food for the voyage. Already some of it was beginning to decay, the smell aggravating the passengers' nausea.

Regan and the other women ran in and out of the women's cabin, trying to get over the trunks, having to walk up and down, over and around for every step they had to take.

By the time she returned to her own cabin, which by contrast looked like a room in a palace, she was more exhausted than she'd ever imagined she could be.

Travis put down his book immediately and gathered her into his arms. "Was it difficult, love?" he whispered.

She could only nod against his chest, so glad to be near someone healthy and strong, glad to be away from the squalor and poverty she'd seen today.

Relaxing against him, half-asleep, she was hardly aware when he put her in a chair and went to answer the door. Even when she heard water splashing, she didn't bother to open her eyes. After all, she'd heard little else all day when she'd washed clothes, babies' diapers, and dirty chamber pots.

Smiling deliciously, she relaxed as Travis's hands began to unbutton her dress. It was nice to be taken care of instead of the other way around. When he gathered her naked form in his arms, she was pleased to be going to bed, but when her bottom hit the hot water, her eyes flew open.

"You need a bath, my smelly little mate," he laughed at her surprise.

The hot water, even if it was sea water, felt wonderful, and she leaned back, letting Travis wash her.

"I don't understand you," she said softly, watching him, feeling his hands, soapy and strong, run over her body.

"What's to understand? I'll tell you what you want to know."

89

"A few weeks ago I would have said a man who kidnapped people was evil and should be put in jail, but you. . . ."

"I what? I kidnap pretty young ladies, ravish them, yet I don't beat them? Not too often anyway," he smiled.

"No," she said seriously. "You don't, but I believe you're capable of anything. I don't understand a man like you."

"And what kind of man do you understand? Your little Wainwright? Tell me, how many men have you gotten to know? How many times have you been in love?"

He wasn't prepared for her answer.

"One man," she said quietly. "I've been in love once, and I can't imagine it ever happening again."

Travis studied her expression for a moment, the way her eyes softened with a faraway look, the gentle way her mouth curved up at the corners.

One moment Regan was thinking of Farrell, how he'd asked her to marry him, and the next she was sputtering as Travis tossed the soap into the water in front of her eyes.

"Finish it yourself, or wait for your lover to come and do it," he growled before slamming from the cabin.

Smiling, feeling she'd at last made him jealous, she left the tub and began to dry herself. She thought that perhaps it was good for Travis to realize that he wasn't the only person in her life, that maybe other people existed in the world. When she got to America and they parted ways, perhaps he'd not be so sure she couldn't make it on her own, maybe even find a man like Farrell, someone who would love her and not think she was an ignorant child.

Climbing into bed, she suddenly felt very lonely. Farrell didn't love her; he'd wanted her for her money. Her uncle didn't want her either, and Travis, this strange, arrogant, kind man, made it clear he only wanted her for the moment. Alone, tired, hungry, miserable, she began to cry.

When Travis pulled her into his arms, she clutched at him, scared that he'd leave her too. "Hush, sweet, be quiet. You're safe now," he whispered, trying to soothe her, but when her lips fastened to his, he no longer thought of comfort.

She had no idea if it was being close to the illness all day or her thoughts of being alone, but she was ravenous for Travis. She didn't think about the fact that she was a prisoner or that she should at least be a reluctant lover. Her only thought was that she needed him desperately, needed for him to hold her, to love her, to make her feel as if she were part of the world and not a useless, unneeded appendage.

Boldly, she put her fingers into his shirt opening, sending a button flying across the room. The hair on his chest was so masculine, reminding her of his maleness. Her fingertips explored, not gently but firmly, roughly even, rubbing the texture of his skin, feeling it grow hot beneath her touch.

Tossing her to the bed, he pulled back to remove the rest of his clothes. His eyes were ablaze, his mouth full and hot. As he turned to sit on the edge of the bed to pull off his boots, Regan was left with his broad, muscular back to her mercies. Her teeth nipped his shoulders while the tips of her breasts lightly and electrifyingly grazed across his spine. Lips soon followed down the deep curve of the bone, kissing, caressing, tasting his flesh. Thumbs digging into his sides, fingertips on his ribs, she stroked the back of him with the front of her. The deep indentations of muscle, his strength, now so quiet under her touch, were heady, making her surge with her own sense of power.

She kissed his earlobe, nipping it sharply, then gave a low, purring laugh. In one swift movement, Travis turned, pulled her into his arms, and was on top of her. She was as eager as he was and more than ready for him.

Travis was blinded by her forwardness, for once not holding back in consideration of her delicate sensibilities. He treated her with all the fire and passion he felt, thrusting hard, massaging her buttocks with his hands, holding her closer and closer.

When at last their release came in a tempest of rapture, they slowly, slowly began to give way to a mass of exhausted, shaking, weak flesh.

"What have you done to me?" Travis gasped, holding her so close he threatened to smother her.

Regan only clutched at him, too tired to think. As she easily fell into a deep sleep, she was unaware of Travis leaning over her, watching her, touching her hair, pulling the sheet a little closer about her. But even in her sleep, she was aware of his arms around her, of his rugged body near her, of the sweetness of his warm breath on her ear. Stirring, she opened her eyes, gave him a sleepy smile, gladly accepted his soft kiss, and then smiled again as he lay his head beside hers and she felt his body relax into sleep.

The next day was a repeat of the same hard, smelly work of helping seasick passengers. In the late afternoon, Travis told her to go to their cabin and rest or she wouldn't be any good for anyone. His tone of voice, always ordering her around, caused her to tell him just what she thought of him.

"You could be helping instead of merely lounging about the deck," she snapped.

"Lounging, am I?" Travis smiled, that half-smile, half-smirk of his that infuriated her.

For the first time she noticed his dress of soiled, sweaty cotton shirt and loose britches reaching to his knees, tucked into soft leather boots. A wide black-leather belt circled his trim waist. Suddenly, several questions were answered for Regan, such as how Travis could afford a private room. In payment, he obviously had to work for his passage.

"How can I help?" he asked. "Although, if you expect me to wipe dirty mouths, I won't."

If Travis had to work for his passage, so did she, and the idea of rest wasn't possible. "This morning two of the upper bunks collapsed. I've talked to the crew, but they just laughed at me."

"They probably laughed because they don't know which end of a hammer is which. What else?"

"We need someone to take care of the older children. I thought maybe you could find Sarah Trumbull. I haven't seen her for days."

"Sarah's busy," he said succinctly, "but maybe I can help with the other problems."

A great burden left Regan's small shoulders because she knew that Travis would keep his word.

"Keep looking at me like that, and I'll build separate houses for each passenger right here on deck."

Giggling and feeling much better, she went back to her duties.

In a very short time, Travis appeared at the door of the women's cabin with carpentry tools in a box. Some of the women squealed in protest because they were in various states of undress, but it didn't take Travis long to make them feel comfortable. He laughed with the women and told them the men were all dying for them to come on deck and make the voyage less tedious. In spite of what he'd said to Regan, he held one woman's head over a bowl and tenderly wiped her mouth. He diapered two babies and rearranged several heavy trunks so there was more walking room, all while he repaired the broken bunks, checked the others, and reinforced several more.

When he left, most of the women were smiling, and it felt as if fresh air had just blown through the stuffy, stinking dormitory.

"Oh my," sighed one woman whose baby Travis had changed. "Who was that glorious man?"

"He's mine!" Regan said, so loudly and with such a challenge in her voice that the women laughed, making Regan blush.

"You don't have to be embarrassed, honey. Just thank the Lord every night for being so good to you."

"Maybe she has other things on her mind at night," someone else said loudly.

Regan was almost grateful when one of the women began to groan and she could run away and escape the women's teasing. But even as she held a pan for the woman, she began to feel angry. He was flirting with all the women, right in front of her! No doubt he liked having all the women drool over him, liked being the only man allowed into the single women's cabins. Allowed! Surely Travis Stanford never did anything so common as ask permission for anything he wanted to do.

Slamming down a pitcher of water, Regan seemed to grow angrier by the moment. Of course, he had no reason to treat her as a lady since all he knew of her was in bed. The big, crude American had no idea how to treat a woman except as something for his own use. To him all women were the same—whether they were sick in bed or dressed in a gown of satin, he seemed to think they were all made for his pleasure.

Near sunset, she went on deck to wash the earthenware basins. There, surrounded by children, were Travis and two sailors showing the boys and girls how to tie knots. One girl, about twelve, seemed to be knotting a piece of fabric while a two-year-old sat on Travis's lap, absorbed in the intricacies of the puzzle of rope Travis was creating. He smiled and waved at Regan before returning to the children.

Haughtily, she put her nose in the air and returned below to the stifling cabin, gritting her teeth against the fact that even the children found him irresistible. She'd told the women he was hers, but she was fully aware that she had no power over him, that she was his captive plaything, and that when they reached America he would dispose of her quickly and no doubt pick up another woman—one not so used. With suspicious eyes, she began to look at each one of the women in the big cabin, wondering if one of them would be her successor.

By the time she was ready to leave the dormitory, she was very angry. Her uncle had said she was mealy-mouthed, an embarrassment to him, but many things had happened to her in the last few weeks, and she was changing.

The cabin she shared with Travis was empty when she reached it, but as she stood watching the stars through the big window, the door opened.

A pewter mug sailing directly toward Travis's head made him duck quickly. "What the—?" he began.

Regan grabbed another mug from a wall cabinet. "You enjoyed flirting, didn't you?" she accused. "You liked having all the women fawn over you. 'Oh what a darling man,' they all drooled." The second mug grazed his shoulder.

As she grabbed the third one, Travis crossed the room and held her hand. Again, that half-amused little smile was on his face. "Don't let your temper get the best of you. Please try to remember that you were once an English lady."

His patronizing tone, added to the fact that he was the one who'd made her fall from being a lady, sent blind rage coursing through her veins. "I am sick of you!" she gasped as she slammed her elbows back into his ribs.

She got some satisfaction from his grunt, but before he could recover she kicked him in the shins.

As he backed away from her, rubbing his shins, his expression was one of bewilderment. "Wouldn't you like to talk about this? What's got you so riled?"

"Riled?" she mocked in her crisp accent. "I am angry because of the way you assume that you have the first right of everything in the world. Did you enjoy the way the women looked at you with great adoring eyes? It was disgusting that you used the babies to get to the women. Are you planning to kidnap one of them when you're through with me?"

"I might," Travis said, his jaw set, a tiny spark of fire in his eyes. "At least one of them might be more grateful for what you have. Why don't you ask who'd like to trade places with you?"

"You are the most vain, arrogant animal ever created!" she seethed. "Did it ever occur to you that I might not want to be held prisoner or that other women might not either? Am I supposed to be grateful that you hold me against my will, drag me onto a ship that's sailing for a country I despise, and threaten to tell everyone our true relationship if I do not remain with you?"

"I told you why I couldn't release you in England." His

voice was quite low. "I've shown you every kindness, given you every stitch on your back, yet you're still too much of a romantic to see the truth. Can't you remember what it was like on the docks when those men came after you?"

It was too much like the things her uncle had said. Someone was always taking care of her, always throwing it into her face. "I'm not grateful," she said quietly. "And I do not want anything more from you. You needn't worry that I'll be attacked on board ship, so I'll leave you now and begin my stay with the single women." Looking down at the simple muslin dress that Sarah had just finished for her last night, she said, "When I get to America I will try to earn enough money to repay you for this dress. Perhaps you can sell the others."

Turning, her chin up, back straight, she started for the door.

It took Travis a moment to realize that she meant to leave him, and she was just stubborn enough to do it. Without thinking what he was doing, he grabbed the back of her dress. With Regan going one way and Travis pulling the other, the thin muslin quickly split from top to bottom, landing in a small heap at Regan's feet.

Instantly, his look changed from anger to desire, his eyes raking her hungrily, feasting on her heaving breasts well exposed above the low-cut chemise.

"No," she whispered, trying with all her might to pull away from his mesmerizing gaze.

His arm, strong and powerful, went around her waist, pulling her to him, bending her backward into an arc.

Weakly, she fought against him, wanting so much to defy

him, to prove to him that she was her own person, but his touch, his lips on hers, drove her senseless.

"You'll do what I say, love," Travis growled, lifting her off the floor, his lips nuzzling her neck. "You're mine for as long as I want you."

Closing her eyes, leaning her head back, giving her body completely to his touch, she had no idea of escaping this man who controlled her so easily. When she heard the sound of tearing cloth, and felt her chemise give, she began to struggle once again.

"Mine," Travis whispered. "I found you, and you're mine."

There was no time for her to think as Travis pushed her back against the wall, her small body pinned there by the strength and size of him.

His kisses became ravenous, as if he meant to devour her. Her own breath was coming faster and faster as her hands clutched at his shoulders, fingertips digging into his flesh through his shirt, trying to pull him close enough to crush her.

One of Travis's hands lustfully traveled down her bare hip, stroked her thigh, and lifted her leg so that it rested on his hip. Eagerly, Regan grasped his body with her legs, her ankles hooked behind him, her weight supported by him as he stroked and caressed her bottom.

His hands moved excitingly, teasingly, driving her to a passionate frenzy. When his clothes fell from the lower half of his body, she didn't know. Only when he lifted her, his hands about her waist, and set her down on his manhood did her eyes open, but only for an instant.

She was completely in his power, unable to move on her own, her back to the wall, her legs clutching his hips, as he began to lift her, to control her movements, guiding her. Feeling his body against her, the undulations of his hips under her thighs, the driving force of him threatened to drive her insane. Clutching his hair in her fingers, she pulled as Travis leaned harder into her, threatening to break her, to merge his flesh with hers, to consume her. With his might he easily picked her up and lowered her, again and again, faster and faster, until she screamed under the pressure of her sweet torment. Crushingly, Travis's mouth came down on hers as he collapsed against her, her legs like a steel vice about him, her body shuddering, weak and helpless, sated, exhausted.

Gradually, she began to become aware of where she was and who she was, her body pliant, boneless against Travis's proud muscularity. He was kissing her damp neck lovingly, his arms under her bottom, supporting her. Carrying her like a child, he took her to the bed and laid her down as if she were the most precious, most delicate substance ever created.

Tiredly, as if he too had no bones left, he removed his shirt and lay beside her. "No supper tonight either," he murmured, but there did not seem to be any regret in his voice. With his last bit of strength, he pulled Regan to him, their skin sticking together from their mutual sweatiness.

"How could I ever let you leave me?" he whispered before they both fell asleep.

Chapter 8

IN THE MORNING, REGAN COULD HARDLY MEET TRAVIS'S eyes. The way he looked at her—so smug, so sure of himself—made her want to toss a knife at him. He seemed to think he knew everything about her, that he had complete control over her, that he merely had to crook his finger and she belonged to him.

How very much she'd like to wipe that expression off his face; just once she'd like to see him not get what he thought was his.

As they were eating, Sarah Trumbull gave a quick knock at the door before entering. "Oh! Excuse me," she said. "Usually the two of you are gone by this time."

"Have some breakfast, Sarah," Travis said, smiling smugly, and looking at Regan as if he understood exactly why she was avoiding his eyes.

But Sarah was more interested in a torn piece of muslin that yesterday had been a dress she had just made the day before. Chuckling, giving Travis a mock look of reprimand, she said, "Travis, if you're going to treat all my handiwork like this, there's no need for me to keep on sewing."

Running his hand through his hair, glancing quickly at Regan's averted face, he laughed. "I'll try to control myself. Now I need to help on deck. The captain is a bit short-handed this trip. Although," he grinned, "I may not have much energy left." He kissed Regan's cool cheek before he left the cabin.

A sigh to rival a hurricane escaped Sarah as she gazed longingly at the closed door. "If there were any more men like him, I might be tempted to get married."

If Regan had known any foul words, she would have used them. "Don't you have work to do?" she snapped.

Regan's tone didn't phase Sarah. "I'd be jealous too if he were mine."

"He isn't—!" she began hostilely, then stopped. "Travis Stanford belongs to no one," she said at last, before beginning to clear the breakfast dishes and put them on a tray.

Sarah decided to change the subject. "Do you know that man in the cabin across from yours?"

"David Wainwright? We met, but that's all. Is he all right?"

"I don't know, but I've been in your cabin for two days now, sewing on your new clothes, and I've never heard a sound from him. I thought perhaps he was helping with the men who are ill."

Frowning, Regan decided to investigate, excused herself to Sarah, and left the cabin. Even though she worked in the stench every day, the smell that hit her when she opened David's cabin was overpowering. The heavy darkness of the room caused her to pause for quite some time on the threshold, her eyes searching for Mr. Wainwright.

Finally, in what looked like a heap of filthy rags, she found him huddled on the window seat, his body shivering. Crossing to him, she saw immediately that he had a fever, that his eyes burned dangerously bright, and, by the tone of his ramblings, that he was delirious.

A noise at the door caused her to turn to see Sarah looking at the room in horror. "How could anyone live in this?"

"Would you tell Travis to send down some hot water, please?" Regan said firmly. "Tell him to send a great deal of it—and I'll need washing rags and soap, too."

"Of course," Sarah said quietly, not envying Regan the task she had ahead of her.

Sunlight filtered through the windows in David Wainwright's cabin, touching on Regan's hair, showing the golden strands intermingled with the darkness. More sun glistened on her soft, sweet-scented muslin gown, highlighting each of the minute, embroidered golden rosebuds. A book was held lightly by her, and as she read from it her words were as soft as the picture she presented.

David lay back against freshly laundered cushions, propped on the end of the window seat, his arm in a sling, his snowy shirt open at the throat. It had been a month since that time Regan had found him alone and ill in his cabin. At the first movement of the ship, he'd become seasick and returned to his cabin. Hours later, he'd fallen from his bunk-bed and landed in such a way that he'd broken his forearm. In pain, nauseated, weak, helpless, he was unable to call for help. In an attempt to return to his bunk, he fell again, and with the new pain he lost consciousness. When Regan found him he had no idea who or where he was, and for days after the bone was set no one was quite convinced he'd live through the ordeal.

And through everything, Regan had never left his side. She scoured the filthy cabin, washed David, sat by him, coaxed him into eating a broth made from salt beef, and, by sheer will-power, kept his spirits up. He was not a good patient. He was sure that he was going to die, that he'd never see England again, that America and Americans were going to be responsible for his death. He spent hours telling Regan how he'd had a premonition that these were going to be his last few days on earth.

For Regan, she was glad of an excuse to get away from Travis's overpowering presence, glad for once in her life to be needed by someone, not to feel as if she were a burden.

"Please, Regan," David said petulantly. "Don't read anymore. I do wish you'd just talk to me." He shifted his injured arm with a great show of distress.

"What would you like to talk about? We seem to have exhausted every topic."

"Every topic about my life, you mean. I still know exactly nothing about you. Who were your parents, where did you live in Liverpool, and how did you meet that American?"

Putting the book down, she rose. "Perhaps we should go for a walk on deck. It's a lovely day, and the exercise will do us both good."

Smiling slightly, David put his feet on the floor, waiting patiently for Regan to help him stand. "My mystery lady," he said, his voice betraying that he rather liked not knowing much about her.

On deck, her arm around David's waist and his about her

shoulders, the first person they met was Travis. Regan couldn't help but notice the contrast, the slim blond young man in his immaculate clothes next to Travis's brawniness, and his clothes smelling of male sweat and the salty air.

"A bit of an airing today?" Travis asked politely, but lifting one eyebrow and giving a mocking grin to Regan.

David nodded curtly, almost rudely, before half jerking Regan forward. "How could you marry someone like that?" he said when they were alone. "You are the gentlest, tenderest woman, and when I think of you having to endure the attentions of that insensitive, oversized Colonial, I am nearly made ill again."

"He is not insensitive!" she said quickly. "Travis is. . . ."

"Is what?" he said with great patience.

There was no answer to that question. Moving away from David, leaning over the rail and watching the water, she asked herself what Travis did mean to her. At night he made her cry in delight, and the way he always had a tubful of hot water ready for her in the evenings convinced her of his kindness. Yet she was always aware that she was his prisoner.

"Regan," David said. "You aren't answering my questions. Don't you feel well? Perhaps you're tired. I know taking care of me isn't the easiest task in the world. Maybe you'd rather. . . ."

"No," she smiled at the familiar complaints. "You know I enjoy your company. Shall we sit here a while?"

Staying with David the rest of the afternoon, she found she couldn't keep her mind on what he was saying. Instead, she kept watching Travis as he agilely climbed the rigging tied along the mast, as he threw great heavy rope into an orderly pile. Several times he stopped and winked at her, always aware of when she was watching him.

That night, for the first time in weeks, she returned to her own cabin ahead of Travis. When he entered, his face was lit, his eyes smiling with happiness.

It seemed he'd grown more handsome in the last few weeks, his face tanned by the sun, his muscles even harder than before.

"You're a welcome sight after a hard day. You think I could have a kiss of greeting, or did you give them all to young Wainwright?"

Her happiness faded. "Am I supposed to take that insult without a word? Just because you force me into an indecent relationship doesn't mean another man can—or even attempts to, for that matter."

Turning away from her, Travis removed his shirt and began to wash. "It's nice to know the pup hasn't tried to take what's mine. Not that he could, of course, but I like to be reassured."

"You are insufferable! And I am not yours!"

Travis merely grinned confidently. "Shall I prove to you that you belong to me?"

"I do not belong to you," she said, backing away from him. "I can take care of myself."

"Mmm," Travis smiled, coming to stand near her. Sensuously, he began to run his finger down her arm, and when her steady gaze flickered he narrowed his eyes. "Can that boy make you shiver with only one finger?"

She jerked away from him. "David is a gentleman. We talk of music and books, things you know nothing of. His family is one of the oldest in England, and I enjoy his company." She straightened her shoulders. "And I will not allow your jealousy to ruin my friendship with him."

"Jealousy?" Travis laughed. "If I were going to be jealous of someone, it would certainly be someone with more than that whining boy." His face turned serious. "But I believe the boy is getting serious about you, and I think you should stop seeing so much of him."

"Stop—!" she sputtered. "Is there no part of my life you don't attempt to control?" She calmed herself. "I am a free woman, and when I get to America I plan to take advantage of my freedom. I'm sure David is the type of man who'd want to get married and not try to make a . . . a slave of a woman."

Calmly, Travis put his hand on her shoulder. "Would you really like to trade me for a boy and a gold ring?"

As he bent to kiss her, she pulled away. "Perhaps I'd like to try," she whispered. "Surely men can't be so different. If David loved me, perhaps we could be compatible in the marriage bed."

Travis's hands on her shoulders were brutal. "If that boy ever touches you, I'll break every bone in his body—and I'll make you watch while I do it." He gave her a sharp push before he slammed out of the cabin.

That night Regan spent alone. She refused to admit to herself how much she missed him, how alone she felt without his arms around her. All night she tossed and turned, trying not to cry, attempting not to be afraid.

In the morning there were circles under her eyes, and Sarah, for once, didn't ask questions. The two women sat quietly in the cabin and sewed. Near sunset, David knocked on the door and asked if Regan would walk with him.

On deck, all she seemed to see was Travis, yet Travis never looked at her.

His ignoring of her made her angry, and as a result she turned all her attentions to David, who was complaining about the length of the voyage and the food. At her look, suddenly turned from disinterest to adoration, he stopped speaking and looked at her.

"You are especially lovely today," he whispered. "The sunlight makes your hair a red-gold."

Just then Travis was passing them, a massive piece of canvas thrown across his shoulder.

"Oh thank you, David," she said, much too loudly. "You make a woman feel like a queen with your fine compliments. I don't know when I've been so flattered."

If he heard, Travis made no sign as he continued past her, his movements not even slowed.

Again that night she was alone in the cabin. She wanted so much to show Travis that it didn't matter to her that he had abandoned her. She wanted to prove to him that she could do something on her own. So, as the days progressed, she flirted more and more openly with David, always when Travis was near.

On the evening of the third night, as David escorted her to her cabin, instead of his friendly goodnight he grabbed her, fiercely pulling her into his arms. "Regan," he whispered, his lips on her ear. "You must know that I love you. I've loved you from the first, yet every night I must lie alone in my cabin while that . . . that animal has the right to touch you. Regan, my dearest, tell me that you feel the same way about me."

With surprise, she found that his kisses and his arms

around her repulsed her. Pushing against him, she tried to free herself. "I'm a married woman," she gasped.

"Married to a man who isn't worthy to kiss the hem of your gown. We'll keep quiet about our love until we dock, and then we'll have your marriage dissolved. You can't think to spend all your life with that poverty-eaten sailor. Come with me, and I will build you a house like that backward country has never seen before."

"David!" she said, pushing in earnest. "Release me this moment!"

"No, my love. If you don't have the courage to leave him, I will tell him myself."

"No! Please, no!" Suddenly she knew that Travis had been right. She didn't want David, and in the last few days she'd been using him to make Travis jealous.

David's fingers turned her face to him, and he planted hot, damp kisses on her face, suffocating kisses, as she twisted her body in an attempt to get away from him.

One moment David was holding her, and the next he seemed to be flying through the air. In astonished disbelief, she watched as Travis's fist smashed into David's face, just before the small man slammed against the wall. As he slid unconscious to the floor, Travis raised his fist again.

With one leap, Regan grabbed Travis's arm, holding on to it, her feet above the ground. "No!" she shouted. "You'll kill him."

The face Travis turned to her was a distortion of his usual countenance. His eyes were hot, black with fury, his mouth grim with his anger. In fear she stepped back from him.

"Did you get what you wanted?" he growled, his heavy brows coming together in a black scowl. Without another word, he turned and left the passageway to return to the deck.

Shaking, Regan looked at David as he was beginning to rouse, blood gushing from his nose. Her first impulse was to help him, but when she saw that he was trying to stand and knew he was all right, she fled to her own cabin. Once inside, she leaned against the door, her heart pounding and tears beginning to roll down her cheeks. Travis had been right! She had used David, toyed with his affections, almost promised what she never meant to give, all in an attempt to make Travis jealous. But Travis could not be made jealous—she was merely a possession to him.

Flinging herself onto the bed, she began to cry in earnest, deeply and sincerely.

Hours later, her head feeling stuffed, her eyes raw, having cried herself to sleep, she was awakened by the violent tossing of the ship. As she lay quietly, trying to understand what was going on, a sudden lurch sent her sprawling out of the bunk and onto the hard floor, where she lay stunned. The cabin door opened, flung back against the wall as the ship plummeted in another direction.

Travis stood in the doorway, wearing a heavy oilcloth slicker, his hair wild and wet. His legs spread as he walked toward her, rolling with the tumbling of the ship. He picked her up in his arms.

"Are you hurt?" he shouted, and until then she hadn't been aware of the tremendous noise about them.

"What's wrong? Are we sinking?" She snuggled against him, so very glad to touch him once again.

"It's only a storm," he shouted down at her. "There shouldn't be much danger since we've been preparing for it for days. I want you to stay here, do you understand? I don't want you to take it into your head to go on deck or to the other passengers. Do I make myself clear?''

She nodded against his shoulder, clinging to him, thinking that perhaps the reason for his absence for the last few days was his preparation for the storm.

Bending, he lowered her to the bed, gave her a look she couldn't fathom, and then kissed her, possessively and forcibly. "Stay here," he repeated, touching the corner of one of her swollen, red eyes.

With that he was gone, and Regan was left alone in the dark cabin. She was much more aware of the rolling of the ship after Travis left. To keep from being thrown from the bunk, she grabbed the sides as best she could. Water seeped in under the door, coating the cabin floor.

Even as she struggled to keep her balance, she began to imagine what was happening on deck. If the water was coming into her cabin, it must be washing over the sides of the ship. Her imagination, always active, began to conjure a picture of horror. Once, when Regan was hardly more than a child, a scullery maid of her uncle's had received a letter saying that her young husband had been washed overboard during a storm, and later a friend of his had come to tell her the full, gruesome story. Every member of the staff, as well as Regan, had gathered around the sailor and heard every gory detail.

Now the story did not seem like a story because above her head were actual waves as tall as a house, waves of such force that they could take a dozen men with them when they returned to sea.

And Travis was up there!

The thought rang through her head. Of course, Travis would never believe he could come to harm. No doubt he was sure even the sea would obey his commands. And it wasn't as if he were a real sailor either. He was just a farmer who'd been on a whaler as a boy, and now he had to work to pay his passage.

An especially violent toss of the ship sent Regan flying out of the bunk again. Travis! she thought, struggling to stand. Perhaps that was the wave that tore him from the decks.

A massive sound of cracking wood above her head sent her eyes upward. The ship was breaking apart! With both hands on the bunk edge, she managed to stand, and she started the long passage toward her trunk, which was fortunately bolted to the floor. First she had to find a cloak, and then she had to somehow make her way on deck. Someone had to save Travis from himself, had to persuade him to return to the comparative safety of the cabin, and if he wouldn't, someone had to watch out for him. If he were washed overboard, she planned to throw him a rope.

Chapter 9

NO STORY EVER TOLD COULD HAVE PREPARED REGAN FOR the blast of wind and sharp salt air that tore into her body as she opened the door under the quarterdeck. It took all her strength to push the door open wide enough to allow her onto the deck, and it slammed hard behind her. A wave of salt spray soaked her immediately, making her wool cape cling heavily to her slight frame.

Bracing herself against the stair railing, using her strength to keep upright, she blinked against the cold, piercing water that seemed to want to drill holes into her and tried to see if she could find Travis. At first she couldn't distinguish men from the parts of the ship, but her interest in the safety of Travis was stronger than the pain caused by the violence around her.

Gradually, her eyes adjusted, and, blinking rapidly to clear the water away, she made out the shadowy figures of men in the midst of the long, wide deck. Before she could make a decision about how to get to that part of the ship, a sudden lurch sent her sprawling, and, like a piece of driftwood, she was knocked down and rolled across the deck. As her body slammed into the side of the ship, she grabbed what was nearest to her—the wooden support of an iron cannon.

When the wave was past, she began to pull herself upright again, and as she did she heard the cracking sound again; only this time she could tell that it was coming from overhead. One of the masts must be breaking. Starting slowly, taking each step by inches, she began to move toward the men and the breaking mast.

Every crewman and, she was happy to see, Travis also, was holding on to a part of the ship and looking up at the splintering wood.

"Get up there, I say!" the captain bellowed, his voice even louder than the fury of the sea.

Wiping her eyes with the back of her hand, Regan could see the sailors take a step backward, and it took her a moment to realize that the captain was ordering someone to climb the rigging. She had half a mind to tell him what she thought of his request, but of course she must keep quiet and not let Travis know she was there.

But one quick look at Travis, and she saw that he'd already seen her and was making his way toward her. The look of rage on his face put the sea to shame, and without thinking Regan started back toward the door under the quarterdeck; her courage had quite suddenly vanished.

Travis's big hand caught her shoulder before she'd gone two steps. He didn't say a word, and since everything was written on his face, he didn't need to.

As the ship lurched and another wave threatened to capsize them, Travis flung his body over hers, pinning her against the railing, holding her securely with his superior strength.

"I may beat you for this," he shouted into her ear when at last the ship righted itself.

But their attention was caught by another, louder, shout from the captain. "Isn't there a man among you?"

It was at that moment, with Travis holding her arm in a painful grip, that Regan saw David and knew immediately that he'd followed her onto the deck. Even in the dim light, through the pounding spray, she could see the bruises on his face where Travis had hit him. Her eyes locked and held with his for a moment, and a wave of guilt passed through her because she saw that he knew she'd used him, that he knew he'd made a fool of himself.

A smaller wave washed across them and broke their eye contact, and when it receded she saw that David had moved forward—but he wasn't looking at her. Walking as straight as he could under the circumstances, he went toward the captain.

Stopping just opposite Travis, he shouted, "I'm a man. I'll climb the rigging."

"No!" Regan screamed, clutching at Travis's arm. "Stop him!"

David held onto the fife rail at the base of the mast and turned his head to Travis. Travis, seeming to understand David's silent plea, nodded once before clasping Regan's hands in his and stilling her.

Regan struggled against Travis, wanting to go to David, to stop him, knowing that what he wanted to do, this attempt at what amounted to suicide, was her fault.

When she saw that there was nothing she could do, she

became very still, like the crew. Travis braced himself between the rail and a cannon carriage, holding Regan tightly, but his eyes never wavered from David's slight form.

The captain, glad to finally find someone brave enough to climb the rigging, was shouting instructions to David while wrapping rope about his waist. From gestures and the few words that could be heard, it was clear that David was to climb the swinging rope rigging to the first and longest yardarm, crawl along its narrow width about halfway until he was suspended over the turbulent water, and bind the splitting yardarm.

Regan could only gasp in disbelief, too astonished even to make a further protest. She knew for sure that she was watching a man go to his death. With fear, she buried her face against Travis, but he pulled her head around and made her look at David, who was poised at the base of the mast, waiting only for Regan to give him a parting glance.

Lifting her hand toward him before dropping it helplessly at her side, she stood straight, her back against Travis's chest, and watched as he grimly started the climb.

His ineptitude was immediately apparent as his feet slipped, quite often losing their grip so that he held on by only one hand. The wind tore at him, pulling his hands away, knocking the rope from under his feet.

Regan put her hand to her mouth and sank her teeth into her own flesh as she watched.

Slowly, with great difficulty at every step, David finally reached the yardarm. Hanging on to it with both his arms, seeming to pause for a moment's rest or perhaps waiting until the next great wave passed, he hesitated. When the water cleared, and the people on deck saw that he was still there, they gave a united gasp of relief.

As the ship righted itself again, David inched forward on the yardarm. A foot before he reached the break, he unwound some of the rope about his waist and put one end into his mouth.

"Look out!" came a shout from near Regan.

But David could not hear the warning as another big wave separated him from the people below.

On deck, the crashing of the wave was mixed with another sound—that of splintering wood. Holding her breath, seeming to wait an eternity before the water cleared, Regan stared fearfully up at the yardarm where David hung so tenaciously. When she could see at last, she smiled because the yardarm was still intact.

But her smile quickly receded when she saw what had broken. Above David's head was the maintop, a large platform where the men kept vigil. This platform had broken away on one side, part of it just over David's head, and from the way he lay without moving, it seemed to have hit him.

Regan clutched Travis to her, her hands holding tightly as she watched David's small, motionless figure high over her head.

She had no idea that Travis was watching her, studying the fear on her face. She was aware of nothing until Travis pushed her away from him, wedged her body onto the deck, and clasped her hands about the heavy, anchored cannon. "Stay!" he commanded, before grabbing rope tied to the fife rail and wrapping it about his waist.

Terror of a new kind surged through Regan, a terror so great that no words would come out of her mouth, and her arms clutching the cold cannon were white with strain.

Scarcely daring to breathe, she watched Travis ascend the rigging, his feet and hands much more sure than David's, agile in spite of the size of him, or perhaps his strength was needed to hold him against the raging storm.

Each time a wave came over her and cut Travis from her view, Regan felt that she died a little bit. By the time he reached the yardarm, her body was as rigid as the iron of the cannon she gripped.

Cautiously, Travis crawled along the yardarm, straddling David when he reached him, leaning over, obviously shouting to the young man, but the fierce wind took the words away.

When David lifted himself and looked up at Travis, several of the sailors shouted encouragement. But Regan felt no relief whatsoever.

Travis and David seemed to talk for quite some time before Travis began moving forward, giving everyone more to fear as he passed David on the narrow projectile. Deftly and quickly, Travis lashed the splintering yardarm together, wrapping it tightly with the rope he carried. Twice he had to stop and cling to the pole as a wave threatened to pull him into the sea.

When he finished, he backed toward David, David handed him the rope from his waist, and Travis tied one end about his own waist. Now they were joined together for whatever fate awaited them in the long descent to the deck.

More talking was done as Travis seemed to be trying to persuade David to move from the piece of wood he held in a strangling grip.

Regan's heart almost stopped beating as she saw Travis pull on the rope, encouraging David to back toward the main mast. It was as if Travis had all the time in the world as he patiently waited for David to begin to move.

Slowly, each muscle at a time, David started backing up,

and Travis guided the young man's feet onto the rope rigging. As if he were a child, Travis helped David, placed his hands and feet in the proper places, and once flung his arms across David, holding them both to the unsteady and flimsy rigging. When the wave passed, they started down again.

Regan began to breathe a bit when they were about twenty feet above the deck. She saw Travis shout at David, saw the young man shake his head, and heard Travis shout again until David nodded his head in agreement. David began to descend alone, Travis holding the rope about his waist, tying one end to the rigging.

Rising from her squatting position, Regan saw that Travis was making sure David was safe, that he was securely fastened so that if the next wave carried Travis over, he would go alone.

Guessing that as Travis glanced out to sea he saw something that the people below couldn't see, she watched, tears coursing down her face. Travis wrapped the rope around his powerful forearm; then, entangling his other arm in the rigging, he kicked out at David, whose head was now even with Travis's feet. David, unsteady and terrified, immediately lost his grip on the rigging, and his slight body swung away, falling for a few precious seconds before the slack was taken up in the hold Travis had on the rope about David's waist.

A high scream of terror escaped David before Travis began to lower him, and the sailors caught him, quickly pulling him to the deck.

But Regan's eyes never left Travis, who, as soon as he saw David was safe, dropped the rope and grabbed the rigging, ducking his head as if in protection. She left the cannon with one swift step, and that was as far as she got before the biggest wave of all hit them. The deck was flooded with cold, salty water, and in protest the ship threatened to turn over.

Regan slammed into the deck, rolled across it, and hit the fife railing with a bone-jarring jolt. Yet, in spite of her pain, all she was aware of was that above her she heard another horrible sound of wood cracking.

In spite of the angle of the deck and the rushing water, she grabbed the railing and tried to pull herself upward. A man's scream and a fleeting glimpse of a body sailing over her head and going past the deck rail did not deter her from her course. It was difficult to breathe, much less see, as she struggled to look up at the rigging where Travis hung.

Had she not been looking so hard, she would not have seen the blurry image of Travis as his hands lost their grip and he began to fall. His foot was caught in the rigging, and this saved him as he appeared to struggle for his senses and find the rope he needed to hold him fast.

The aftershocks of the big wave tossed the big ship like a child's top as Regan clung and prayed and watched Travis struggling to hang on. She could see that something was wrong with him, that he was fighting more than the sea.

With one arm hooked about the rail, she wrenched a piece of rope as big around as her arm from the pins and then inched toward the bottom of the rigging.

All around her, men were shouting, and the wind and water played tricks with sounds, but Regan only saw Travis as he painfully lowered himself. Still holding on as best she could, she climbed up the rigging until she was able to touch Travis's foot.

Scared but knowing there was no other way, she wrapped the rope around his ankle and the rigging. The rope was too long and too big for her to knot properly, so all she did was wrap it, hoping she'd have time before the next wave came.

She was unprepared for the slash of a wave while hanging above the deck on just a bit of rope. She tangled her body in the rope and hung on for dear life.

After this wave, she was too frightened to move, and with her hand clasping the end of the big rope attached to Travis's ankle, she was afraid to open her eyes. She'd done all she could to save him, and now she couldn't bear to look to see if he was there or not.

It seemed to her a long time that she hung there, half-sitting, half-suspended, before she heard shouts below. Still afraid to open her eyes, she kept them wrenched shut.

"Travis!" came the clear call from below her, actually seeming quite near.

"Mrs. Stanford," called a voice that could only be the captain's.

With trepidation, she opened her eyes, still afraid to look to her left where Travis might or might not be.

Later, no one could remember who was the first to start laughing. Perhaps it wasn't a laughing matter, but the sailors were so relieved to have finally left the storm behind them, the last two waves having knocked the ship out of its path, that the sight above them was hugely entertaining.

Regan, ten feet above deck, was practically sitting in the rigging, clad only in a very wet muslin dress, her bare legs through the knotted rope squares wrapped tightly, hugging her own body, as were her arms. In one hand was an enormous rope attached to the leg of Travis, a man twice her size, who now lounged in the rigging as if he were sleeping. For all the world she looked like a little girl leading some sort of strange animal.

"Stop your yammering and get them down!" the captain bellowed.

Encouraged by their laughter, Regan dared to look toward Travis, and at this close range she could see the blood seeping at the side of his head.

When three of the sailors had climbed to her and saw Travis's condition, they no longer laughed.

"You saved his life," one of them said, awe in his voice. "He's not even aware we're here. He couldn't have hung on without you tyin' him."

"Is he all right?"

"He's breathin'," the sailor said, but would say no more.

"No," she said when he touched her. "Get Travis down first."

Now that the seriousness of what Regan had done reached them, the sailors glanced up at her in amazement for a moment before turning away and respectfully not looking openly at her fine, bare legs.

With some dignity, Regan was able to descend the rigging with the help of a sailor. She was startled at how high up she'd gone and at the difficulty she had in getting down.

Finally on a solid surface again, she followed the men carrying Travis to their cabin. As they passed David's cabin, one of the men murmured that the young gentleman was sleeping. Regan only nodded as her thoughts were completely with Travis.

The ship's doctor came to Travis quickly and examined his head wound. "The maintop must have hit him when it broke away." The doctor turned appraising eyes toward Regan. "I hear you kept him from being washed overboard."

"Will he be all right?" she asked, not caring about his praise.

"No one can tell with these head wounds. Sometimes they live, but their minds never work again. All you can do is try to get him to drink water and stay quiet. I'm sorry I can't be of more help than that."

Regan only nodded as she smoothed Travis's wet hair from his forehead. The ship was still rolling frantically but seemed calm after the last several hours. Turning, she asked one of the sailors still in the room to get her some fresh water.

When she was alone with Travis, she started to work, undressing him first, which was no easy task considering the weight of Travis's inert body. Wrapping his naked body in dry, warm blankets that she got from a trunk, she stopped to answer a knock at the door.

Sarah Trumbull stood there. "One of the sailors came to get me, told me some wild story about you tying Travis to the sail. The man said Travis was hurt and you might need help. And he sent this."

Regan took the water she offered. "I don't need help," she said, her voice tight. "Maybe you can help the other passengers." She gave a brief nod toward David's closed door.

Sarah had only to look at the fear apparent on Regan's face to know that something was dreadfully wrong. "You have the prayers of everyone on board," she whispered, giving Regan's hand a quick squeeze.

Alone again with Travis, she began to bathe his head. The cut wasn't long, but it seemed to have been a hard knock as Travis was completely unconscious. Once he was clean and warm and he still didn't move, she stretched out on the bed beside him and cradled him in her arms, hoping to bring him back to life by sheer force of will.

Hours later she awoke, having fallen asleep from exhaustion, and her teeth were chattering with cold. She'd been unaware that she still wore her wet clothes. Travis lay still, deathlike, his skin pale, his vitality gone.

Rising quietly, she peeled away her sodden, cold dress and noticed absently that somewhere she'd lost her new wool cape and that the muslin gown was torn in several places. Poor Travis, she thought with a smile. He was going to have to buy her a new wardrobe before the first one was even finished.

The thought sent her hand to her mouth and tears to her eyes. Perhaps Travis wouldn't live to see her new clothes; perhaps he'd never wake up from his death-sleep. And all because of her! If she hadn't flirted with David, the young man wouldn't have felt compelled to show Travis that he was indeed a man. If only . . . she thought again but made herself stop.

Going to the chest, she pulled out a dress of heavy maroon corded silk, piped about the waist, neck, and cuffs with pink satin. Once dressed, she went to Travis again, bathing his cool face and washing the cut on his head which still seeped blood.

At midnight he began to move and thrash about on the bed, and Regan tried hard to restrain his flailing arms to keep him from hurting himself. Her strength was no match for his, so all she could do was throw herself on top of him, using her body weight to hold him.

By morning he grew tired again and seemed to fall asleep, although for the most part he kept his eyes closed. As the sun was entering through the window, Regan sat on the edge of the bed, her head on Travis's shoulder, and fell into a deep sleep.

What woke her was Travis's hand stroking her hair gently, calmly touching her hair and her neck. Instantly, she was fully awake, her head coming up to look at him and see if there was some lucidity in his gaze.

"Why are you dressed?" he asked hoarsely, as if that were the most important thing in the world.

She had no idea how rigidly she'd been holding her body for the last several hours, but now so much tension left her all at once that she was shaking, trembling. Great fat tears rushed to her eyes and glided down her cheeks. Not only was Travis going to get well, but his mind was unharmed.

He put a finger to her cheek, touched a tear. "The last thing I heard was the maintop breaking away. Did it hit me in the head?"

All she could do was nod, and the tears came harder. "Was that yesterday or the day before?"

"Before," she mouthed, the lump in her throat so large she couldn't speak.

Travis began to smile, winced once with pain, and then the smile returned. "So those tears are for me?"

Again, all she could do was nod.

His eyes closing once again, he kept smiling. "It was worth a little bump on the head to see my girl shed tears for me," he whispered before falling asleep.

Regan put her head back down on his chest and gave herself over to tears. She cried for all her fear at seeing Travis climbing after David, at having gone after Travis herself, and for the last several hours when she hadn't known whether he was going to live or die.

Travis was a wonderful patient, so wonderful in fact that Regan was exhausted within forty-eight hours. He took to being spoiled and pampered more easily than a new colt takes to walking. He wanted every meal spoon-fed to him by Regan, constantly needed her help in dressing, and wanted a sponge bath twice a day. Every time Regan suggested he try walking in order to regain his strength, Travis suddenly developed an even more severe headache than the one that plagued him constantly and needed Regan to run cool cloths over his forehead.

On the fourth day, when Regan was about to tell Travis she wished he had been washed overboard, she answered the door to find David Wainwright standing there.

"May I come in?" His arm was still bandaged, and there was a fading greenish bruise on his jaw.

With more strength than he'd shown in days, Travis sat up in bed. "Of course you can come in. Have a seat."

"No," David said quietly, not looking directly at Regan. "I came to thank you for saving my life."

Travis studied the young man for a moment. "I only did it out of shame because you made the rest of us look like cowards."

David's eyes widened, and he was well aware of the way he'd been paralyzed atop the yardarm and how Travis, patient even in the midst of the storm, had gotten him down to safety. Yet he also saw that Travis had no intention of repeating the story to anyone. David's shoulders straightened a little, and he gave a faint smile. "Thank you," he said, his eyes telling more than his words. Quickly, he left the cabin.

"How kind of you," Regan said, bending and kissing Travis's cheek.

His arm flew out and caught her about the waist. "Your aim's off," he growled, pulling her across him and kissing her on the mouth.

Regan's arms went around his neck, responding to him fully, her body well aware of the many days since she'd touched him in any way except an impersonal one. Pulling away from him, as his teeth gently chewed on her lower lip, she gave a deep chuckle. "An hour ago you were too weak to get out of bed."

"I still don't want to get out of bed, but it has nothing to do with weakness," he said, his hand at the back of her dress.

Instantly, she jumped out of bed. "Travis Stanford, if you tear another one of my lovely dresses, I'll never speak to you again."

"I don't care if you do speak to me," he said as he threw back the covers and showed her that he was more than ready for her.

"Oh my," she breathed, her hand unbuttoning buttons faster than anyone's hands ever had before or since.

Gleefully, naked, she sprung into bed with him, running her legs up and down his body, her face buried in the soft skin of his neck. She had waited quite a long time for him to return to her bed, and she was as ready as he was. Yet, when she tried to pull him on top of her, he wouldn't budge.

"No, my little nurse," he chuckled, and put his hands about her waist, lifting her like a doll and setting her on top of his manhood.

Gasping in surprise, it took Regan a moment to recover from her first sense of shock, but as Travis pushed her forward and took her breast in his mouth, her surprise gave way to delight. His hands ran up and down her back as his mouth teased the front of her. Never had she felt so many sensual areas touched at once. His strong hands moved back to her waist and lifted her, slowly, before setting her back down.

Regan did not think twice before she caught the rhythm herself. Her strong legs, muscled from walking about the constantly moving ship, moved her body up and down. She soon learned that she liked controlling the rhythm, fast or slow, bending to rub her breasts across Travis's chest, leaning over him, watching his handsome face turn to an angelic expression.

But her interest in watching him faded quickly, and as her passion mounted she began to move faster and faster. Travis grabbed her in a hard clasp and, never leaving her, rolled her onto her back, where he thrust hard and deep until the wave of release and delight swept over both of them.

Weak, he collapsed on top of her, his body coated in sweat, every muscle relaxed. Under him, Regan smiled and hugged him close. It added to her pleasure to have control over him, to be able to take someone as strong as Travis and turn him into this pliable, calm man atop her.

Still smiling, she fell asleep.

Chapter 10

REGAN LAY BACK AGAINST THE CUSHIONS ON THE NARROW bunkbed, weak and trembling, while Travis pressed a cold cloth to her forehead. Looking up at him in gratitude, she smiled as best she could. "What a time to get seasick," she murmured.

Travis said nothing as he picked up the chamber pot containing the contents of Regan's stomach and went out on deck to empty it.

Regan was quiet, too weak to move as she lay there in the bed. Personally, she felt that this new sickness had something to do with what was going on in her mind. Of course she couldn't mention it to Travis, but she was quite scared of arriving in America, of being on her own in a strange country with people whose language she sometimes had to strain to understand.

It had been nearly a month since the storm, and since then she'd done little except help Sarah sew on her new clothes.

There were no more flirtations with David Wainwright, no more attempts to make Travis jealous. Instead she'd spent her time with Travis, eating with him, making love with him, and talking to him. She found he was a wonderful storyteller, entertaining her with long narratives about his friends in Virginia. There were Clay and Nicole Armstrong, of whom Travis told an extraordinary story of how Clay had been married to one woman, a French aristocrat, and engaged to another woman. The way Travis told the story made Regan laugh until she cried, especially at the antics of Clay's niece and nephew.

He told her about his little brother, Wesley, and it took Regan days to figure out that Wes was a young man and not a child. Silently, she offered a prayer of support for any person who had to live under Travis's thumb. Then there were the Backes and all the other people up and down the river.

Regan listened with interest, adding to his stories with her imagination. Picturing these people, she conjured small, crude houses; the women in their simple calico gowns, even smoking corncob pipes; the men plain farmers hard at work in the fields. Smiling confidently, she hoped the people would not treat her as royalty merely because of the beautiful, expensive clothes she wore.

All of Travis's stories, and her own fantasies added to them, had made the long journey fly past, and it wasn't until this week that she'd begun to worry. She didn't know if the worry caused her vomiting or the other way around. All she knew was that suddenly she'd become very ill and weak, lying on the bunk, idly watching the ceiling, her stomach rolling.

Travis had been wonderful since she'd become ill, watching her quietly, holding her head over the pot, washing her face, and seeing that she rested. He'd even stopped working with the crew, not leaving her alone for more than a few minutes.

And Regan knew that all his attention was a way of saying goodbye to her. The pretty clothes and the last-minute attention were his final reward for the pleasure she'd given him on the voyage to America. Now he could be free of her, go back to his family and friends, and never have to see her again. No more would he have to put up with her flirting with other men, or her uselessness.

Tears began to trickle down her face. Why couldn't he have left her in England where at least she knew the customs of the people? Why did he have to force her to come to this strange place and then abandon her like so much rubbish?

She planned to tell him what she thought of him, but as soon as Travis returned to the cabin her stomach started heaving again, and her anger was abandoned.

"We've just sighted land," Travis said, holding her in his arms, her head cradled against his warm, comforting chest. "By this time tomorrow we should be docked in Virginia Harbor."

"Good," she whispered. "Perhaps I won't be seasick once we're on land."

This statement seemed to amuse Travis, who hugged her quickly and stroked her hair. "I think your seasickness will be over very soon."

The next few hours were a frenzy of activity. Sarah put the last of Regan's new clothes in the trunk, and Travis paid her and the other women who'd helped with the sewing. There were tears shed as Sarah and Regan said goodbye. Sarah planned to stay on the ship and travel north to New York to be with her family. All of the many women whose heads Regan had held got together and presented her with a gift of a child-sized quilt done in the Rose of Sharon pattern.

"We figured you'd need it soon," one woman said, her eyes teasing and glancing up at Travis.

"Thank you so much," Regan said, pleased more than the women could know, there being no way of telling them that they were her first friends.

That night she lay awake in Travis's arms, looking at him in the moonlight. She wished he hadn't come to mean so much to her, that she could hate him as she had once done or even find him contemptible, but now all she felt was an overwhelming loneliness that she was losing so much—this big, overpowering man whom she'd come to depend on, as well as other women who considered her a friend, who didn't think she was useless.

By the next morning she was deathly quiet. Doing her best to smile, she stood on the quarterdeck and waved goodbye to her friends, all of them glad to be off the ship, excited about coming home or entering a new land.

Travis had left her alone while he ordered the unloading of goods. When she'd awakened this morning, after sleeping very late, she'd found the ship already docked and some people already disembarked. After a quick kiss, Travis said he'd be busy until afternoon, explaining that the storm had blown them closer to America, and since they were several days earlier than expected no one was there to meet them.

Them! Regan thought with disgust as she watched Travis ordering some sailors in the stacking of crates.

"Mrs. Stanford?"

Turning toward the timid voice, she saw David Wainwright behind her. He looked thinner than she remembered, and his eyes darted to gaze at a space somewhere to the left of her head.

"I want to wish you and your husband the best of everything," he said quietly.

"Thank you," she said. His face showed all of the fear she felt, and she only hoped hers didn't look the same. "I hope we both like America more than we thought we would."

He wouldn't take her hint at the conversations they'd once shared; his embarrassment was too deep. "Tell your husband. . . ." He didn't seem able to finish but grabbed her hand, placed a hard kiss on it, met her eyes for a moment, gasped "Goodbye," and then was gone, hurrying down the gangplank.

Warmed by David's sentiments, she leaned over the rail and saw Travis frowning up at her. Raising her hand, she waved gaily at him and thought for the first time that perhaps she could make it alone in this new country. After all, she'd made friends on board ship. Perhaps. . . .

Travis gave her no more time to think, because minutes later he was telling her to hurry up and eat, to wear something sturdy, to finish putting her clothes in the trunk—in general, running her life.

He couldn't wait to get rid of her, she thought, obeying him but with a slowness Travis found maddening.

"Either you finish that in two minutes or I carry you out of here," he warned. "I have a wagon waiting for us, and I'd like to get there before sundown."

Her curiosity won out over her resentment. "Where are we going? Did . . . did you find me employment?"

Pausing, the trunk across his back, Travis grinned at her.

"I found you a great job! One you're especially good at. Now, come on, let's go."

Using all her strength, Regan tried not to let his words upset her but followed him down the gangplank, her head held high.

He tossed the trunk into the ugliest, most dilapidated vehicle she'd ever seen.

"Sorry," he laughed at her obvious disgust. "I told you we were early, and this was all I could get. We're driving to a friend of mine's tonight, and tomorrow I'll borrow a sloop."

Nothing Travis said made sense to Regan. She knew a sloop was some sort of ship but didn't have any idea why Travis would want to borrow one. Grabbing her waist and plunking her down on the half-rotten wagon seat with as much ceremony as he'd used with the trunk, he climbed up beside her and clucked for the two tired-looking horses to go.

The country they traveled through looked wilder, more forbidding than England, and the road was atrocious, really little more than a rutted path. As her jarring teeth attested, Travis hit all of the ruts.

Chuckling, he watched her. "Now you see why we travel mostly by water. Tomorrow we'll be in a smooth little sloop, with no holes to fall into."

She had no idea where she'd be tomorrow as Travis seemed to want to keep her employer a secret—and she wasn't about to ask him for details, not when she knew her questions would earn that infuriating look of his.

The sun was just setting when they stopped at the first house they saw—a neat, clean, whitewashed little clapboard. Early spring flowers graced the front path, a warm breeze gently bending the colorful petals. It was a plain house but certainly of a higher caliber than Regan had expected in America.

Travis's knock was answered by a plump, gray-haired woman wearing a calico apron over her muslin dress. "Travis," she said. "We thought something was wrong. The man you sent said you'd be here hours earlier."

"Hello, Martha," he said, kissing her cheek. "It just took us longer than I thought. The Judge here?"

Martha laughed. "You're as impatient as ever. I take it this is the young lady."

Possessively, Travis put his arm around Regan. "This is Regan, and this is Martha."

Gulping once at Travis's crude manners, Regan held out her hand. "I am happy to meet you, Mrs.—?"

"Just Martha," she smiled. "You're in America now. Come into the parlor. The Judge is waiting for you."

Swept forward by Travis's arm around her, Regan was propelled into a pleasant room with clean, well-worn furniture covered in a soft green, the windows draped in a fabric of the same color. Before she could say any more, she was introduced to the Judge, a tall, nearly bald man who seemed to have no name besides Judge.

One moment Regan was shaking hands, and the next she heard the words, "Dearly Beloved, we are gathered here today in the sight of our Lord. . . ." Bewildered, thinking her hearing was faulty, she looked at the people around her. Martha was smiling angelically at her husband, who had a book open in front of him and was reading a marriage ceremony. Travis, holding her hand, had an astonishingly solemn look on his face.

It took Regan several minutes to realize what was going

on. Without having been asked if she agreed, she was being married to Travis Stanford! She was standing in front of these strangers, wearing a dark green traveling dress of heavy linen, her face dirty, tired, her brow creased with worry about her future—and she was going through a marriage ceremony! Glancing up at Travis's solemn profile, she thought that for once he'd gone too far. When she got married, she was going to be asked, and she was going to wear her prettiest dress.

She realized that everyone was watching her. The Judge smiled and said, "Regan, wilt thou take this man for your husband?"

Looking up at Travis with the sweetest, most lovesick smile she could muster, she whispered, "No."

It was a moment before anyone reacted. Martha gave out a giggle that showed she knew Travis's domineering ways well, while the Judge hurriedly looked at his book. His face aflame with anger, Travis grabbed Regan's upper arm and half dragged her into the entrance hall, closing the parlor door behind him.

"Just what the hell was that little display supposed to mean?" he growled, his face very near hers.

Involuntarily taking a step backward, Regan tried to keep her courage up. She was in the right, and she had that on her side. "You never even asked me if I wanted to marry you. You didn't ask if I wanted to come to America either. I'm tired of your making all my decisions for me."

"Decisions!" he gasped. "There are no decisions to be made by either one of us. Fate has made them for us."

At her look of consternation, he groaned. "I'd try to shake some sense into you, but I'm afraid it'd hurt the baby."

"Baby?" she whispered.

Closing his eyes for a moment, Travis seemed to be praying for strength. "You can't be so damned starry-eyed that you didn't realize that what we do in bed creates babies." At her silence, he continued in a quieter tone. "You didn't really think you'd been seasick these last few weeks, did you?"

Gently, he caressed her cheek. "Sweetheart, you're carrying my baby, and I make it a rule always to marry the mother of my children."

Stunned, Regan could form no coherent thoughts. "But employment," she whispered. "And I can't get married in this dress, and I have no flowers, and . . . and . . . oh Travis! A baby!"

Gathering her in his arms, he held her tightly. "I thought you knew. I thought you were just trying to keep it from me. I wouldn't have known either, except my friend Clay's wife threw up right in front of me one day. She told me a lot of women did that the first few months. Now, love," he said, lifting her chin. "Will you marry me?"

When she hesitated, he continued. "You can do all the work you want at my place," he smiled, "so you can satisfy any need you have to earn your keep. And as for your dress, I like you better wearing nothing, so whatever dress you wear is fine, and, besides, it's only Martha and the Judge here. For flowers I could pick some from Martha's garden."

"No," she whispered, blinking back tears. His words were so logical. Of course she was going to have a baby, and of course she'd marry him; there wasn't much else she could do because she knew she couldn't escape Travis when she had something he owned. As for her clothes, what did they matter? If she could get married without love, she could certainly do so without a pretty dress.

"I'm ready," she said grimly.

"It's not an execution," he chuckled. "Maybe tonight I can make up for today."

As she walked ahead of him into the parlor, she knew he'd never understand. A wedding was supposed to be a woman's greatest moment, a time when she felt everyone loved her and wished her great happiness. For the rest of her life she'd remember this secretive, dreary little ceremony, surrounded by strangers, the marriage taking place not because of herself but because of what she carried in her stomach. Mechanically, at the proper time, she said she would take Travis for her husband and ignored the searching look he gave her. When it came time for him to place a ring on her finger, Martha offered her own, but Regan shrugged and said politely that a ring didn't matter.

By the end of the ceremony no one was smiling, and when Travis turned to kiss her, Regan offered him her cheek. She barely tasted the wine the Judge offered and made no comment when Travis said they must leave.

Trying her best to smile, Regan bid them farewell and thanked them as Travis helped her back onto the wagon seat. The tension of the day, the wedding—if it could be called such—had exhausted her, and as she slumped in the seat Travis pulled her close to him.

"It wasn't much of a wedding, was it?" he asked heavily. "Not something a girl can tell her grandchildren about."

"No," she said simply, not daring to say any more or she'd start crying. All she wanted now was to go to sleep, and perhaps tomorrow she could think happy thoughts about her baby and about being Travis's wife.

By the time the wagon stopped, she was almost asleep, barely waking when Travis lifted her down and carried her up some stairs.

"Are we home?" she murmured.

"Not yet." His voice was serious, without its usual hint of laughter. "We're at an inn. In the morning we'll start home."

She merely nodded and snuggled against him. At least this was her wedding night. If Travis didn't know how a wedding should be conducted, at least he knew how to make the night the best a woman could imagine.

Lying on the bed where he'd left her, she listened as he carried their trunks up the stairs. Perhaps it wouldn't be so bad being married to Travis; at least now she didn't have to worry about being abandoned.

Smiling, she felt his warm lips on her cheek. "I'll be back in a little while," he murmured, sending little shivers down her spine. "You rest, because you're going to need it."

As the door closed behind him, she stretched, put her hands behind her head, and looked up at the ceiling, but she didn't really see it. Tonight was her wedding night. Last year one of the kitchen maids had gotten married, and the next day everyone teased her mercilessly, but the girl had been so radiant that nothing anyone said bothered her. Now Regan understood why.

Suddenly, she sat up. She may be expecting his baby and far from being a virgin, but tonight she certainly felt like one. With one adoring look directed toward the closed door, she thought how kind it was of Travis to give her this time alone to prepare herself. Hot water waited for her on the old dresser at the corner of the small room, and she guessed he must have sent someone ahead to prepare for them. He'd even left the keys to the trunks on the dresser.

Hurriedly, because she knew Travis would be an impatient bridegroom and wouldn't stay away very long, she opened her trunk and began to rummage through the beautiful clothes she and Sarah had sewed. Toward the bottom was a gown of gossamer silk with a bit of silver sheen to the surface. It was translucent, allowing just a hint of her hand beneath it to show through, revealing yet secretive. She'd been saving this lovely bit of moonlit silk for just such a time as this.

Quickly, she unbuttoned her linen dress, not dwelling on the fact that this traveling dress had been her wedding gown. At least she'd be able to wear something elegant for her wedding night. Naked, she began to wash, laughing all the while. Then she slipped into the gown, shivering in delight as the silk touched her skin. The feel of it was heavenly, soft, caressing, clinging to her curves in just the right places. Moving to the mirror, she was a bit startled to see the way her breasts impudently lifted the lovely fabric, the rosy crests barely visible yet somehow emphasized. Oh yes, she thought. Travis would love this gown.

Out of the trunk came the silver-backed hairbrush Travis had given her, and she pulled the pins from her hair, allowing it to cascade down her back, wispy curls about her face. She was glad she'd never cut her hair short as so many women had since the revolution in France. After only a few quick strokes of the brush, she hurried to the bed, knowing she'd taken long enough, feeling just as impatient as Travis must be.

Once in bed, she arranged herself in what she hoped was a seductive pose, half-reclining against the pillows, one arm extended, the other with fingertips grazing her shoulder. With what she hoped was a sophisticated look, she gazed languidly toward the door.

It was late and the inn was quiet, yet every time a board so much as creaked, she found herself smiling, imagining the look Travis would have when he came through the door. Each time she thought of him she arched her back a little more, thrusting her chest forward. She kept remembering how Farrell had said he dreaded the wedding night with her, that she'd probably cry and pout like a two-year-old. Tonight, although of course Farrell would never know about it, she'd prove him wrong. Tonight she'd be a temptress, a seductress, a woman who knew what she wanted—and got it. Travis would be on his knees, trembling like a bit of calves'-foot jelly, and she'd be his master.

Perhaps it was the awkward position of her back arched so far forward that first caused her pain; then she realized her arms ached and one side of her hip was asleep. Moving a bit, lowering her arm to her lap, she began to return from her dream world. She was a master at being able to escape from reality for long periods of time, and now she wondered how long she'd been in this position.

Glancing about the room, she saw there was no clock, and neither was there any moon outside the window—and the candle by the bed, which had been new, was inches shorter.

Where was Travis? she wondered, throwing back the covers and going to the window. Surely he couldn't believe she needed this much time to get ready for him. A bolt of lightning flashed and for an instant illuminated the empty courtyard below. Within minutes a soft rain began to fall, and Regan shivered as cold air came in through the poorly fitting window.

Getting back into the warmth of the bed, she looked about her, idly thinking that this room was very much like the one where Travis had held her prisoner in England. Then she'd been his slave, and now she was his wife. Of course, she had no ring, and the paper the Judge had signed was with Travis, but, she thought smiling, she had Travis's child and he'd certainly come back for that.

The thought that he might not come back made her frown. Why had she even let such an absurd idea cross her mind? Travis was an honorable man, and he'd married her.

Honorable, she murmured. Did honorable men kidnap women and take them to America against their will? He'd given her reasons for his forcing her to accompany him, but maybe all he'd really wanted was someone to warm his bed on the long voyage across the sea. And she'd certainly done that! They'd nearly set the bed on fire, and now she carried the product of that fire with her.

The rain started falling more heavily, lashing against the dark window, and with it Regan's despair began.

Travis had never wanted her. He'd said so himself a hundred times. Even once they were on board the ship, he'd still been trying to find out who she was so he could rid himself of her. He was the same as Farrell and her Uncle Jonathan—they'd never wanted her either.

The tears began to fall down her cheeks on a par with the turbulent rain outside. Why did he marry her? Had Travis somehow found out about her inheritance? He'd taken her to America, married her immediately, and now that he had that piece of paper and could claim her money he wanted nothing more to do with her. He'd abandoned her in a strange country with no money, no help, and maybe a baby to care for.

She began to cry furiously, fists beating into the pillow,

sobs tearing through her. When her first passion was gone, the tears became slower, flowing out of her quietly as her anger turned to hopelessness as she asked herself why she was so unworthy of love.

The rain outside turned to a hard, steady downpour, and, after hours, her grief began to be lulled by the sound as she fell into a deep, deathlike sleep. When the first heavy steps sounded on the stairs she did not hear them, and it was only the pounding on the door that was finally able to wake her.

Chapter 11

"OPEN THIS DAMNED DOOR!" BELLOWED A VOICE THAT could only belong to Travis. Obviously he was unconcerned about waking the other occupants of the inn.

Her head feeling as heavy as a piece of granite, Regan tried to sit up, staring through her swollen eyes at the door that threatened to break under Travis's pounding.

"Regan!" Another shout came that sent her flying to the door.

Turning the knob, she said dazedly, "It's locked."

"The key's on the dresser," Travis replied, his voice heavy with disgust.

The door was barely open before Travis burst into the room—but Regan could hardly see him, for he was buried behind the most flowers she'd ever seen in her life. As an amateur gardener, she recognized many of them—tulips, daffodils, hyacinths, irises, violets, three colors of lilacs, poppies, laurel, and beautiful, perfect roses. There was no order to the flowers as they trailed behind Travis, hung down in front of him, some tied together in bundles, some loose and falling, a few covered in mud, others beaten by the rain. Even as he stood there, they fell about him like a colorful riot of lovely raindrops.

Going forward, scattering more flowers, walking on some, he tossed the whole mass on the bed and exposed himself as a man covered in mud—and his face showed his anger.

"Damned things!" he said, pulling a bunch of violets from his shirt collar and throwing them onto the bed. "I never thought I could hate flowers, but tonight I may change my mind." As he removed his hat, water poured onto the floor. Disgustedly, he pulled three dwarf irises off his hat and tossed them with the others.

So far he had barely glanced at Regan, and his anger was so great that he didn't even notice her sheer gown or the way the early sunlight made her body glow beneath the gossamer silk.

Heavily, he sat down in a chair and started to remove his boots, but first he lifted himself and with a grimace removed a thorny rose from beneath him.

"All I planned was a simple trip north," he said as he pulled a boot off, pouring water out of it. "I have a friend who has a glasshouse, and he only lives five miles north of here. And of course a bride should have flowers, so I thought I'd just get you some."

Still, he didn't look up as he began removing his soaked, filthy coat. A flood of flowers fell from inside his jacket; crushed, falling apart, they cascaded to the floor.

Travis ignored them with a determined aloofness. "I was halfway there when it started to rain," he continued his

146

story. "But I kept on, and when I got there my friend and his wife got out of bed and personally cut the flowers for me. They cleaned out the garden and the glasshouse."

His shirt, soaked to his skin, came off next, and more flowers drifted to the already considerable pile at his bare feet.

"It was on the way back that the trouble started. The damned horse threw a shoe, and I had to walk in that strip of mud Virginia calls a road. I couldn't stop and have a new shoe fitted and miss my own wedding night."

Fascinated, Regan could only watch him, her heart beginning to heal with every word he spoke.

"Then lightning flashed, and the horse reared and knocked me in the mud. If that animal lives two more days, it won't be because I allow it," he threatened. "I would have let it go, but the damned flowers were on the saddle, so I had to spend two hours in the storm looking for that animal, and when I found it the saddle was gone."

Angrily, he stripped off his pants. "Another hour went by before I found the saddle and all these . . . these. . . ." he said, pulling what was left of a peony from his pants and giving a crooked smile as he slowly crushed it before letting it drop. "The bags were broken, and there was no way to carry them, so I started stuffing them wherever I could." His eyes locked with hers for the first time. "There I was, a grown man, standing in the middle of one of the worst storms of the year, filling my clothes with these thorny, itchy, smelly flowers. Do you know how much a fool I felt like, and what the hell are you crying about?" he said in the same breath and tone.

Picking up a slightly damaged and very wet rose from the

bed, she held it to her nose. "A bride should have flowers," she whispered. "You did this for me."

Bewilderment and exasperation showed on Travis's wet face. "Why else would I go out on a night like this, on my own wedding night, for God's sake, unless it was for my bride?"

Regan couldn't answer, just kept her head down, tears beginning to flow.

After a moment's silent thought, Travis came to her, lifted her chin in his hand, and studied her face. "You've been crying a lot," he said quietly. "You didn't think I was coming back, did you?"

Jerking away from him, she walked to the head of the bed. "No, of course not. It's just—"

A soft chuckle from Travis made her turn. He was naked, standing like some god of old in a wealth of fragrant flowers, and she began to smile too. He had returned to her, and he'd gone to a great deal of trouble to give her what she wanted.

Travis's eyes, looking at her in the sheer gown, turned hot with desire. "Don't I get a reward for all my work?" he whispered, opening his arms to her.

With one giant leap, Regan flew at him, her arms going about his neck, her legs around his waist.

Surprised for a moment, Travis caught her. "How could you think I'd leave you after all the trouble I've gone through to get you?" he murmured before fastening his lips to hers.

The feel of his bare skin, cool and damp between her legs, made her shiver with pleasure as she tightened her legs about his middle until she threatened to sever him in half. Only the thin bit of silk between them kept their skin apart as she rubbed against him, her breasts nearly crushed by the hard mass of his chest.

Her hands went to his hair, pulling on the wet thickness of it, her fingers disappearing into it as her lips made a hot trail across his mouth. He was here; he'd come back to her, and he was her husband, hers to do with as she wanted.

In glee, feeling powerful, she bit his earlobe much too hard.

Within an instant she found herself pulled from Travis and being flung through the air, landing in an explosion of flowers of hundreds of shades and hues and a swirl of delicate silk. Brushing four daffodils off her face, she smiled up at Travis as he stood over her, hands on hips, muscles bulging, manhood towering.

"Now that's the way a bride should look."

"Stop talking and come here," she laughed, holding her arms up to him.

But instead of going to her, he knelt and kissed her toes, one by one, his tongue teasing the soft pads. His hot mouth moved to the bottoms of her feet, and as he raked his teeth along the arch she jumped as a nerve inside her tightened, jolting her entire body.

Travis laughed, a deep rumbling sound that touched her foot, traveled up her leg, and reverberated in the center of her being.

"Travis," she gasped, lifting herself and reaching for him. Flowers under her crackled and released their heady fragrance. But he ignored her as his lips moved upward to her knees, exploring, kissing, caressing.

Regan, ready for him, actually eager for him, felt she would go insane as he toyed with her senses. His mouth tortured one leg, and as if that weren't enough, his hand, so strong yet so sensitive, caressed the muscles of the other leg until she was weak with helplessness. Yet at the same time she felt like a tigress, wanting to claw and bite, wanting to tear at this man who threatened her sanity.

When he reached the center of her with his hands and lips, she nearly screamed, rolling her head in agony at what he was doing.

"Please, Travis, please," she begged.

Within seconds he came to her, his mouth hard on hers, but no harder than hers as she attempted to devour all of him. When he entered her, she arched high, completely off the bed, supporting him, needing him, using her hips to drive him onward.

His passion was as great as hers and his need as violent. After only a few powerful, deep, filling thrusts, his body jerked, and he clutched her to him in a bone-crushing hug as spasms racked both their bodies.

It was several moments before Regan realized she couldn't breathe, that Travis seemed to be trying to pull her inside him, and that she wanted him to.

As he relaxed his grip but still held her, his face buried in her neck, she opened her eyes and saw a long line of crushed flower petals clinging to his sweaty skin. Turning her head, breathing deeply of the lovely fragrance, she began to laugh as she put out her hand, grabbed some flowers, and playfully tossed them into the air.

One eyebrow lifted, Travis moved to look at her. "And what is so amusing?" he asked.

"Flowers for the bride!" she laughed gaily. "Oh Travis, I meant a bouquet, not a whole garden."

Leaning across her, he grabbed a handful, catching the flowers upside down and sideways, and he held out the funny bouquet. "I'm sure you could find what you wanted in this."

She moved out from under him, rolling in the flowers, tossing clumps into the air, and then began pelting him with them. "She wants flowers," Regan laughed in a mock deep voice. "I'll give her flowers. Oh Travis, everything you do is so . . . so big!" she laughed, trying for the right word. "Everything is so oversized, blown out of proportion, over-powering, domineering." Sitting up, watching him, looking at that magnificent body reclining lazily on a bed of flowers, her heart seemed to turn somersaults.

"Perhaps," she said in a cat-soft voice, "not all of you is overpowering all the time."

After a sharp intake of breath, Travis grabbed her by a handful of silk, but a short, sharp scream from Regan stopped him.

"Don't you tear one more piece of my clothing," she warned, but flung the silk gown off before he could disobey her.

"Orders and taunts," he said, his eyes narrowing as he lifted himself up onto all fours and began to stalk her like some great beast of prey.

With a squeal of delight, Regan backed away from him, bombarding him with flowers as he slowly came toward her. When she was backed against the wall, she threw her hands up in surrender. "Oh, kind sir," she said in mock fear. "Do what you will with me, but do not take my virtue."

Her skin alive, anticipating Travis's delicious pounce, she was startled when he uttered a heartfelt "Damn!"

Turning her head, she saw that he'd sat up, holding his knee. "How can you crawl around on these damned things without injury? Look at that! Have you ever seen a thorn that big?''

Regan burst into laughter so hard her stomach threatened to split. Her knees drawn up, she rolled in laughter.

Pulling the thorn from his knee and angrily tossing it onto the floor, he gave her a nasty glare. "I am glad I afford you some amusement."

"Oh Travis," she cried. "You are so, so romantic."

He stiffened at her sarcasm, his mouth turning into a straight line. "Why the hell did I get you all these goddamn flowers if I wasn't the very soul of romance?" he demanded seriously.

This statement, and especially the way he said it, sent Regan into new spasms of laughter, and it took some minutes before she became aware that she was hurting his feelings. He really had tried, she admitted to herself. It wasn't his fault if he didn't understand that a bunch of violets was often more romantic than enough flowers to fill a wagon. She'd said she wanted flowers, and he had gotten them for her. And neither was it his fault that a thorn in his knee forced him to interrupt a lovely little romantic game.

As he started to leave the bed, she put her hand on his shoulder and swallowed her laughter. "Travis, the flowers are lovely. I really do like them." When he didn't respond and she saw the muscles standing rigid on his neck, she really was sorry that she'd laughed. He'd done what he did to please her, and all she did was laugh.

"I'll wager I can make you stop being angry with me," she whispered, nuzzling his ear, her teeth running along the cartilage edge, her tongue touching the lobe. "Maybe if I kiss your sore knee, it will stop hurting," she murmured, running her lips down his arm.

"It might," Travis said, his voice especially deep. "I'd sure like to try it."

Regan, aware of how he'd tried to please her, wanted to please him. Pushing him gently, she found he was putty in her hands, and the look of wonder and pleasure on his face was intriguing. The strength of him surrendering to her was a powerful feeling.

Beginning at his knee, her lips traveled upward, her hands trailing behind, massaging his leg, glorying in the great muscle there. When she reached the center of him, Travis groaned, whispering her name. With one fluid motion he pulled her up in the bed, his eyes black and hot as he roughly threw her down beside him and mounted her in moments. He was not his usual, calm self, but a man driven beyond endurance with his blinding lust.

His violent need of her was exciting, especially because she knew she'd driven him to it. Lifting her body under him as if she were a rag doll, he thrust hard and long, pulling her, pushing her—owning her.

When at last the fury died in one massive flash, Regan was limp, weak from the raw tempest of their wild, savage lovemaking. Exhausted, they fell asleep in each other's arms.

"Get up!" Travis commanded, slapping her firm, lovely buttocks. "If we don't get started, we'll never make it to Clay's house, and if you think I'm going to spend a night on that little sloop with you, you're wrong."

Having no idea what he was talking about, she didn't make a comment but pushed her hair out of her eyes and pulled a tulip petal from where it was stuck to her cheek. "Why wouldn't you spend the night on a ship with me?"

she asked idly, sitting up, feeling dazed and drained—but happy.

"It's not a ship," he answered, "but a tiny little boat, and we'd probably sink it with your acrobatics."

"My—?" she began, trying to look haughty, but sitting naked in the midst of the large pile of crushed flowers, her cheeks pink, her eyes liquid and lazy, she couldn't look like more than a tempting little wood-sprite.

Travis, his cheeks covered with shaving soap, looked at her in the mirror, and his glance made her smile and start to lean back on the bed. "Oh, no you don't," he cautioned, immediately changing his look to a threatening one. "If you don't get out of that bed this minute, I'll see that we have separate bedrooms at my house."

That absurd threat made her laugh, but just the same she got up and began to wash. She felt so good that she couldn't seem to do anything in a hurry, yet Travis wouldn't help her get dressed but stood to one side impatiently waiting for her.

When at last she was ready to leave, he half-pushed her down the stairs and to a chair where an enormous American meal awaited her. Travis set to the food like a starving man, grumbling that he never got regular meals anymore and that she was wearing him out in the prime of life, but his eyes danced with merriment.

In very short order their trunks were stowed on the little boat, they were heading up the James River toward Travis's home, and Regan began bombarding him with questions. Before, she had fought so hard against going to America that she hadn't thought much about where Travis lived.

"Is your farm very large? Do you plow the fields yourself, or do you have employees? Is your house as nice as where the Judge and Martha live?"

Looking at her in bewilderment for a moment, Travis began to smile. "My . . . ah . . . farm is a good size, and I do have a few employees, but I sometimes plow my own fields. And I believe my house is rather nice, but then maybe that's because it's mine."

"And you built it with your own hands," she said dreamily, trailing her hand in the water. Perhaps in a simple country like this, her lack of experience in household management wouldn't be so devastating. Farrell had said he knew she couldn't manage his estate, and she was sure he was right. But with a little place like Travis's, maybe a one- or two-room house, she could manage.

The increasing warmth of the sun and the pleasant thoughts soon made her drop off to sleep.

Quite a while later, she woke with a start as a shot rang out over her head. Practically falling into the water, she jumped and saw Travis holding a smoking pistol pointed toward the sky.

"Did I wake you?" he asked.

From the excitement on his face, she knew something was about to happen and didn't answer his silly question. Stretching her cramped body, she looked around as Travis reloaded the pistol, but all she saw was the river and the lush greenery on each side.

"We're near Clay's place," he said as he fired into the air again.

After a glance at the dense trees around them, she wondered how anyone could build a house there, but even as she thought it she saw the trees abruptly stop just ahead on the left.

Protruding into the water was a large wooden wharf with two boats, both bigger than the one they rode in, and as they sailed closer many buildings came into view. There were large and small houses, gardens, fields neatly plowed, workers everywhere, horses, wagons, and in general a great deal of activity.

"Is your house in this town also?" she asked as Travis maneuvered them toward the wharf.

A low chuckle she didn't understand came from Travis. "This isn't a town. It's Clay's plantation."

To her knowledge, she'd never heard the word before. As she opened her mouth to start asking questions, she was interrupted as a squeal of children's laughter took Travis's attention. Quickly, he leaped from the boat and hauled Regan onto the wharf after him, just in time to catch two of the prettiest children she'd ever seen.

"Uncle Travis!" they laughed as he twirled them about. "Did you bring us anything? Uncle Clay was getting worried about you. What's England like? Mama had two babies instead of one, and we have a new litter of puppies."

"Mama, is it?" Travis laughed.

The boy gave his sister a disdainful look. "She means Nicole. Sometimes it's hard to remember that she's not our mother."

Close behind the children came a man, tall and slim, with dark hair and eyes, sharp cheekbones, a look of great happiness on his face. "Where the hell have you been?" the man demanded, holding out his hand to Travis and then hugging him exuberantly.

"I'm weeks early, and you damn well know it!" Travis answered. "No one was there to meet me, and I had to store my goods and borrow this sorry excuse for a boat."

Gesturing offhandedly toward the boat, Travis caused Clay to notice Regan, who was standing quietly on the edge of the wharf. But before the man could ask any questions, Travis gave a long sigh.

"Here's who I wanted to see." Hurrying forward, he caught a deliciously pretty young woman in his arms, kissing her heartily on the mouth. Instantly, the other man's attention left Regan and went to the two of them. He seemed to be working at controlling some inner emotion.

Within moments Travis was leading the woman toward the wharf. "I have someone I want you to meet," he was saying.

At close range the woman was even prettier than from a distance, with a heart-shaped face, big brown eyes, and a sensual mouth. After a quick assessment, Regan saw she was wearing a dress of deep purple muslin, with tiny green ribbons under the high waist. So much for wanting to show the Americans the new fashions! This woman's gown could be worn at court.

"This is my wife Regan," Travis said gently, looking at Regan with pride. "And this is Clayton Armstrong and his wife Nicole. And these scamps," he grinned, "are Clay's niece and nephew, Alex and Mandy."

"How do you do?" Regan said quietly, still puzzled by these people. They were far from her idea of what Americans were like.

"Won't you come to the house?" Nicole said. "You must be tired, and I doubt if Travis has let you rest much."

To that, Travis snorted and Regan held her breath, hoping he wouldn't say something crude.

When Regan merely followed Nicole docilely, Nicole smiled. "It's a bit overwhelming, isn't it?"

Regan was looking about her, trying to understand just what sort of place she was in.

A big, broad, blonde woman came running toward them, her skirts lifted high above her ankles. "Was that Travis what just come in?" she shouted before she even reached them.

"Yes, and this is his wife Regan. Regan, this is Janie Langston."

"Wife?" Janie asked, surprised. "He did do it! That Travis is a wonder. He said he was going to England and bring back a wife. Honey," she said, putting her hand on Regan's arm. "You got your work cut out for you being Mrs. Travis Stanford. I hope you got courage enough to stand up to him."

With that, she started running toward the wharf.

Chapter 12

"WHO ELSE LIVES HERE?" REGAN ASKED NICOLE.

"Quite a few people, really. There are field workers, weavers, the dairy people, gardeners—all the people needed to run a plantation."

"Plantation." Regan whispered the strange word. They were entering a long row of box hedges, and her view of the buildings around them was obscured. "Travis said you were going to have a baby, and the children said something about two babies."

A lovely smile crossed Nicole's face. "Twins seem to run in Clay's family, and four months ago I had a boy and a girl. Come inside, and I'll gladly show them to you."

Looming above them was a large brick house, about the same size as Weston Manor. Regan hoped shock wasn't showing on her face. Of course there were wealthy people in America too, and of course some of them would have mansions. It was just that in England people spoke of America as being so young that there hadn't been time to really build much of anything.

Inside the house, the rooms were startlingly lovely, large, spacious, the furniture upholstered in silk, the wallpaper hand-painted, portraits on the walls. Fresh-cut flowers graced tables and desks.

"Shall we go into the drawing room? I'll bring the children down."

Left alone in this room, Regan was further amazed at the elegance of it. A Sheraton desk with delicate inlay was against one wall, a gold-framed mirror above it. Facing it was a tall cabinet of leather-bound books.

She'd only known Weston Manor, and by comparison the English house was shabby and poor. Here everything sparkled with cleanliness and care. There was no chipped woodwork, worn upholstery, or scuffed surfaces.

Her attention left the room's furnishings when Nicole returned, a baby in each arm. At first Regan was afraid to hold either one of the children, but Nicole persuaded her she could do it. Within moments Regan had the little boy smiling and cooing back at her, hardly noticing when Travis entered and sat beside her on the sofa. They were alone in the room.

"Think we could make two at a time?" he asked quietly, taking the baby's hand and letting him grip his finger.

The expression on Travis's face as he watched the baby was one of joy. "You really want a child, don't you?" she asked.

"For a long time," he said seriously, then added with his usual bluntness, "I never much wanted a wife, but I could surround myself with children."

Frowning, Regan wanted to ask him why he'd saddled

himself with a wife now, but she knew the answer. He wanted the child she carried. Later she would show him that she was of more use than for breeding stock. Together they'd work and build up his farm. Perhaps it would never be as nice as the Armstrong plantation, but someday it could be very comfortable.

"What do you think, Travis?" Clay asked from the doorway, his chest expanded several inches in pride, Mandy by his side, Alex behind him, and the second baby in the crook of his arm. Regan thought he looked as happy as anyone alive.

"Clay," Travis began. "How did those new cows work out? And did you have any mold on last year's hay?"

As the two men seemed to want to talk business and both of them were happy with the babies, Regan handed Travis the baby she held and stood up. Travis showed no qualms about taking the child, unlike Regan who'd been afraid she'd drop him. "I think I'll find Nicole," she said, and Clay gave her directions to the kitchen. Outside the room she heard Clay say, "She's prettier than I ever thought you could get," to which Travis only snorted.

Her head held high, she went through the flower-bedecked hallway and out the back door, turned left, and headed for the kitchen, which was in a separate building. Inside the big room everyone was bustling about, and Nicole, her arms covered in flour, was directing all of it. When a young girl accidentally dropped a basket of eggs, shells and all, into a bowl of batter, it didn't upset Nicole at all. Two children, dressed plainly but cleanly, ran through the building, and Nicole just caught a pail of milk before it overturned. Even as she righted it, she looked up, saw Regan, and smiled warmly.

Wiping her hands on her apron, she came forward. "I'm sorry I had to leave you, but I wanted to see that a nice supper was prepared for you."

"Is it always like this?" Regan asked, half in horror.

"Most of the time. There are an awful lot of people to feed." She started to untie her apron. "I need to cut some herbs, and maybe you'd like a little tour before supper. If you're not too tired."

"I slept most of the way here," Regan smiled. "And I'd love to see the . . . the plantation."

Later, Regan didn't believe anything could have prepared her for what Nicole showed her. A man hitched a two-wheel wagon for them, and Nicole drove them about the plantation, pointing out each of the dependencies. Regan had been right in her first estimation. The plantation was a village of sorts, but all owned by one man. Nearly everything needed for living was made, grown, or caught on the plantation. Nicole pointed out the dairy, dovecote, loom house, stables, tannery, and carpenter shop, and around the kitchen was a smokehouse, malt house, and wash house. Nicole showed her the acres and acres of fields planted with cotton, flax, wheat, and tobacco. And across the river was a mill where their grain was ground. Cattle, sheep, and horses grazed in separate areas.

"And you manage all of this?" Regan asked in wonder.

"Clay helps some, too," Nicole laughed, "but, yes, it takes a lot of work. We don't get away much, but then we don't have to since everything we could ever want is right here."

"You're very happy, aren't you?"

"I am now," Nicole answered. "But it hasn't always been easy." Her eyes went to the mill across the river.

"Clay and Travis have been friends since they were boys, and I hope we'll be friends too."

"I have never had a girlfriend," Regan said, looking at this woman who was the same small size she was. They had no idea what a striking pair they made, Nicole with her black hair, and Regan's dark brown with its red-gold highlights.

"Neither have I," Nicole said. "Not a real girlfriend I could talk to and confide in." With a smile she flicked the reins, and the horse started to move. "Someday, when we have a lot of time, I'll tell you how I met Clay."

Blushing, Regan thought that she could never, never tell anyone how she met Travis. For one thing, no one would believe her story.

"I'm hungry. How about you?" Nicole asked. "And I can feel that those babies of mine are about to starve."

"And without a doubt Travis is hungry," Regan laughed.

"Is she as young as she looks?" Clay asked, jostling his son on his arm and looking through the window at Nicole and Regan pulling away from the house in the buggy.

"Would you believe I don't know how old she is? And that is one question I'm afraid to ask. It'd be my luck that she'd turn out to be sixteen."

"Travis, what on earth are you talking about? How did you meet her? Couldn't you have found out from her parents how old she was?"

Travis had no intention of telling the story to anyone. Years ago, when Clay's older brother James was alive, he might have confided in him, but now he couldn't bring himself to tell of kidnapping his wife.

Clay seemed to understand, for there were things he

didn't want to tell about himself—and what had gone on between him and Nicole. "Is she always so quiet? I don't mean to pry, but the two of you seem an incongruous pair."

"She can hold her own," Travis smiled, eyes twinkling. "To tell you the truth, I don't know what she's like. She seems to change every minute. One moment she's a little girl with dreams of romance, and the next she's. . . ." His voice trailed off as he remembered early this morning, her lips moving up his inner thigh. "Whatever she is, I find her fascinating."

"And what about Margo? I don't believe she's going to be too happy to welcome your little wife."

"I can handle Margo," Travis said in dismissal.

Old memories, only half-healed, clouded Clay's eyes. "Watch her with your wife. A woman like Margo eats sweet little things like Regan for breakfast. I know," he added softly.

"Margo can't do a damned thing, and I'll let her know it. I'll be around to protect my wife, and Regan ought to know what I feel about her. I married her, didn't I?"

Clay didn't say any more. There was a time when people had given him advice, but he hadn't listened, and he knew how easily marriage vows could be made—and just as easily broken.

That night, as Regan slipped into the canopied bed beside her husband, she told him some of her impressions of the day. "I never knew anything like this existed. It's as if Clay and Nicole were the sole owners of an entire town."

He pulled her close to him. "Then you like our plantation system?" he murmured, relaxing into sleep.

"Of course, but I am glad there aren't many of them. I

don't see how Nicole can run a place this size. Thank heavens you are just a poor farmer.''

When she received no reply, she looked over at Travis and saw that he was asleep. Smiling, she snuggled closer to him and drifted into a quiet, gentle sleep.

The next morning parting was surprisingly difficult as they all stood on the wharf and said goodbye. Nicole promised to visit Regan very soon and to give her any help she could. Clay and Travis exchanged comments about this year's crops, and then all too soon they were climbing into the little boat and heading upriver.

Regan found she was very excited about seeing the place where Travis lived and wondered if it could possibly be as big and wild and crude as he was. She hoped she could refine his home as she wanted to refine him.

After a while of slow, easy sailing, they came to another break in the trees. An enormous wharf with more ships could be seen in the distance.

''This isn't another plantation, is it?'' she asked, moving to stand beside Travis. This looked many times larger than Clay's place, so surely this was a town.

''It certainly is!'' Travis said with a big smile.

''Do you know the owners of this place?'' As they sailed nearer she could see that this plantation looked like a blown-up version of Clay's. By the wharf was a building as large as Clay's house. ''What is that?'' she pointed.

''It's the ship's store and the warehouse. The captains can replace sails and damaged gear at the store, and goods waiting transport are stored in the warehouse. The assessor's house is that smaller building.''

There were three small craft tied at the wharf, two barges,

and four shallops as Travis called them. To her bewilderment Travis steered the little boat to this wharf.

"I thought we were going home," she said in consternation. "Do you want to see friends here?"

Travis leaped onto the wharf and pulled her up before she could say another word. Taking her chin in his warm hand, he lifted her face to meet his. "This," he said quietly, his eyes locked on hers, "is my plantation."

For a moment she was too stunned to speak. "All . . . all of it?" she whispered.

"Every blade of grass. Now come on and let me show you your new home."

Those were the last words they were allowed each other before a mob of people descended on them. Shouts of "Travis!" and "Mr. Stanford!" echoed from one building to another. Travis never released Regan's hand as he shook hands with what seemed like hundreds of people who came running from every corner of the plantation. And he introduced her to every person, saying this man was head carpenter, this one the second assistant gardener, this woman third upstairs maid. On and on the list went, and all Regan could do was to stand and nod at them while her mind kept repeating, They are all employees. They all work for Travis—and for me.

Somewhere during all the introducing, Travis declared the day a holiday, and before long the field hands were coming to greet Travis too. Great, thick, muscle-bound men came laughing and smiling, teasing Travis that he'd probably gotten soft while he was away. A swift wave of pride shot through Regan as she saw that none of the men was any more muscular than her husband.

As they started walking away from the river, greeting

people along the way, some of the employees began asking questions. It seemed that half the plantation was falling apart.

"Where's Wes?" Travis demanded, walking so fast Regan was nearly running.

"Your Uncle Thomas died in Boston, and Wes had to go to straighten out his affairs," said a man who was an overseer.

"And what about Margo?" Travis frowned. "She could have handled some of these problems."

"About twenty of her cows are down with some sort of disease," the man answered.

"Travis," said a sturdy, red-haired woman. "Three of the looms are down, and every time I tell a man to fix them he says it's not his job."

"And Travis," another woman said. "The Backes have some new chickens from the East. Could you authorize some money to buy some?"

"Travis," said a man smoking a pipe. "Something's got to be done about that smallest sloop. Either it has to be repaired or scrapped."

Suddenly, Travis stopped and held up his hands. "All of you stop right here. Tomorrow I'll answer all your questions. No!" he said, his eyes lighting and reaching for Regan's hand. "I have a wife, and tomorrow she'll take over the women's duties. Carolyn, you ask her about the looms, and Susan, you ask my wife about chickens. I'm sure she knows more about them than I do."

Regan was glad Travis was holding her hand, because otherwise she might have turned and run away. What did she know about looms and chickens?

"Now," Travis continued. "I plan to show my bride my

house, and if I get asked one more question today I will call off the holiday," he said in mock fierceness.

If Regan hadn't been so depressed, she would have laughed at the speed with which the people left them, all except for one old man standing quietly in the background.

"This is Elias," Travis said with pride. "He's the best gardener in Virginia."

"I brought something for your new missus," Elias replied, and held out a flower such as Regan had never seen before. It was a shade of purple that was at once bright and soft. The center was a sort of frilled horn with large tear-shaped petals behind it.

Putting out her hand, she was almost afraid to touch it.

"It's an orchid, ma'am," said Elias. "The first Mrs. Stanford had them brought to her whenever the captains went to the South Seas. Maybe you would like to see the glasshouses when you have time."

"Yes," she answered, wondering if this place of Travis's did without anything. After thanking him, she followed Travis as he kept walking away from the river, and for the first time she noticed the tall, sprawling brick house rising before them. Even from this distance it looked as if you could put Weston Manor and Clay's Arundel Hall in one wing.

Travis was proudly bragging about the house he obviously loved, telling her how his grandfather had built it and how all the Stanfords loved it. But with each step Regan's fear grew. Nicole's responsibilities had seemed overwhelming, but now she was wishing she was going to be living in a small place like that. How was she going to manage this monstrous house, let alone the other duties Travis seemed to expect of her?

The house, when they reached it, was larger than it

seemed. A massive square center section of brick, four and a half stories high, towered over her, with two L-shaped wings radiating to each side. Travis led her up wide stone stairs to the first floor and once inside began the hurried tour of his extensive house.

He took her through a blue room, a green room, a red room, and a white room and showed her the schoolroom and housekeeper's room. Storage rooms were as large as her bedroom at Weston Manor.

With each room—each exquisitely furnished, beautiful room—Regan's fear climbed higher in her throat. How could she possibly manage a place the size of this?

Just when she thought she'd seen every room a house could contain, Travis half-dragged her up the east stairs. The rooms on this second, main floor put the ones below to shame. There was a dining room with an attached parlor for ladies' teas, another parlor for the family, a library for the men, two more sitting rooms for whatever anyone wanted them for, and an enormous bedroom with an attached nursery.

"Ours," Travis said, before pulling her into the ballroom.

Here, Regan was stunned. She'd said very little since they'd entered the house, but now she felt her legs give way under her. Collapsing onto a sofa in the corner, she stared in awed silence.

If nothing else, the sheer size of the room would have been overwhelming. Seventeen-foot-high ceilings made one feel small, insignificant. The walls were paneled, painted the palest blue, and the oak floors were polished to a gleam. There seemed to be a great many pieces of furniture—six couches covered in rose-brocaded satin, innumerable chairs with seats upholstered to match, a harp, a pianoforte, and numerous tables—but they were all set about the border, leaving the floor open, covered in a long rug from the Orient.

"Of course we roll up the rug when we have parties," Travis said proudly. "Maybe you'd like to give a party. We could invite a couple of hundred people to spend the night, and you and Malvina—she's the cook—could plan all the food. You'd like that, wouldn't you?"

It was all much too much. Tears in her eyes, her stomach aching, Regan ran through the ballroom toward the opposite door. She had no idea how to even get out of the house as she ran down a long passageway, finally opened a door, and fled into a lovely, small, blue and white room. She couldn't even remember all the names of the rooms, much less where they were.

Flinging herself to the floor, her head in her arms on the seat of a blue and white couch, she began to cry. How could he do this to her? How could he not have told her?

Within seconds Travis was beside her, pulling her into his arms as he sat on the couch. "Why are you crying?" he asked in a voice of such longing and hurt that she began to cry harder.

"You're rich!" she blurted, tears closing her throat.

"You're crying because I'm rich?" he asked in astonishment.

Even as she tried to explain, she was sure he'd never, never understand. Travis was so sure he did everything right; it had never occurred to him to doubt that he could accomplish anything. He didn't know what it was like to be useless. Now he expected her to manage the house, the dependencies, servants, and, by the by, give a party for a couple of hundred friends.

"I can't help you if you don't tell me what's wrong," Travis said, handing her his handkerchief. "You surely can't be angry because I'm not some poor farmer."

"How . . . ," she sobbed. "How can I . . . ? I've never even seen a loom!"

It took Travis a moment to piece that together. "You don't have to do the weaving; just tell someone else to do it. The women will bring their problems to you, and you'll fix them," he said. "It's all very simple."

She would never make him understand! Jumping out of his arms and off his lap, she ran from the room, down the passage, back into the ballroom, through it, and into another passage, until at last she found their bedroom and collapsed on the bed in a flurry of muslin dress and petticoats.

Even over her sobs she could hear Travis's slow, heavy footsteps as he approached. Pausing at the doorway, he seemed to study her for a moment before deciding that she needed to be left alone. As his steps retreated she began to cry harder.

Hours later, a maid, softly knocking on the door, asked her what she would like for supper. When she nearly replied "Yorkshire pudding," Regan realized she didn't even know what foods were available in America. Finally, she told the girl she didn't feel like eating and to please go away. Perhaps she could stay forever in this room and never have to face the outside world.

Chapter 13

No matter what Regan's first impression was of how difficult it was to run a plantation, she was far from the reality of it. Travis left their bed before the sun rose, and within minutes there were women in her room asking her questions. When she had no idea what answers to give them, she could see the way their eyes slid to one side. Once she overheard a maid mutter something about how a man like Travis could marry a nothing like her.

And everywhere she heard the name Margo.

A weaver showed her patterns Margo had given her. A gardener set bulbs from Miss Margo. In the blue room she found dresses that she was told belonged to Miss Margo, because she stayed here so often.

In the evenings at dinner, she asked Travis about this woman, but Travis only shrugged and said she was a neighbor. After having been away from his plantation so long, he was buried in work. Even during meals he went over papers with his two clerks, computing figures of goods received and goods exported. Regan didn't have the heart to add to his burdens by telling him her problems.

And then one day Regan's world came to a screeching halt. Travis had just returned to a quick dinner, talking to her with his mouth full about the arrival of a new ship from England, when the clatter of a horse's hoofs on the brick drive outside made him start. The crack of a whip was followed by the shrill scream of a horse, and Travis was at the window instantly.

"Margo!" he bellowed down. "You strike that horse again, and I'll use that whip on you."

A deep, seductive laugh seemed to fill the dining room. "Better men than you have tried, Travis, my love," a woman's voice purred, followed by another crack and another scream from a horse.

The entire house shook as Travis tore downstairs.

Regan, her eyes wide, put her napkin on the table and went to the window. Below her was a ravishingly beautiful red-haired woman wearing a tight emerald-green habit over an awesome figure. Her large, jutting breasts, small waist, and round hips made Regan glance down at her own slight curves.

But in seconds her attention was again on the woman atop her black stallion as it pranced angrily in the courtyard. The woman seemed to be easily in control of the monster of an animal, her eyes on the front of the house, and when Travis appeared she gave that low laugh again and raised her whip.

Within seconds Travis made a leap, grabbing at the whip in the woman's upraised hand. He caught it, but she dug her heels into the horse, sending it rearing, and Travis, clutching the pommel, held on. She never seemed to lose balance or confidence as the horse's front hoofs flailed at the air, and when the animal came down she started to give it another kick.

But Travis was too fast for her. He grabbed her arm with one hand and the reins with the other. For a moment there was a tug of war, the woman's laugh filling the air, sounding like moonlight during the day. She was a large, strong woman, and with the added strength of the horse beneath her she gave Travis an excellent fight.

When at last he pulled her from the horse, she slid down him liquidly, running her breasts across his face and down his chest, and when she was in range she opened her mouth and pressed it to his in a kiss that even from Regan's position, high above, looked as if it might devour him.

She wouldn't have guessed she could fly downstairs as quickly as she did, and when she reached the front stairs the kiss was only just ending.

"Still planning to use a whip on me?" Margo said huskily but loudly enough for Regan to hear. "Or could I persuade you to use something a little smaller—a very little bit smaller, if I remember correctly," she added, rubbing her hips meaningfully against his.

Travis took her arms and set her away from him. "Margo, before you make a complete fool of yourself, I think you should meet someone." He turned around, seemingly aware of Regan's exact whereabouts. "This is my wife."

Many expressions went across Margo's classically beautiful face. The arched eyebrows drew together, and the green-gold eyes caught fire. Patrician nostrils flared, and the sensual lips curled. She seemed to start to say something, but no words came out. With one look at Travis she gave him a slap that echoed against the towering house. In another second she was on her horse, jerking savagely at its mouth and already whipping it viciously as she headed east.

Travis watched her for a moment, muttered something about "No right to treat animals that way," flexed his injured jaw, and turned back to his wife. "That was Margo Jenkins, our closest neighbor." With that calm statement he seemed to dismiss the whole episode.

Regan, stock-still, her body rigid, could see the vivid print of Margo's hand on his cheek as he bent to kiss her.

"I'll see you tonight, and why don't you take a nap? You look a little pale. We want a healthy baby, remember?" With that, he nodded for his clerk, standing behind Regan, to follow him, and he went toward the west wing of the house where his office was located.

It took Regan what seemed like an hour before she recovered enough to return to the house. The vision of the haughty, splendidly lovely Margo haunted her all day. Twice she paused before a mirror and looked at her own reflection, at her wide-set eyes, her slim figure, and her overall look of sweetness. There was nothing sweet-looking about Margo Jenkins. Sucking in her cheeks, Regan tried to imagine herself more sophisticated, a superior beauty, but with a giant sigh she gave it up.

For the next few days she began to listen when Margo's name was mentioned and found out that it had been understood for years that Travis would marry her. When Travis and Wesley were both away, Margo managed their enormous plantation as well as her own.

With every word she heard, Regan became a little less sure of herself. Had she broken up this love match when she ran into Travis on the London docks? Why had Travis married her, except because she was going to have a baby?

When she tried to ask Travis these questions he just laughed. He was too busy with spring planting to be able to spend much time talking, and when they were alone together his hands on her body made her forget everything else.

A week after Margo's visit, Regan was in the East Passage, dreading her journey to the kitchen. It was time to look at the menus for next week—and time to face Malvina, the cook. The old woman had taken an instant dislike to Regan, muttering under her breath constantly. One of the maids mentioned that Malvina was a cousin to the Jenkins family, and of course she had expected, as everyone had, that Travis would marry Margo. Gathering her courage, Regan went through the long passage to the kitchen.

"I ain't got time to do nothin' else now," Malvina said before Regan could speak. "A shipload of men just come in, and I have to feed 'em."

Regan refused to back down. "That's perfectly all right, I'll just have a cup of tea, and we can discuss menus some other time."

"Ain't nobody got time to make tea," the cook snapped, giving warning looks to her three young helpers.

Straightening her shoulders, Regan walked toward the smelly, smoke-emitting cast-iron stove set along one wall. "I can certainly make my own tea," she said in what she hoped was a scathing voice, and did not reveal that she had no idea how to make a cup of tea. Turning just slightly to give the cook a lofty look, a deprecating smile on her lips, Regan picked up the tea kettle.

The smile left instantly as she gave a little scream, dropped the scalding-hot kettle, and then had to jump backward as boiling water splashed to the floor. Behind her, the cook's malicious chuckle rang out, and all Regan could do was stare helplessly at her burned palm.

"Here," said one of the kitchen maids with kindness as she pressed cool butter into Regan's injured hand. "Leave this on it, and go sit down. I'll bring you your tea." This last she said with a whisper, one eye glancing toward the cook.

Silently, her head down, Regan left the kitchen, with her fingers extended and the butter melting against the throbbing surface. She wanted to go straight to her bedroom, but a young man informed her that a guest waited for her in the parlor. Regan was just wondering how she could escape when Margo appeared at the head of the stairs, looking radiant in a blue satin dress.

"Whatever have you done to yourself, child?" she asked, sweeping down the stairs. "Charles, bring bandages to the parlor, and have Malvina send us tea. With sherry! And tell her I want some of her fruitcake."

"Yes, ma'am," said the young man, who hurried away.

Margo took Regan's wrist and led her up the stairs. "What were you doing to burn your hand so badly?" she said sympathetically.

With her pride hurt as well as her hand, Regan was glad for the sympathy. "I picked up the tea kettle," she said meekly, embarrassed.

Margo didn't blink an eye as she led Regan to a couch. Within seconds a maid Regan was sure she'd never seen before appeared with bandages and clean cloths. "And where have you been, Sally?" Margo asked sternly. "Have you been up to your old tricks and getting out of work?"

"Oh no, ma'am. I help the mistress every morning, don't I, ma'am?" she asked, boldly looking at Regan.

Regan didn't say a word. She'd met so many people in the last few weeks.

Margo grabbed the bandages. "Get out of here, you little slut! And be careful I don't have Travis turn your indenture papers over to me."

After one wild look of fear, the maid left the room.

Margo sat down beside Regan on the couch. "Now let me see your hand. This is really a bad burn. You must have held that kettle quite some time. I do hope you tell Travis about the house servants. He lets them do as they please, and as a result they think they own the place. And Wes is certainly no better. That's why Travis has been planning for so long to get a wife. He needs someone strong who can take care of the duties of a plantation this size."

All the time she was talking, she was tenderly bandaging Regan's hand. When she was finished, the man, Charles, entered the room bearing a tray large enough to hold a pony. On it was an exquisite Georgian silver tea service, a crystal decanter of sherry with two glasses, and an astonishing array of tiny cakes and sandwiches.

"Not Malvina's best," Margo said, looking down her nose at the tray. "Perhaps she doesn't consider me a guest any longer. Tell her," she said, glancing at Charles, "that I'll speak to her before I leave."

"Yes, ma'am," Charles bobbed before he left the room.

"Now," Margo said, smiling at Regan. "I shall, of course, pour since you have that dreadful hand."

With the greatest of ease, Margo poured tea, added a good dose of sherry, and chose a cake for Regan.

"I really came to apologize," Margo began as she poured herself sherry, forgetting the tea. "I can't imagine what you must have thought of my unforgivable rudeness last week. I was really too embarrassed to return and ask you to receive me after what happened.''

Regan was pleased at this regal woman's humility. ''I . . . you should have come,'' she said quietly.

Margo looked away and continued, ''You see, Travis and I have been sweethearts since we were children, and everyone assumed we would someday marry. So, of course, it was a shock when he introduced someone else as his wife.'' She looked back at Regan, her eyes soft and pleading. ''You do understand, don't you?''

''Of course,'' Regan whispered. How alike Margo and Travis were, so sure of themselves, so confident. They were the rulers of the world.

''My father died two years ago,'' Margo said, and there was such pain in her voice that Regan winced. ''And since then I've run my plantation alone. Of course, it is nowhere near the size of Travis's place, but it is adequate.''

Regan felt that here was a woman who could run an entire plantation alone, while she couldn't even prepare a cup of tea. At least there was one thing she could do correctly. Lowering her head and smiling, she said, ''Travis hopes our children will help him work the plantation. Of course, that will take time, but this one has a good start already.''

When Margo was silent, Regan looked up and saw fire in the larger woman's eyes.

''So that's why Travis married you!'' she said in a voice that came from deep inside her.

A wave of shock ran through Regan.

''Forgive me again!'' Margo said, putting her hand on Regan's wrist. ''I never seem to say the right thing. It's just that I had wondered why, since we were practically engaged. Travis is so honorable that, of course, he'd feel he had to marry a woman who was carrying his child. You know,'' she laughed, ''I should have thought of that. Perhaps if I'd, well, you know, and gotten myself pregnant, he would have married me.

''Oh my!'' Margo said. ''I seem to be doing it again. I wasn't by any means insinuating that you were *enceinte* before Travis married you. Of course you weren't.''

She rose, and Regan stood beside her. ''I really must go,'' Margo said. ''I can't seem to say anything right today.'' She patted Regan's hand. ''I'm sure Travis fell in love with you, and that's why he chose you. This isn't the Middle Ages. Men marry women of their own choosing and not because they're going to have babies. Of course, Travis always said he'd like to have children but without a bossy wife to put up with. Of course, you, dear sweet child, could never be bossy. Now I really must go. I hope we will become the closest of friends. Perhaps I can help you with learning about Travis's likes and dislikes. After all, we've been very close all our lives.''

She kissed the air beside Regan's cheek before turning to leave. ''I'll leave word for the tray to be removed,'' she smiled. ''So you don't have to worry your sweet little head about it. You just go and rest and take care of that baby Travis wants so much.''

With that she left the room, and Regan collapsed onto the couch, feeling as if she'd just left a storm. It was a few minutes before she began to think about Margo's words. Choice? Travis did not choose her; she ran into him. He would gladly have released her, but she wouldn't tell him her uncle's name. Honor! Travis's honor forbade him releasing her into the streets of London, and later his honor made him marry her. What had he said at their wedding? He always married the mother of his children.

Had she forced him to marry her? Obviously their marriage had nothing to do with love. How could a man like Travis love a child who couldn't even make tea without practically crippling herself?

The days began to pass, and with each one she seemed to fall farther behind in work. The household staff seemed to take delight in changing daily. When Regan spoke to them they were insolent, and at last she found herself rarely leaving her room.

Travis came home, swept her into his arms, tossed her above his head, and tickled her until the sadness left her face. Constantly, he asked her what was wrong. He invited her to tour the plantation with him, and she went, ashamed at how much she wanted his protection. She could never admit how much of a stranger she felt in this country.

Travis never complained about her lack of authority, and no one dared be insolent with him, but he did notice that certain areas of the plantation were not being supervised properly. One day she heard him shouting at the dairymen, asking why they were slack in their job.

Twice Margo visited, and each time she talked softly to Regan before setting into the house staff for their negligence of the gracious house. After she left Regan felt drained and worse than useless.

She never let Travis know of her problems with the staff or of her hundreds of thousands of tears during the day.

One afternoon, while Regan was in the library trying to concentrate on a book, Travis entered.

"There you are," he smiled. "I thought you'd disappeared."

"Is something wrong?"

Over his clothes he wore an oiled cloth, like the sailors on board ship had worn.

"A storm is brewing, lightning cut one of the fences down, and about a hundred horses are out."

"Are you going after them?"

"Just as soon as I can get Margo, I am."

"Margo?" She closed the book. "What does she have to do with horses getting out?"

Travis laughed at her expression. "Some of them belong to her, and, besides, she can outride most of the men in the county. The plain fact, my green-eyed little wife, is that I need her."

Standing, she looked up at him. "But what can I do?"

He smiled indulgently and kissed her nose. "Not worry your pretty little head for one thing, keep my baby safe for the second, and, last but definitely not least, warm my bed." With that, he left the room.

For a moment Regan stood where she was. Her first impulse was to cry, but she was sick to death of crying! She was *not* going to sit alone and keep Travis's baby safe. Surely there must be more to life than just living for the few moments alone with a man who only cared about what she carried in her stomach.

When he really wanted something, he went to the woman he'd always gone to—Margo—Margo with her pride and arrogance, Margo with her confident ability to do anything in the world.

Without another thought, she went to their bedroom and began throwing clothes into a cloth case. The idea of doing something—anything—made her hurry. In a case on the chest of drawers was a bracelet of sapphires and a pair of diamond earrings. They'd belonged to Travis's mother, and he'd given them to her. With only a moment's hesitation, she slipped them into the bag.

Putting on a heavy cloak, she went to the door, made sure no one saw her, and started toward the stairs. At the head, she paused and looked back at what had once been hers. No! It never had been hers. With a fresh burst of resolution, she ran back to the library and scribbled a note to Travis, telling him that she was leaving and he was free to have the woman he loved. Then, opening a drawer, she emptied the contents of a tin box of cash into her pocket.

It was easy to escape the house without notice. The workers were busy securing windows and doors in preparation for the storm that hung in the air like damp wool. The house faced the river, but behind it ran a rutted path that Travis said was a road. Most Virginians traveled by water, and Regan felt sure she would escape detection if she took this route.

She walked for an hour, the air heavy with the storm, before the rain began. The path turned to mud that sucked at her shoes and made walking nearly impossible.

"Want a ride, young lady?" someone called.

She turned to see a wagon behind her, an old man atop it.

"Not much protection from the wet, but it beats walkin'!"

Gratefully she put up her hand, and he pulled her onto the seat beside him.

Margo stormed into the house, her clothes dripping, her hair in a bedraggled mess down her back. Damn that Travis! she thought. He sends for me as if I were some field hand to help him round up horses, while that precious, brainless wife of his stays at home! There was hardly a day when she didn't remember that awful morning alone with him.

The day before, she had gone to greet him on his return from England, expecting him to take her to his bed as he usually did, but instead he'd introduced that colorless child as his wife. The next morning she'd confronted him, demanded to know just what the hell he thought he was doing. Travis hadn't said much until she began enumerating Regan's faults—which she'd been told in full by Malvina, her cousin.

Travis had raised his hand to hit her but recovered himself in time. In a voice she'd never heard him use before, he told her Regan was worth two of her and that he didn't give a damn if his wife couldn't control an army of servants. He also said that if Margo ever wanted to be welcome at his house she'd better ask Regan's permission.

It had taken Margo a week to swallow her pride and go to that simpering brat. And what had she found there? The child was in tears, unable even to treat her own burned fingers. But at least Margo had found out why Travis had married her. It all made such perfect sense. Her submissiveness, combined with Travis's aggression, had gotten him what he wanted and had gotten her pregnant. Now all Margo had to do was show Travis what a waste it was to spend his life— and money—on that useless bit of fluff.

Now, angry as she always was in the last weeks, she started up the stairs. Travis had asked Margo to look in on his little china-doll wife on her way home, as Travis was going to have to spend tonight and maybe tomorrow night at Clay's house. Lightning had struck Clay's dairy, and they needed help in rebuilding it. Margo could have struck Travis when she saw the look on his face. You would have thought that spending two nights away from that brat was a tragedy.

Taking a deep breath to calm herself, she opened the bedroom door, surprised to find the room empty—and a mess. Looking at open drawers and clothes strewn over the bed, she knew it was too much to hope that a thief had entered the house and carried off the little princess. Snatching at a satin dress in a delicious shade of ripe peaches, Margo snarled. If one looked closely, there were worn places on all of her own gowns.

She threw the dress down and went through the familiar house, banging doors open, thinking that all this should have been hers. In the library, a single candle guttered over a simple note on Travis's desk. The handwriting, with all its open a's and o's, disgusted Margo.

But, as she read it, her mind began to clear. So! The runt had left Travis to the "woman he loved." Perhaps now was the time to do something about Travis's infantile infatuation with the girl.

Slipping Regan's note into her pocket, she wrote one of her own.

Dear Travis,

  Regan and I have decided to become better acquainted, so we're going to Richmond together for a few days. We both send our love.

  M.

Smiling, Margo hoped "a few days" was enough time to cover Regan's tracks. No doubt, the girl would be as clumsy in trying to run away as she was in everything else she attempted. But Margo could change that. By slipping a little money here and there, she could persuade people they'd never seen the runt.

It was four days later when Margo finally returned, alone, to the Stanford plantation. She was disgusted when Travis ran to greet her, jumping into the carriage and turning feverish-looking eyes up to her. "Where is she?"

Later, Margo was proud of her acting. She'd shown Travis her anger at being stood up by Regan, saying the dear woman had never shown up for their journey.

Travis's anger was frightening. She'd known him all her life, and never had she seen him really lose his self-control. Within moments he had his entire plantation mobilized in a search for his wife. Friends from everywhere came, but on the second day, when a piece of one of Regan's dresses was found at the river's edge, many people gave up the search and went home.

But not Travis. He made a circle of a hundred-mile radius around his plantation and asked questions of everyone within the circle.

Margo held her breath and prayed she'd done her work well. She was rewarded when Travis returned in a month, weary, thin, aged. Smiling, Margo remembered all the money this deception had cost her. With her plantation already in debt, she couldn't afford too many errors, so she'd taken what cash she had and bribed men and women all over the countryside. Some people told Travis they'd seen Regan and then gave him incorrect directions. Some who had seen her said they hadn't. And a few who couldn't be bribed told the truth, but further along the trail there were others who swore they'd not seen the young lady.

Gradually, Travis returned to the working of his plantation, allowing his brother Wesley to take over more and more of the running of it. And Margo went about picking up the pieces of Travis's life.

Chapter 14

REGAN FOUND THE FIRST LEG OF THE JOURNEY ALMOST pleasant. She kept imagining Travis's face when he found her. She would, of course, bargain with him before she returned to his home. She'd insist he fire the cook and hire a housekeeper. No! Regan would choose her own housekeeper, someone loyal to her.

The man on the wagon let her off at a stage stop, and Regan mustered her courage and went into the small inn, which seemed more like someone's house than a public establishment.

"It used to be our house," the landlady said. "But after my husband died I sold the farm land and started taking in guests. It was a lot easier than cookin' for my ten children while they was growin' up."

The landlady swept Regan under her arm and gave her a friendly lecture about traveling alone. As she ate alone in a high-sided booth, she thought of how Travis would ask this woman for directions.

In the morning Regan asked the landlady four times where the next stage was heading, in order, she realized guiltily, to impress on the woman's mind her destination.

On the second day in a stage she grew quite tired and kept glancing out the window. The storm had gone, leaving the air heavy enough to cut, and her dress clung to her. Once a horse and rider came thundering down the road toward them, and at the sound Regan smiled, sure the rider was Travis. She had her head half out the window, her hand raised in recognition, when the man on the horse galloped by. Embarrassed, she sat back in the stage.

That night there was no friendly landlady but only a querulous old man serving a stringy roast and hard potatoes for supper. Sad and tired, she went upstairs to the bedroom that, as a single woman, she shared with ten other women.

Before the sun came up she awoke and began softly crying. When the stage was ready to leave, her head ached and her eyes were swollen.

The four other passengers tried to talk to her, but she could only nod at their questions. Everyone kept asking her the same question: Where was she going?

Staring out the window in an unseeing gaze, she began to ask herself the same question. Had she run away from Travis just to show him she could be independent? Had she really believed he wanted Margo?

She had no answers for her questions but just traveled on one stage after another, watching the passing scenery, not even upset by the lack of decent food, beds, or rest.

It was in a daze that she stepped down from the stage one

afternoon into a barren little place that was little more than a few houses.

"This is the end of the line, lady," the stage driver said, offering his hand to her.

"I beg your pardon?"

He looked at her with patience. For the past two days she'd been half in a stupor, and he thought perhaps she wasn't completely right in the mind. "The stage line stops here. Past Scarlet Springs is nothing but Indian country. If you want to go into that, you'll have to hire a wagon."

"Could I get a room here?"

"Lady, this ain't even a town yet. It don't have hotels yet. Look, you either go on or you go back. There ain't nowhere to stay here."

Go back! How could she go back to Travis and his mistress?

A woman's voice came from behind the stage. "I have room. She can stay with me until she makes up her mind what she wants to do."

Regan turned to see a short, voluptuous young woman with honey-blonde hair and big blue eyes.

"I'm Brandy Dutton, and I have a farmhouse just down the road. Would you like to stay with me?"

"Yes," Regan said quietly. "I can pay you. . . ."

"Don't worry about it. We'll work it out." Grabbing Regan's bag, she led the way down the street.

"I saw you standing there, and you looked so little and lost that my heart just went out to you. You know, I must have looked the same about three months ago. Both my parents died and left me alone with nothing but an old farmhouse and not much else. Here we are."

She led Regan inside an unpainted, rundown, two-story

house. "Sit down, and I'll make you some coffee. What's your name anyway?"

"Regan Stanford," she said before thinking, then shrugged because what did it matter if she didn't hide? Travis obviously wasn't interested in having her back.

Regan sipped the coffee, not really liking the taste of it. But it helped revive her, although she could feel tears growing behind her eyes.

"You look like you've had your share of tragedy, too," Brandy said as she cut a piece of cake and handed it to Regan.

A man who wanted to marry her in spite of the fact that he despised her, an uncle who detested her, a man who married her because of the child she carried—she could only nod to Brandy's question.

When she only picked at the cake, Brandy looked at her sympathetically and asked if she'd like to lie down. Once alone in the little bedroom, Regan began to cry in earnest, as she'd never cried before.

She didn't hear Brandy enter the room, only felt the woman's arms around her. "You can tell me about it," she whispered.

"Men!" Regan cried. "Twice I've loved them, and both times—."

"You don't have to say any more," Brandy said. "I am an expert on men. Two years ago I fell for a man, decided he was worth more than anyone else on earth, so one night I slipped out the window of my bedroom, didn't even leave my parents a note, and ran off with him. He said he was going to marry me, but there never seemed to be the right time, and six months ago I found him in bed with another woman."

This statement started Regan's tears harder.

"I didn't know where to go," Brandy continued. "So I came home, and my wonderful parents accepted me back and never said a word about what I'd done. Two weeks later they were dead of scarlet fever."

"I . . . I'm sorry," Regan sniffed. "Then you're alone, too."

"Exactly," Brandy said. "I own one farmhouse that's about to fall down around my ears, and I have every man coming through here swearing he can make me the happiest woman in the world."

"I hope you don't believe them!" Regan snapped.

Brandy laughed. "You're beginning to sound like me, but it's either marry one of them or starve to death here."

"I have some money," Regan said, emptying her pockets onto the bed. To her chagrin, there were only four silver coins left. "Wait a minute!" she said, going to her bag and pulling out the sapphire bracelet and diamond earrings.

Brandy held them up to the light. "One of your two men must have been good to you."

"When he was with me," Regan said stiffly. Suddenly, her face changed, and she grabbed her stomach.

"Are you sick?"

"I think the baby just kicked me," she said in wonder.

Brandy's eyes opened wide just before she began laughing. "Aren't we a pair! Two rejected females who at this moment hate the whole male race"—her tone left no doubt that that opinion would change—"with a couple of pieces of jewelry, four silver coins, a falling-down house, and a baby on the way. How are we going to put food on the table this coming winter?"

It was the way she said "we" and the hint of their being

together this winter that made a spark of interest shoot through Regan. Travis didn't want her, yet she had to survive. At another kick from the baby, she smiled. She hadn't thought much about her baby in the last few months. Travis was so overpowering that she could see nothing but him.

"How about more cake and let's talk?" Brandy said.

It wasn't with glee that she thought about her future, but she had to plan something for her and the baby.

"Did you make this?" Regan asked, hungrily digging into the cake.

With pride, Brandy smiled. "If there's one thing I can do, it's cook. By the time I was ten I was doing all the cooking for my parents."

"At least you have some talents," Regan said grimly. "I'm not sure I can do anything."

Brandy sat down at the old table. "I could teach you to cook. I was thinking of baking things and selling them to the people who pass through Scarlet Springs. We two could make enough to get by on."

"This is Scarlet Springs? That's the name of this place?"

Brandy gave her a look of sympathy. "I take it you just got on a stage and went to the end of the line."

Regan only nodded as she finished her cake.

"If you're willing to try and willing to work, I'd certainly like your company."

They shook hands in agreement.

It took Brandy a week before she really began to believe that Regan could not cook, but it was ten days before she gave up.

"It's no use," Brandy sighed. "You either forget the yeast or half the flour or the sugar, or something." Dumping

194

a hard loaf on the table, she tried to stab it with a knife but couldn't.

"I'm so sorry," Regan said. "I really try, I do."

Eyeing her critically, Brandy said, "You know what you're really good at? People like you. There's such a sweetness about you and you're so damned pretty that women like you and want to take care of you, and so do the men."

Travis had once wanted to take care of her, but it hadn't lasted long. "I'm not sure you're right, but what sort of talent is that?"

"Selling. I'll cook; you sell. Look sweet on the outside, but drive a hard bargain. Don't let anyone get away with paying less than we ask."

The next day the stage brought six people to meet others who camped outside Scarlet Springs, waiting to start the journey West. On impulse, Regan raised the prices of the baked goods, and no one questioned them but bought everything.

That afternoon she spent all the money she and Brandy had. Three of the settlers traveling West had overloaded their wagons, and they meant to throw their excess lanterns, rope, and a few pieces of clothing into the river. They were angry and wanted to make sure no one could use what they'd paid for. Regan offered to buy all of it. After running all the way to the farmhouse, she grabbed all their money from the box and paid it to the settlers.

When she returned with the merchandise, Brandy was furious. They had no money, their supplies were nearly empty, and they had a room full of equipment no one wanted.

For three days they lived on apples pilfered from an orchard four miles away, and Regan was ridden with guilt.

On the fourth day, new settlers came to Scarlet Springs, and Regan sold all the goods for three times what she'd paid for them. Crying in relief that everything had worked out, Regan and Brandy hugged each other and danced around the kitchen.

It was the beginning of everything. With this first good sale they gained confidence in themselves and each other. Both women began to look ahead to what they could do.

They struck a bargain with the farmer who owned the apple trees and purchased all his fallen apples in exchange for very little money and a loaf of bread a week from Brandy for the next six months. At night Brandy and Regan peeled and sliced apples and put them out to dry in the next day's sun. When they were dry they sold them to the westward-traveling settlers.

Every penny they made, every bargain they struck, increased the size of their business. They were up before dawn, to bed very late. Yet sometimes Regan felt she'd never been happier. For the first time in her life she felt as if she were needed.

It was during the fall that they began taking in boarders and serving meals. People came to Scarlet Springs too late to go West and had no wish to return to where they'd once lived. One man explained that his hometown had given him a going-away party, and he couldn't face returning, saying he'd missed the wagons.

Regan and Brandy looked at each other, smiled contentedly, and told the man they'd take care of him. By Thanksgiving they had six boarders, and they were all jammed on top of one another.

"Next year I'm putting down pickles and kraut," Brandy said, looking in disgust at a meal of little else but wild meat. She stopped her complaints when she looked at Regan.

Regan stood unsteadily, her stomach well out in front of her. "If you will excuse me," she said in the quietest possible voice, "I believe I'll go upstairs and have a baby."

Brandy, angered, grabbed her friend's arm and helped her up to the bedroom they now shared. "No doubt you've had pains all day. When are you going to stop feeling like you're a burden and start asking for help?"

Awkwardly, Regan sat on the bed, leaning back on the pillows Brandy shoved behind her. "Could you lecture me later?" she asked, her face contorting.

In spite of Regan's small size, it was an easy birth. Her water broke all over Brandy, and they laughed together for just a second before a large, perfect baby girl came flying into the world. She screwed up her face, clenched her fists, and started screaming. "Just like Travis," Regan murmured before reaching for her daughter. "Jennifer. Do you like that name?"

"Yes," Brandy said, cleaning Regan and the room. She was too exhausted to consider what the baby's name was. Glancing at Regan cuddling her baby, she felt she was the one who'd been through the worst ordeal.

Within a month the women had settled in to the new routine of running the boarding house and caring for the baby. When spring arrived, so did hundreds of new settlers. One man, whose wife had died on the journey to Scarlet Springs, decided to remain with his two young children in the sparse little settlement and began building a large, comfortable house.

"This town's going to grow," Regan murmured, her

baby on her arm. Looking back at the drafty old farmhouse, she began to see it with a fresh coat of paint, and, as her imagination took over, she saw an addition on the front, something with long porches.

"That's a funny look," Brandy said from behind her friend. "Mind sharing what's causing it?"

Not yet, Regan thought. She'd had too many dreams in her life, and all of them had fallen through. From now on she was going to concentrate on one goal, and she was going to work hard at achieving it.

Weeks later, when Regan did finally, tentatively, talk to Brandy about her ideas for remodeling and enlarging the farmhouse into a full-size hotel, Brandy was somewhat shocked.

"It . . . sounds like a wonderful idea," Brandy hesitated. "But do you think we—I mean, us two women—can do something like that? What do we know about a hotel?"

"Nothing," Regan said in all seriousness. "And don't let me consider what I can do versus what I want to do, or I'll never even try it."

Laughing, Brandy didn't know how to address that statement. "I'm with you," she said. "You lead; I'll follow."

That was another statement Regan didn't want to consider. In fact, she wanted to keep so busy that she had no time to think. Two days later she had found a wet nurse for Jennifer, unearthed the jewels from their hiding place, and boarded a stage heading north. She went to three towns before she found someone willing to pay a decent price for the bracelet and earrings. And everywhere she went she visited the local inns. She found that an inn was not only a place for wayfarers but a social and political gathering place as well. She drew sketches and asked questions, and her earnestness and youth gained her many hours of discussion and answers to her probings.

When she returned home, tired but exhilarated and more than eager to see her daughter and her friend, she had a fat leather case filled with notes, drawings, and recipes for Brandy. And sewed inside her clothes were bank drafts for the jewelry. From that moment on there was never any doubt about who was the leader in this partnership.

Chapter 15

FARRELL BATSFORD STEPPED OFF THE STAGE IN THE BUSY little town of Scarlet Springs, Pennsylvania, on a cool March morning in 1802. Dusting himself off, smoothing the rich blue velvet of his coat, he tugged at the lace at his cuff.

"This where you stoppin', Mister?" the stage driver asked from behind the slim, tailored man.

Farrell didn't bother to look at the driver but merely gave a brief nod of acknowledgment. Seconds later, he twirled about as the first of his two large, heavy trunks were tossed to the ground from the top of the stage. With a wide smile, the driver blinked at Farrell angelically.

"You want me to take those to the inn for you?" a burly young man asked.

Again Farrell only nodded curtly, ignoring as best he could the entire American race. As the stage pulled away, Farrell got his first glimpse of the Silver Dolphin Inn. It was three and a half stories high, with double porches across the front and tall white columns reaching to the steep roof. After tossing the young man a quarter, Farrell decided to walk about the town.

There's money here somewhere, he thought as he viewed the clean, neat buildings. Across from the inn were a print-shop, a doctor's office, a lawyer, a druggist. Close by were a blacksmith shop, a large mercantile shop, a school, and at the other end of town a tall, well-kept church. Everything was prosperous, fat-looking.

Turning his attention back to the inn, it was easy to see that the manicured building was the dominant one in the town. In the back was an additional wing, a well-tended older part of the building. Every window was sparkling clean, all the shutters newly painted, and even as Farrell watched many people came and went into the obviously thriving establishment.

Once again he took a worn newspaper article from his pocket. The article stated that a Mrs. Regan Stanford and Brandy Dutton, a spinster, practically owned an entire town in Pennsylvania. At first Farrell had thought it couldn't possibly be the Regan he'd been looking for for so many years, but a man he had sent to the town came back with a description that just could be the Regan he once knew.

Again, he thought of that night nearly five years ago when Jonathan Northland had thrown his niece from her own house. Poor, simple Regan had never realized that Weston Manor was hers, and, instead of her living on her uncle's income as Jonathan said that night, it was Northland who was living on the interest off Regan's fortune. Smiling, Farrell wondered if Northland ever realized who had alerted the executors of Regan's estate to what her uncle had done. It was a small but not adequate revenge for the things Northland had said about Farrell that night when the executors tossed Jonathan out of Weston Manor without so much as a penny. Six months later, Jonathan Northland was found stabbed to death in a wharfside gin shop, and finally Farrell's revenge was complete.

As the months and years passed, Farrell began to think more and more about Regan's millions, just lying in a bank, growing daily through the careful, wise investing of her executors. He began looking for a bride, someone with money enough to support him and his estate in a gentlemanly manner, but all the young women fell short of having the money Regan Weston possessed. Any women of her wealth wanted nothing to do with a penniless, titleless gentleman of dubious habits.

After two years of fruitless searching, Farrell persuaded himself that Regan had jilted him and had ruined his reputation with women. Therefore, the honorable thing to do was to find the child, marry her, and let her money mend his damaged reputation.

It had taken a while to trace Regan's old maid, Matta, to Scotland where she was living with relatives. The old woman suffered permanently from the pain of a misaligned jaw bone, a bone Jonathan Northland had broken for her when she tried to answer an American's questions about a young girl he'd found.

Drooling, slurring her words, drinking constantly to dull the pain, Matta disgusted Farrell until he could hardly bear being near her. Her memory was cloudy, and it took hours to get what he wanted from her, but he left with some idea of where to look.

Following one answer to another, he soon realized that Regan had sailed for America. It wasn't easy to make the decision to go after her, but he was fully aware that after years in that uncivilized country she'd probably be dying to return home.

America was larger than he'd imagined, and there were a few isolated points of civilization, but the people were disgusting, never aware of their station in life, each man believing he was a member of the peerage.

He was almost ready to return to England when he saw the small article in the newspaper. When the man he had hired to go to Scarlet Springs returned, he described a woman very like Regan in looks, but she did not seem to be the simpleton he remembered.

Now he walked across the green lawn that made a lush oval between the two main streets and entered the inn.

A large reception hall lined with white-painted paneling greeted him. Several well-dressed men and women were just entering a room to his right, and he followed them to an even larger room furnished with comfortable chairs and sofas and, along one wall, a deep, wide stone fireplace. All the furniture was newly upholstered in dusty rose and pale green striped satin. A taproom—rustic, he thought, with its oak chairs and tables, but obviously doing a brisk trade—adjoined the common room.

An enormous public dining room was across from the common room, two private dining rooms next to it. Finally, returning to the front of the inn, not touring into the old part of the building, he looked into a cozy library that smelled of leather and tobacco. Across the hall was the reception room, where a clerk politely assigned him a private bedroom upstairs.

"How many bedrooms do you have?"

"An even dozen," the clerk replied. "Plus two with sitting rooms and, of course, the owners' private apartments."

"Of course. I take it you refer to the young ladies."

"Oh, yes, sir, Regan and Brandy. Regan lives downstairs at the end of the old part, and Brandy is upstairs, just over her."

"And these are the ladies who supposedly own most of the town?" Farrell asked.

The clerk chuckled. "The preacher says that the only building they don't own is the church, but everyone knows they paid for it. They do hold the mortgages on all the other buildings. If a lawyer came through, Regan would give him the money to build a place and he'd stay here, then a doctor, and pretty soon this place became a town."

"Where might I find Mrs. Stanford?" Farrell asked, not liking the man's use of Regan's first name.

"Anywhere," he said quickly as a couple came in to register. "She's everywhere at once."

Not wanting to cause a scene, Farrell allowed the insolent man's abrupt dismissal of him. Later he'd have to speak to the manager, whoever she was.

Upstairs he found his room clean and well furnished, with warm sunlight sparkling through the window. A small fireplace was along one wall. After changing his dusty clothes, he went downstairs to the dining room. It galled him to eat in the public room, but he knew he'd be more likely to see Regan there. The menu was extensive, serving seven meats, three fish, plus cold dishes, relishes, vegetables, game, and a formidable list of pastries and puddings. Arriving quickly, the food was hot, well prepared, and delicious.

While he was sampling something called Moravian sugar cake, a woman entered the room, and every eye, male and female, glanced up at her. It was not just her extraordinary beauty that made them look, but her presence, her sense of self. This woman—small, wearing an exquisite gown of forest green muslin—knew who she was. She walked with confidence, easily speaking to first one person and then another. She looked to be a gracious lady welcoming people to her home. At one table she stopped, looked at a dish, and sent it back to the kitchen. At another table two women rose and hugged her briefly, and for a few moments she sat with them, laughing happily.

Farrell could not take his eyes off her. Superficially, she resembled the awkward girl he'd once known. The eyes were the same color, the hair the same shiny brown, but this woman, with her firm curves and her ease with people, was not at all like that simpering, terrified-of-her-own-shadow child to whom he'd once been engaged.

Leaning back in his chair, he waited calmly for her to come to him. When she saw him she smiled, but there was no recognition. A full minute later, as she was speaking to a couple across from him, her eyes lifted and met his. It was an appraising look she gave him, and Farrell gave her his most charming smile in return. He was extremely pleased when she turned and rather quickly left the room. Now he was sure there was some feeling, whether good or bad, left in her concerning him. Hate or love, he didn't care which, just so she remembered him.

"Regan, are you all right?" Brandy asked from the other side of the big oak kitchen table, where she was supervising three cooks.

"Of course," Regan snapped, then drew a deep breath and smiled. "I just saw a ghost, that's all."

The two women exchanged looks as Brandy drew Regan to a corner of the big room. "Jennifer's father?"

"No," Regan said quietly. Sometimes there didn't seem to be a moment of her life when she didn't think of Travis. Every time she looked into Jennifer's big brown eyes, she saw him. Sometimes a heavy step on the stairs made her heart skip a beat.

"Remember the man I was engaged to years ago? Farrell Batsford?" There were no secrets between the two friends. "He's sitting in the dining room."

"That bastard!" Brandy said with feeling. "What's he eating? I'll douse it with poison."

Regan laughed. "I should feel the same way, I guess, but I wonder if anyone gets over their first love. Seeing him brought back such a rush of memories. I was so frightened of everything, so eager to please, and so very much in love with him. I thought he was the most handsome, elegant man I'd ever seen."

"And now how does he look?"

"He's certainly not ugly," Regan smiled. "I guess I should invite him to my office for a talk. It's the least I can do."

"Regan," Brandy warned. "Be careful. It isn't a coincidence that he's here."

"I'm sure of that, and I have a good idea what he wants. In less than a month I'll be twenty-three, and the money my parents left me is mine."

"Don't forget that for a moment," Brandy called after Regan.

Regan went to her office next to the kitchen and sat down in the leather chair behind her desk. It wasn't that Farrell had affected her so much, but the sight of him brought back so many memories. Like a wave of cold water, she remembered the awful night she'd heard the truth from her uncle and her fiancé. One memory piled on top of another—Travis holding her, Travis telling her what to do, Travis making love to her, Travis bigger than life, and Regan constantly terrified. In the past four years, a hundred times she'd started to write him, to tell him about his daughter, to let him know they were both well and prospering. But she was always a coward in the end. What if Travis wrote her that he didn't care, which was surely the case since he'd never tried to find her? Over the years she'd learned to stand on her own two feet, but could she do so with Travis around? Would he bully her back into becoming the tearful, frightened girl she once was?

A knock on the door brought her back to the present. At her answer, Farrell opened the door.

"I hope I'm not intruding," he said, smiling, his eyes showing how much he enjoyed the sight of her.

"Not at all," she answered, rising, offering him her hand. "I was just going to send you a message asking you to join me."

Lowering his head, he kissed her hand ardently. "Perhaps you couldn't bear to face me so soon," he murmured lovingly. "After all, we meant so much to each other so long ago."

It's a good thing Farrell couldn't see Regan's face at that moment. Sheer shock was the expression that immediately registered. Why, you pompous little dandy! she thought. Did he really believe she had no memory of that hideous night so long ago, that she didn't remember the reason he wanted to marry her?

By the time he'd lifted his head, Regan was smiling. She

hadn't become a wealthy woman by letting her feelings show. "Yes," she said sweetly. "It has been a long while. Won't you sit down? Could I get you something to drink?"

"Whiskey if you have it."

She poured him a water-glass full of Irish whiskey and smiled innocently when he blinked at it. Settling herself in a chair across from him, she asked, "And how is my uncle?"

"Deceased, I'm afraid."

Regan didn't respond to that, unsure of her own emotions. For all he had done to her, he was still her relative. "Why have you come here, Farrell?"

He took a while before answering. "Guilt," he finally answered. "Although I had no real say in what your uncle did to you that night, I still felt somewhat responsible. In spite of what you may have thought you heard, I did care about you. I was concerned that you were so young, and I was displeased with your uncle for keeping you in such ignorance." He laughed as if they exchanged some private joke. "You must admit you were not the most inspired of dinner companions. I've never been one for robbing from the schoolroom. Perhaps other men like that sort of thing."

"And now?" Regan smiled seductively.

"You've changed. You're . . . not a child anymore."

Before she could answer him, the door burst open and Jennifer ran in, a handful of stemless flowers clutched in a dirty hand. She was a pretty three-year-old, with Regan's smallness and Travis's eyes and hair. She'd also inherited her father's sureness in life, never cringing from anything as Regan had done at her age. "I brought you some flowers, Mommie," she grinned.

"How sweet of you! Now I know spring is really on its

way,'' Regan answered, giving her sturdy daughter a fierce hug.

Jennifer, never shy, was staring openly at Farrell. "Who's he?" she said in a stage whisper.

"Farrell, I'd like you to meet my daughter Jennifer, and this is an old friend of mine—Mr. Batsford."

Jennifer managed to get a "How do you do?" out before she left the room as quickly as she'd entered it.

Regan gave an adoring glance at the door her daughter had just shut much too loudly, before looking back at Farrell. "I'm afraid you've seen my daughter for as long as any of us see her. She has the run of the inn and the grounds and makes use of every moment."

"Who is her father?" he asked, wasting no time.

Regan gave the lie she always gave, saying quickly that she was a widow, but, perhaps because today she was thinking so hard about Travis, her eyes betrayed the lie. She caught Farrell's quick look but said nothing more because to emphasize the lie would make it weaker.

"I must let you get back to your work," he said quietly. "Perhaps you will have dinner with me tonight?"

Still flustered over Farrell's catching of her lie, she agreed readily.

"Until tonight then," he smiled, and left the room.

Farrell went immediately to the kitchen to speak to the head chef about a very special dinner. When he was introduced to Brandy and saw the hostility in her eyes, he knew she'd been told Regan's story. Instantly, he turned on his most charming manner and asked if she'd show him the town. Feeling helpless to do otherwise, Brandy agreed and set out on one of the most charming afternoons of her life. If there was one thing Farrell had learned in the last several years in his pursuit of a rich wife, it was how to charm women. By the end of the afternoon he had Brandy believing he was an innocent victim of Jonathan Northland's greed. He told a long, complicated story of what he'd gone through to find Regan, how his conscience had eaten at him over the years. When he returned to the hotel, he had Brandy singing his praises, and he had more—the name and whereabouts of Regan's husband. By the time he was ready for dinner, a man had been dispatched to Virginia to find out the truth about Travis Stanford.

Chapter 16

TRAVIS LOUNGED AGAINST THE COUNTERTOP OF THE GLASS case in a Richmond dress shop, waiting with little grace while Margo tried on yet another dress.

"And how is this one, darling?" she said, returning from behind the dressing-room curtains. Very little of her large breasts were left to the imagination by the rust-colored muslin. "It's not too daring, is it?" she asked in a low voice as she walked closer to him, grazing his chest.

"It's fine," he said impatiently. "Haven't you bought enough? I'd like to get home before the sun sets."

"Home!" she said in a pretty pout. "You hardly ever leave that awful ol' plantation anymore. You used to take me dancing. You . . . used to do a lot of things with me."

Removing her hands from his chest, he gave her a tired look. "That was before I was a married man."

"Married!" she gasped. "Your wife ran off and left you!

She proved she didn't want you, and what other man stays faithful to his wife, whether she's with him or not?''

"Since when was I like other men?" he answered, giving her a look of warning. They'd had this argument many times before.

The jangling of the bell on the shop door stopped Margo's next words as they both turned to see Ellen Backes enter. She was a neighbor and a friend of Travis's family. "I thought I saw you, Travis," she said cheerfully. "Margo," she added curtly, letting it be known what she thought of Margo's pursuit of a married man. She'd never met Regan, but she'd heard about her from Nicole, Clay's wife. Having known Travis for years, she felt she knew why Regan had run away.

"The oddest thing just happened," Ellen continued. "I was in the church delivering fresh flowers for Sunday, and a man—a rather shabby little man, I might add—started asking the pastor all sorts of questions about you."

"Probably wants a job," Travis said in dismissal.

"At first I thought that, too, and of course I wasn't listening very carefully, but I swear I heard the name Regan."

Instantly, Travis stood upright. "Regan?" he whispered.

"I was going to wait until the pastor had finished, but I was afraid I might miss you."

Without another word, Travis left the room and immediately jumped into a carriage, yelling at the horses to go faster.

"Damn!" Margo said vehemently. "You would have to go and spoil my day."

"Oh, I am sorry," Ellen said with a radiant smile as Margo flounced toward the dressing room. Turning back toward the window, Ellen offered a silent prayer that Travis would find out something about his wife.

The horses hadn't come to a full stop when Travis leaped from the carriage in front of the church. Just leaving was a small man who looked as if he hadn't gone without a drink for more than a few hours in his life.

Travis, never one to stand on formalities and too angry to consider consequences, grabbed the man's shirtfront and slammed him against the clapboard wall. "Who are you?"

"I didn't do nothin', Mister, and I ain't got no money."

Travis pushed him harder into the wall. "You the one's askin' questions about me?"

Wincing from pain, trying to breathe against Travis's big fist pressed against his throat, the man gasped, "He paid me. I was just supposed to find out if you was alive or not."

"You'd better start talking. Who is he?"

"Some English dandy. I don't know his name. He said you were a friend of his but heard you were dead, wanted me to find out when you died and then tell him."

Travis pushed his fist harder into the man's throat. "You mentioned Regan."

Bewilderment crossed the man's face. "I said the man was stayin' at Regan's place."

For a moment Travis let up on the pressure. "Regan who? And where's her place?"

"Scarlet Springs, Pennsylvania, and she's Regan Stanford, like your name. I asked the preacher if you were related to her."

Instantly, Travis dropped the man and had to catch himself to keep from collapsing. "Get in the carriage. We're going to Scarlet Springs, and on the way you're going to talk."

Before the man could seat himself, Travis whipped the horses forward. As he flew past the dress shop where Margo stood outside, he didn't even slow down. At the livery stable he pulled to a halt.

"Jake," he called. "Give me a decent wagon, something that'll hold up for a longer trip, and here." He tossed money on the seat. "See the owner of this rig gets it back."

Jake barely glanced up. "If you're in a hurry, you better get goin' 'cause it looks to me like a storm's about to descend on you." Nodding in the direction of a very angry Margo, he dropped the horse's hoof he'd been cleaning and went to hitch a wagon for Travis.

Turning to the little man still on the buggy seat, Travis gave him a warning. "You move, and it'll be the last move you make." He'd hardly finished the words before Margo flew at him.

"How dare you drive past me like that!" she gasped, breathless from practically running down the street, chasing him.

"I don't have time to argue right now. I'm leaving in about five minutes."

"Leaving! Well I guess I've completed my shopping, but you'll have to stop at the four shops and pick up my purchases."

"Jake!" Travis bellowed. "Is that wagon ready yet?" He turned back to Margo. "I'm not going home, and you'll have to find someone else to take you. Get Ellen to give you a ride, and stop off and tell Wes I'll be away for a while."

Turning, he saw Jake bring the heavy wagon to the front of the stable. "Get on it," he commanded the nervous little man on the borrowed buggy.

"Travis," Margo hissed. "So help me, if you don't—."

She broke off as Travis leaped onto the wagon. "Where are you going?" she screamed as he started to move away.

"Scarlet Springs, Pennsylvania, to get Regan," he yelled and then was gone in a hail of gravel and dust.

Coughing and cursing, Margo looked back at the stableman, who was grinning broadly. She knew her pursuit of Travis was a joke, and the more people laughed, the angrier she grew. But even as she was fuming, a plan began to form in her mind. Scarlet Springs, was it? Poor dear Travis left without a stitch of clean clothing. Perhaps she should pack and take him a few things. Yes, the more she thought about it, the more she was sure he needed clean clothes.

Regan was at her desk in her office, going over accounts, when Brandy walked in.

"And how is everything?" Brandy asked.

"Going quite well," Regan answered, looking at the books. "Next year we should be able to put up a couple of new buildings. I was thinking of a cabinet shop. Don't you think Scarlet Springs needs its own furniture maker?"

"You know I'm not talking about finances. How is it going between you and Farrell? You had dinner with him last night again, didn't you?"

"You know very well that I did. But to answer you, Farrell is always a delightful companion. His conversation is excellent, his manners are impeccable, and he knows how to make a woman feel like a crown princess."

"You're bored to tears by him, aren't you?" Brandy said with a sigh, sitting down.

"In a word, yes. There are no surprises with Farrell. He's so . . . I don't know, he's too perfect, I guess."

"Jennifer likes him."

Regan gave a little laugh. "Jennifer likes his gifts. Can you imagine giving a child as active as Jen a French porcelain fashion doll? She wanted to use it for target practice with the bow and arrow set you gave her."

Brandy smothered a giggle. "Perhaps Farrell expects little girls as well as big ones to be ladies."

Regan stood behind her desk. "Have we any new guests? I haven't looked this morning."

"There was some man getting out of a wagon a few minutes ago. Good-looking guy. Big."

"Brandy, you are incorrigible," Regan laughed. "But I'll go and welcome him."

Outside her office, she met Farrell. "Good morning," he said, raising her hand to his lips. "You are sweeter than the early sunshine on the drops of dew on a rose petal."

She didn't know whether to laugh or groan. "Thank you for such a lovely compliment, but I really must go now."

"Regan, dearest, you work too much. Come spend the day with me. We'll take Jennifer and go on a picnic, just as if we were a family."

"It's a tempting offer, but I really must go now."

"You can't escape me that easily," he smiled, and took her arm as they walked toward the reception area.

Regan felt Travis's presence before she saw him. He stood in the doorway, blocking the light with his big body. Her body went rigid as her eyes locked with his.

Neither of them moved; they just stood looking at each other. Wave after wave of emotion went through Regan until a loud crashing sounded in her ears. After minutes, hours it seemed, she turned on her heel and, skirts flying, fled back toward her office.

Farrell wasn't sure what was going on between Regan and

this man, but he had a good idea. He didn't like this kind of reaction from her. Losing no time in following her, he was inches behind her.

"Regan, love," Farrell said as he put his hands on her shoulders. She was shaking so badly she could hardly stand.

But Regan was barely aware of him. All she heard was the pounding of her heart and the slow, heavy steps moving deliberately toward her door. Trembling, the blood gone from her head and hands, she clutched at the edge of her desk and leaned toward Farrell's strength.

The door to her office was pushed open with brutal force, slamming back against the wall.

"Why did you leave me?" Travis demanded in a low whisper, his eyes drilling into hers.

As he came closer she could not speak, could only look at him wildly.

"I asked you a question," Travis said.

Farrell stepped between them. "Now see here. I don't know who you are, but you have no right to anything from Regan."

He didn't finish what he had to say because Travis idly grabbed the smaller man's shoulders and tossed him to the far side of the room.

Regan barely noticed, only aware of Travis coming ever closer to her.

When he was inches from her, he gently touched her temple with his fingertips, and Regan felt her knees go weak. Before she could collapse, he caught her, lifted her in his arms, and buried his face in her neck. Without a word exchanged, he carried her toward the door, turned right, and went toward her apartment at the end of the hall. After two days of talking to the man Farrell had hired, Travis knew the entire floor plan of the Silver Dolphin Inn.

Her mind too full to think at all, she never considered what she was doing or committing herself to. All she knew was that Travis held her, and, more than life itself, she wanted him to make love to her.

Gently, as if she might break, he laid her on the bed and then sat beside her, his hands holding her face, fingertips caressing her cheeks and temples. "I had almost forgotten how beautiful you are," he whispered, "how delicately lovely you are."

Her hands went up his arms. How magnificent it felt to feel his strength once again, to feel the nearness of him! Her trembling began again as desire flooded her, coursing through her blood hotly.

"Travis," she managed to whisper before his mouth covered hers.

Desperate, frantic, turbulent, they began to tear at each other. There was no desire for sweetness, only a violent need that had to be fulfilled. Clothes tore away, buttons flew across the room, a handful of laces burst, and delicate stockings shredded. As they came together like a clap of thunder following a burst of brilliant lightning, they clawed and clung, drove each other deeper and deeper, trying to satisfy their overpowering, uncontrollable need of each other.

Violently, in a blinding flash, they arched together as spasms twisted their bodies. Clinging in a breathless crush for full minutes before their muscles relaxed, they finally surfaced and looked at each other, their eyes seeming to try to devour each other.

It was Regan who broke the spell—by laughing—for Travis, his chest and one arm bare, wore one shirt sleeve alone.

Glancing down at what she was laughing at, he grinned delightedly.

"The pot shouldn't call the kettle black," he said as he nodded pointedly toward the remnants of her attire.

A petticoat was bunched about her waist, while a torn one lay under them. Her stays, half on, half torn off, were crumbled under one arm, while her dress was about twelve feet across the room, dangling by a button from the corner of a picture frame. Rising on her elbows, she glanced down at her feet and saw that one stocking and its pretty lacy garter was intact while the other, with holes in it, was tangled in her toes.

Travis wore the one sleeve of his shirt and his boots and nothing in between.

With one look at Travis—his eyes dancing, his delicious body so near—she started laughing, her arms going out to him, pulling him to her as they began to roll about the bed, laughing gleefully, while Travis quite expertly tore away the remnants of her clothes. Never seeming to leave her, he took his boots off, and a loud crash of breaking china as one of the boots landed somewhere in the room caused new hilarity.

Sharp, teasing, nipping little bites on her shoulders and arms made her stop laughing and turn serious as she gave herself over to his lovemaking. Their first passion was gone, and they could spend more time reexploring, rediscovering each other. As Travis's mouth traveled down her body, she closed her eyes, gave herself over to her senses. Running her hand down his arm, she caught his hand, raised it to her lips, and began to taste those broad fingertips that gave her so much pleasure. Scraping them against her teeth, gently chewing on the soft pads, running her tongue across his knuckles, she was so aware that this was the hand of a man—scarred, hard, callused, broad, yet delicate and sensitive. She bit hard in the palm, wanting to devour him.

Travis pulled his hand away to run it over her legs, to massage, to kiss and caress, until she kicked her legs in impatience, wanting him again. When he brought his head up again, she pulled his mouth down to hers and threatened to swallow him whole.

Travis gave a low, seductive laugh and pulled her to him, both of them on their sides, facing, as he manipulated her legs around him and groaned when he entered her softness. Holding him tightly, staying with him as he moved her body, he prolonged her ecstasy for minutes, days, weeks, years, a century, as her head lolled backward, rolling, unaware of who or where she was.

When she thought she would go insane, he abruptly pushed her to her back and thrust into her long and hard until their bodies at last found release.

Without a word, exhausted, sweaty, sated, they fell asleep in each other's arms.

Regan was the first to awaken, surprised to see the sun setting outside her window. Stretching, moving away to look at Travis sprawled across the bed, she wondered if she'd ever have any sense when it came to him. For the first time in years she'd completely forgotten her responsibilities to her daughter, her friend, and her business. Quietly, so as not to disturb him, she left the bed and dressed, grabbing what was left of her mutilated garments from the furniture. Before she left the room she planted a kiss on Travis's hair and covered the lower half of him with a light quilt.

Silently, she left the room and headed toward the kitchen. Brandy must be wondering what had happened to her.

Travis awoke slowly, feeling as if he'd slept well for the first time in years. With a smile on his lips, he turned his head to look at his wife, but, instead of Regan, he encountered a pair of solemn brown eyes watching him intently.

"Hello," Travis said quietly to the little girl. "What's your name?"

"Jennifer Stanford. Who are you?"

Even before she spoke, Travis had an idea of who she was. There was a look about her of his younger brother, and the arch of her eyebrows was very like their mother's. "Is your mother's name Regan?"

Seriously, the child nodded.

Sitting up on the bed, pulling the quilt across his lower half, Travis was also serious. "What would you say if I were your father?"

Jennifer traced a pattern on the bedspread. "I might like it. Are you my father?"

"I think it would be safe to say I am."

"Are you going to live with us?"

"I was planning for you to live with me. If you were to come sit by me I could tell you all about where I live. Last year I bought four ponies just the right size for my daughter."

"You'd let me ride a pony?"

"It would be yours to care for, to ride, and to do whatever you wanted with it."

After just a moment's hesitation, Jennifer climbed onto the bed beside her father, far away at first, but as Travis's storytelling increased, soon she was sitting in his lap.

And that is how Regan found them, cuddled together, fascinated by each other. It was a charming picture.

As soon as Jennifer saw her mother, she started bouncing on the bed with glee. "This is my daddy, and we're going to go live with him, and he has a pony for me and pigs and chickens and a treehouse and a swimming pond, and we can go fishing and everything!"

After one quick look at Travis, Regan held out her arms for her daughter. "Brandy has supper ready for you in the kitchen."

"Can Daddy come too?"

"We need to talk," Regan said sternly. "He'll see you later—that is, if you eat what Brandy gives you."

"I will," Jennifer promised, waving to her father before scampering out the door.

"She's a beauty," Travis said. "I couldn't be prouder. . . ." He stopped when Regan turned to look at him in fury. "Did I do something?"

"Did you do something?" she mocked, trying to control her temper. "How dare you tell *my* daughter we're going to live with you!"

"But of course you'll return now that I've found you. It just took me a while, that's all."

"Did it ever occur to you that I've always known where you were?" she fumed. "At any time that I wanted, I could have returned to you and that monstrosity of a plantation of yours."

"Regan," Travis said, his voice low. "I don't understand why you left, but I can tell you that you and my daughter are returning home with me."

"Right there is why I left," she said. "From the moment I met you you've told me what to do and how to do it. I wanted to stay in England, but you wanted me to come to America, so I came to America. You initiated a wedding ceremony without even asking me if I wanted to marry you. And then at that plantation of yours! I was left in charge of a hundred people who did everything they could to defy my authority. And all the while you were . . . out chasing horses with your dear Margo."

At the last, Travis smiled. "Jealousy, was that why you left me?"

Regan threw up her hands in despair. "Haven't you heard anything I've said? I don't want you to run my life, or Jennifer's. I don't want her growing up and being told when to do something and how to do it. I want her to learn to make her own decisions."

"When have I ever stopped you from making decisions? I gave you half a plantation of decisions to make, and I never interfered."

"But I didn't know how to make them. Can't you understand? I was so afraid, in a new country around strangers who constantly told me I didn't know how to do anything. I was *afraid!*"

Travis's eyes were twinkling. "From what I've heard, you've done very well here. You didn't seem to be afraid of Americans here, so why were you there? I admit I have a fairly harsh group of judges working for me, but if you did it here, why couldn't you have done it then?"

"I don't know," she answered honestly. "Here I had to

do something or starve. At your place I could have stayed in my room and never come out.''

"Which you did most of the time, if I remember correctly.''

She gave him a sharp look because she'd had no idea he'd known what she did during the day. Had he any idea how terrified she'd been during those months?

He continued, "After starting from scratch and buying and building a whole town, my place should be easy to run. I have a wagon here. We could pack Jennifer's clothes and yours and leave tomorrow. Or, better yet, let's leave now. You have clothes at home, and I'll buy my daughter everything new.''

"Stop it!" she shouted. "Right this moment! Do you hear me? You are *not* going to start running my life for me again. I like having some power of my own. I like deciding what I want to do rather than having you or my uncle or even Farrell making my decisions for me.''

His head came up. "Who's Farrell?"

With a look of disgust, she answered, "The man you so blithely tossed across the room this morning.''

"So what's between you two?" he asked, his eyes in a hawklike gaze.

"I knew Farrell in England. In fact, I was engaged to him once, and he came to America to find me.''

For a moment, Travis was quiet. "You said you'd been in love with a man once. Was he this Farrell?"

She was startled at his memory. "I believe so. I was lonely, and he paid attention to me for a while, and I thought I loved him. It was so long ago, and I was a different person then.''

"And how do you feel about him now?"

She walked about the room. "I don't know how I feel about anything right now. For years I was scared of everything, and then I suddenly was totally alone, and I had to sink or swim. For the last four years all I've done is balance ledger sheets and buy and sell property. Men have not been part of my life. Now all at once Farrell turns up, and I'm reminded of that unloved little girl I once was, and here you are, just like always, making me ache to touch you yet terrified you may make me into a crying child as I once was. Can't you understand, Travis? I can't return to your plantation and be smothered by you. The only way I can be myself is to stay away from you."

In spite of her best intentions, she began to cry. "Damn you!" she said. "Why did you have to come back and upset me like this? Go away, Travis Stanford! Go away and never, never come near me again." With that, she slammed out of the room.

Leaning back against the headboard, Travis smiled. When he'd first met her, he'd seen just a hint of the woman she could be, but he wasn't sure how to help her become that woman. Maybe she was right and the plantation was too much to handle. When he'd heard how the staff was treating her, it was all he could do to keep from throttling the lot of them, but he knew she needed to find her own strength.

Now, closing his eyes, thinking about her, he was overwhelmed at the woman she'd become—sure of herself, sensible, her dreams put into action, made into reality. She'd taken what was little more than a wide spot in the road and built a thriving town, and she'd raised an intelligent, sensible little daughter. No one need worry that Jennifer was going to retreat to her room and cry.

With a loud laugh of pure happiness, he tossed aside the quilt and began to dress; at least his pants and boots were in one piece. Although Regan thought she'd matured enough to resist him, he knew she hadn't. What was that old saying? Age and treachery will win out over youth and talent every time. He planned to use every means, every aid ever learned to win her back. With resolve, he left the room, wearing only the snug dark pants and tall boots.

Chapter 17

TRAVIS STOPPED AT THE OPEN KITCHEN DOOR, DRAWN TO the smells coming from within. Chuckling, he remembered how Regan had always made him miss meals. With one glance about the room, he knew the luscious bit of curves and blonde hair in the corner was Brandy Dutton. He'd heard a lot about her from the weasel he'd met in Richmond.

"Excuse me," he said loudly. "I wonder if I might get something to eat in here. I'm not exactly dressed for dining in public."

"Oh my," Brandy said in such a way, smiling openly at Travis's wide chest and brawny arms, that Travis knew what he'd heard about her was true; Brandy was far from celibate.

She recovered herself. "So, you're the man who put roses in Regan's cheeks," she said heartily, coming forward.

"I put roses somewhere," he said quietly, for Brandy alone and not her staff, who were gaping unabashedly.

With a throaty laugh, Brandy took his arm. "I think we're going to get along quite well. Now sit down, and I'll get you something to eat. Elsie," she called over her shoulder. "Run down to the mercantile store and get Mr. Stanford a couple of new shirts, the biggest Will has. And take your time getting back. We have a lot to talk about."

Brandy fed Travis a meal such as he'd never had before. The more he ate of her food, the more she liked him, and between his shirtless state, the food, and his answers to her questions, she was practically in love by the end of the meal.

"Yes, she's lonely," Brandy said in answer to Travis's question. "All she does is work. It's like she's been driven to prove something to herself. For years I've tried to get her to slow down, but she'll never hear of it. She goes and goes all the time, buying more and more. She could have retired a year ago."

"No men?" he asked, his mouth full of mince pie.

"A few hundred have tried, but no one has succeeded. Of course, when you've had the best. . . ."

He smiled at her, took the new shirt from the chair back, and rose. "Regan and Jennifer are going to leave Scarlet Springs to return with me. How is that going to affect your partnership?"

"There's a new lawyer here from back East, and he could handle selling the properties and investing the money. With my half, I might like to travel, maybe see Europe. Tell me, have you told Regan she's leaving here?"

Travis only smiled in such a way that Brandy laughed. "Good luck," she called as he left the kitchen.

For two days Regan managed to avoid Travis, or at least she was able to avoid another out-and-out argument. But no one could miss him physically. Jennifer seemed to think her father was her personal playmate, and the two of them never left each other's sight. Travis even took over the task of washing his daughter's long, snarled hair, and Regan was disgusted not to hear one screech of pain or protest from Jennifer. He took her riding and tree climbing, and she was impressed at her father's agility. Jennifer showed him the whole town, announcing that he was her daddy and that she was going to go live with him and his horses.

Regan did her best to ignore Travis and his seduction of her daughter, as well as the countless questions from the townspeople.

Regan had not seen Farrell since the day Travis had arrived, and she was startled to realize, when he reappeared, that she had not thought of him in his two-day absence.

"May I speak to you privately?" he asked.

He looked tired and very dirty, as if he'd been traveling for days without sleep.

"Of course. Come to my office." When they were inside the office, door closed, she turned to him. "You look as if you have something important to tell me."

Collapsing into a chair, he looked up at her. "I have been all the way to Boston and back in two days."

"It must have been urgent business," she said, pouring him a drink. "I take it I and my father's money are involved."

"Yes, or at least your father's will. There was a copy filed in an attorney's office in Boston. I had it made and sent to America some time ago, just in case I did find you. I thought I was sure of one point in it, but I went to Boston to have it confirmed. I have here a letter," he said, removing an envelope from his inside coat pocket.

Regan took it, held it for a moment. "Perhaps you could tell me what it says."

"Your parents died when you were very young, and perhaps you don't remember, but at that time your father's brother was still alive. He was to be your guardian, and you did stay with him for a few months, but he died soon after your parents."

"I remember only Uncle Jonathan."

"Yes, he was the only other relation you had, so the executors of the will, your parents' bank, put you into his care. They, of course, had no idea what sort of a man he was. At the time the will was written, your parents thought you would be safe with your father's brother."

"Farrell, please get to the point."

"The point, my dear, is that you could not get married without your guardian's permission. Perhaps they didn't want you marrying a fortune hunter, or perhaps they didn't want to see you go through the hell they did when they were cut off by her family without a penny."

"Is that all? Surely there's more to this," she said.

"Regan, you don't understand. You were married to Travis Stanford without your guardian's written permission, and you were only seventeen."

"Seventeen! No, I'd been eighteen for months."

"In the letter is your actual date of birth. Your uncle tried to forge the date ahead so he could marry you off and get his money."

Feeling a bit stunned, Regan leaned back against the desk. "You're saying that my marriage to Travis isn't valid, aren't you?"

"Worthless. You were underage, a minor without your

guardian's consent. You are not, nor have you ever been, married to anyone, Miss Weston.''

"And Jennifer?"

"I'm sorry to say that she is illegitimate. Of course, if you were to marry again, the husband could adopt her.''

"I don't think Travis would like someone else adopting his daughter," she said quietly.

"To hell with Travis," Farrell said, jumping up to stand before her. "I've waited for you for years. I've loved you for years. You can't blame me for shying away from a seventeen-year-old child. Instinctively I must have sensed your tender years, and you can't blame me for not wanting a child for a wife. At least I didn't force you to my bed as that man who is Jennifer's father did.''

He paused, taking her hand in his. "Marry me, Regan. I'll make a good, faithful husband to you. Haven't I loved you for many years already? And I'll be a good father to Jennifer.''

"Please, Farrell," she said, pulling away from him. "I must think about this. It's come as a shock finding out I've lived in sin with a man for so many years. And this could hurt Jennifer badly.''

"That's why—," he began, but she put up her hand and cut him off.

"I need to be alone to think about this, and you," she smiled, "need a bath and some rest.''

It was several more minutes before he left and Regan was finally alone to read what was inside the packet Farrell had brought her. A half-hour later, when she put it down, she smiled. It was true she'd never been married to Travis. How he was going to rage at this news! For the first time in years she lapsed into one of her daydreams, imagining how he'd react when she told him he had no power over her, that, legally, Jennifer was no man's daughter. For just once in her life she was going to win over Travis Stanford, and it was going to be a wonderful experience.

As for Farrell's proposal, she dismissed it. The silly man thought Regan really believed his protestations of love. He wanted her married to him before her twenty-third birthday when she would come into her parents' fortune. He'd learn soon enough that she was going to live her own life.

With a smile, she began to write Travis a note, asking him to join her for a private dinner that night.

The private dining room was set with tall, fragrant candles, cut crystal glassware from Vienna, porcelain dinnerware from France, silver from England. The wine was a delicacy from Germany, and the food was American.

"I'm glad to see that you've come to your senses," Travis said, buttering a biscuit. "Jennifer will be much better off around friends instead of all these strangers. Has she always been given the run of this place? I can't see that it's good for a child playing in the corridors of a public inn."

"And you have such a vast experience with children that you, of course, know exactly what is right for them," Regan retorted.

He shrugged, enjoying his food. "I certainly know enough to be certain there is a better place for a child than this. At my place you can spend more time with Jennifer and"—he smiled—"our other children."

"Travis—," she began, but he interrupted her.

"I can't begin to tell you how relieved I was when you finally came to your senses. But really, I was expecting more of a fight. You've grown up more than I thought."

"What!" she sputtered on her wine. "Finally came to my senses? Grown up? What are you talking about?"

He caught her hand in his, caressed her fingers, and when he spoke his voice was deep and low. "This dinner was such a surprise to me because I knew what you wanted to say." He kissed her fingertips. "I want you to know that I realize how difficult a decision it's been for you, and I'll never use it against you. You've done a brave and generous thing in agreeing to return with me. Perhaps you'd like to stay here in your little town for a while longer, but Jennifer needs more than a houseful of strangers—she needs a home, which I can, of course, give her." Again, he kissed her fingers. "You've made a wise decision."

Taking deep breaths to calm herself, as well as a deep drink of wine, Regan gave him a radiant smile. "You vain, pompous farmer," she said conversationally. "I do not plan to return to your house, and my 'little town,' as you call it, is home for my daughter."

In spite of her good intentions, her voice was rising. "I invited you here, not to tell you I was returning with you as you so arrogantly assumed, but to tell you that I am not and never have been married to you."

It was Travis's turn to sputter. Regan, for the first time during the meal, began to eat. It felt good to win over Travis!

Grabbing her wrist, he started to pull her from her seat.

"What are you doing?" she demanded.

"I assume you have a preacher in this town. He can marry us now."

"He will not!" she hissed. "And if you don't sit down I just may take Jennifer away again."

Hesitating, but not wanting to risk such a punishment, he sat down. "Tell me the whole story," he said bleakly.

Regan lost some of her cheerfulness when she saw Travis's look, and when she told him his daughter was not legally his, she almost said she'd marry him then and there. But it was at the mention of Farrell's name that his look changed.

"That two-bit piece of scum told you this?" he demanded. "He's certainly gone to a lot of trouble. What's in it for him?"

Regan was well aware that Travis knew nothing of the money she was due to inherit, money that would mean nothing to Travis but meant everything to Farrell. But, truthfully, she didn't like Travis's insinuation that Farrell had a motive besides love.

"Farrell wants to marry me," she said haughtily. "He says he loves me as well as Jennifer and wants to adopt my daughter."

"You wouldn't be such a fool," Travis said smugly. "Why would any woman want a weakling like that?"

The implied second part of that statement was, "When you could have someone like me?"

Glaring at him, Regan almost snarled. "Farrell is a gentleman. He knows how to make a woman feel like a lady. His courting is . . . exquisite," she said with feeling. "All you Americans know is how to make demands."

Travis snorted. "Any American can outcourt any weakling Englishman."

"Oh Travis," Regan smiled serenely. "You know nothing of courting. Your idea of seducing a woman is to drag her about by her hair."

"There've been a few times when you've liked being dragged about," he answered.

She lost her serenity. "That is an example of your Colonial crudity."

"And you, my dear, are an English snob. You said your birthday is in three weeks. You'll marry me on that day, and you'll do it willingly."

With that, he left the room before he heard Regan gasp, "Never!"

Early the next morning, Regan, in her office, was bombarded with news from Brandy. First there were accusations because Travis had left the inn last night, and this morning he still hadn't returned. Brandy's looks showing her opinion that Regan was in the wrong were followed by a word of warning, for a tall, red-haired woman had just registered at the inn and was asking for her fiancé, Mr. Travis Stanford.

"Looks to me like you've got some trouble," Brandy sighed.

"Oh good," Regan answered in a tired voice. "Just what I need. Doesn't anyone realize that it's not easy to run an inn this size? I have days of work piled on my desk, and, by the way, Farrell has already informed me that Travis has left, and, before him, my daughter told me. Farrell, I'm sure, has much more to say to me, but Jennifer may never say another word in my presence. Now, the redhead has got to be my dear friend Margo Jenkins. Just let me have a few minutes to collect myself and I'll be able to deal with her."

Brandy nodded and left the room.

For several moments, Regan stood quietly in her bedroom, letting her mind take her back to that time of Margo's visits to Travis's plantation. Then, Regan had been so grateful to Margo for not being angry with her, for helping with the household staff, that Regan had not seen Margo's insults for what they were. That Malvina! Regan thought. How she'd like to get her hands on that foul-tempered, lazy cook now. And Margo! Dear Margo lording it over the poor, insecure little wife, pretending to help but actually destroying what little confidence she did have.

Smiling, Regan left her office, stopped by the kitchen, and asked Brandy to prepare midmorning tea for two women. She ignored Brandy's remarks about looking ready to do battle and then sent an invitation to Margo, asking her to tea in the library.

Margo appeared in an astonishingly short time, and Regan saw things she hadn't seen before; years of dissipation were showing on Margo's face and body. Late nights, rich food, overindulgence of every sort showed in lines and dark places, a thickening of the waist in spite of the tight lacing of her stays.

"My, my, it's the little English flower," Margo said as she entered. "I hear you own this place now. Who bought it for you?"

"Won't you have a seat?" Regan said politely. "I've ordered some refreshments. Yes, I do own the inn." Smiling innocently, she continued, "As well as the printer's building, the lawyer's, the doctor's, the mercantile store, the blacksmith's, the schoolhouse, the druggist's, plus four farms outside the town and three hundred acres."

Margo's eyes blinked once, but otherwise she showed no change of expression. "And how many men have you slept with to get all that? Travis, I'm sure, would like to know."

"How kind you are to say you think I'm worth so much," Regan said enthusiastically. "But alas, I'm afraid I don't have your skills of selling myself to get what I want. I had to use old-fashioned intelligence and hard work to get what I own. Whenever I had a spare bit of change, I didn't spend it on a new gown but used it to bargain with to buy more land and more building materials.''

She stopped to answer the door to a very curious Brandy who was holding a large tray.

"How's it going?" Brandy whispered.

Regan smiled smugly, making Brandy laugh as she handed her friend the tray.

When they were alone again, with the tray on a low table between them, Regan poured tea.

"Shall we begin again?" Regan asked. "It's no use pretending that we're friends. I take it you are here because you want my husband.''

Margo collected herself. This was not a battle she wanted to lose. "I see you have learned to pour tea," she said.

"I have learned a great many things in the last few years. You'll find I'm not so trusting as I once was. Now tell me what you want.''

"I want Travis. He was mine until you jumped into his bed, got yourself pregnant, and forced him to marry you.''

"That is one way of looking at the situation. Tell me, has Travis said he'd marry you if he were free of me?''

"He doesn't have to tell me," Margo said. "We were almost engaged when he met you, and the only problem is that he's infatuated with you. He's never had a woman leave him before, and it's driving him wild.''

"If that is the case, if Travis likes women who leave him, why did you follow him here? Wouldn't it have been better to stay away and let him return to you?''

"Damn you, you little bitch!" Margo snarled. "Travis

Stanford is mine! He was mine long before you were out of short dresses. You left him! You stole his mother's jewels and just walked off and left him. If I hadn't found that note—.'' She stopped abruptly.

Regan caught Margo's eyes for a moment, her mind concentrating. All these years she'd wondered why Travis had never found her. She'd left a trail a child could have followed, but Travis had never even bothered. But if Margo had found the note first. . . .

"Did he look for me for very long?" Regan asked quietly.

Standing, Margo glared down at her. "You don't really expect me to tell you anything, do you? Just be warned. Travis is mine. I don't believe you're woman enough to fight me. I get what I want.''

"Do you, Margo?" Regan asked calmly. "Do you have a man who holds you at night while you cry or one you can tell your deepest secrets to? Do you know what it's like to share, to love and be loved by someone?" Turning her head, she looked up at Margo. "Or do you think of people in terms of dollars and cents? Tell me, if you owned Scarlet Springs, would you be so interested in my husband?''

Margo started to speak but seemed to change her mind as, silently, she left the room.

When Regan put the teacup to her lips, she was surprised to find she was trembling. The questions she'd asked Margo were what she'd been asking herself and had not been aware of them. What did owning a town mean, anyway? She had friends here, people she'd come to love, but were they any substitute for one special person, someone who loved you even when you weren't in the best of moods, someone to hold your head when you were sick, a special person who knew all your ugly parts and still loved you anyway?

Remembering Travis's plantation and Stanford Hall, she knew that Jennifer should grow up there. Travis's hundreds of relatives' portraits were on the walls, and they were Jennifer's ancestors, too. She deserved that sort of continuity, a place that was filled with security and peace, not the ever-changing interior of an inn.

Smiling, she leaned back against the chair. Of course, it wouldn't be easy to tell Travis he'd won. No doubt he'd gloat and tell her he knew he'd win. But who cared? It meant more to spend her life with the man she loved than to give it all up because of her silly pride. Besides, there'd be ways to repay him. Oh yes, she thought. She'd make him sorry he had ever bragged about anything.

"You certainly look pleased with yourself," Brandy said.

Regan hadn't heard her friend enter the room. "I was just thinking about Travis."

"That would make me smile, too. So when are you leaving with him?"

"And what makes you assume—?" Regan began, then stopped at Brandy's laugh. "I know what you're thinking, and it's all true. You know, for years I was afraid of Travis, afraid his personality would devour me and I wouldn't exist any longer."

"But now you know you can hold your own," Brandy said.

"Yes, and I realize he's right, that his plantation is a better place for Jennifer. And what about you? How is it going to affect you if I leave Scarlet Springs? Should I get someone else to help run the inn?"

"No, don't worry about it," Brandy said, holding up her

hand. "Travis and I have arranged it all. There'll be no problem."

"Travis and you! You mean you . . . and my husband . . . ? Behind my back?"

"The last I heard, he wasn't your husband any longer. And of course I knew you'd leave here. Travis is not a man a woman can resist very long. Did you know what hell he went through trying to find you after you left? And that he's been celibate since you left him?"

"What?" Regan asked as warmth spread over her. "How do you know any of this?"

"While you've been working, I've spent some time with Travis and Jennifer, and if you weren't curious, I certainly have been. Would you like to hear some of what that dear man's been through in the last few years?"

Brandy didn't wait for Regan's answer before she started on the long, detailed story of Travis's ordeal. Most of his friends believed Regan had drowned, but Travis kept searching for her in spite of everyone telling him to give it up. At one point a preacher was urging him to conduct a funeral for his dear departed wife, thinking perhaps that would rid Travis of his obsession with her.

An hour later, Regan left the library, her head in the clouds. Ignoring Farrell, who called after her, she kept looking for Travis, eager to tell him she loved him, wanted to marry him, and would return to his home with him.

By the end of the day, when he still hadn't appeared, some of her enthusiasm left her. Distractedly, she refused Farrell's dinner invitation and spent the evening with her daughter. When the second night passed and she still hadn't seen Travis, her euphoric state broke. Jennifer was sulking and shooting angry looks at her mother, Farrell was becoming quite persistent in his invitations, and Margo constantly asked Regan where Travis was.

By the third day, she wished she'd never heard of Travis Stanford. He couldn't have left her after all he'd done to find her! Could he? Oh, please God, she prayed, flinging herself onto the bed that night. Please don't let him have left me. For the first time in years, she began to cry. Damn you, Travis! she gasped. How many tears had that man made her shed?

Chapter 18

AT FIVE O'CLOCK THE NEXT MORNING, REGAN WAS AWAK-
ened by someone knocking on her door. Sleepily, she rolled
out of bed and pulled on her dressing gown.

Standing in the hallway was Timmie Watts, the son of
one of her farm tenants. Before she could say a word, the
little boy handed her a long-stemmed red rose and vanished
down the hall.

Yawning, not awake, Regan looked down at the exquisite, fragrant flower. Attached to its stem was a bit of paper
which she unfurled to read, "Regan, will you marry me?
Travis."

It was a full minute before her mind understood what her
eyes saw, and then she gave a squeal of delight, hugged the
rose to her breast, and jumped into the air three times. He
hadn't forgotten her after all!

"Mommie," Jennifer said, rubbing the sleep from her
eyes. "Is Daddy home?"

"Almost," Regan laughed, grabbing her daughter and waltzing her about the room. "This rose, this lovely, perfect rose, is from your daddy. He wants us to go live with him."

"We are," Jennifer laughed, clutching her mother as she began to get dizzy. "We can ride my pony."

"Every single day from now on and forever!" Regan laughed. "Now let's get dressed, because I'm sure Daddy will be here very soon."

Before Regan settled on a gown of gold velvet, she threw everything she owned onto the bed. It was while she was in the midst of this mess that someone again knocked on her door. Flying to it, hoping to see Travis, she flung the door open.

Standing there was Sarah Watts, Timmie's sister, and she was clutching two pink roses. Puzzled, taking the roses, Regan watched as Sarah fled down the hall.

"Was that Daddy?" Jennifer asked.

"No, but Daddy sent us two more roses." Attached to each one was a curl of paper in Travis's handwriting, saying, "Regan, will you marry me? Travis."

"Is something wrong, Mommie? Why doesn't Daddy come see us?"

Heedless of the clothes on the bed, Regan sat down. It was just a tiny, lurking suspicion, but the extra roses made her wonder what Travis was planning. With one glance at the clock, she saw that it was just after five-thirty. One rose had been delivered at five, two at five-thirty. No, she thought. It couldn't be.

"Nothing's wrong, sweet," Regan said. "Would you like these roses for your room?"

"They're from Daddy?"

"They certainly are."

Jennifer took the flowers, holding them as if they were priceless, and carried them to her room.

At six, when Jennifer and Regan were dressed and going down to breakfast, three more roses were delivered to Regan.

"How lovely," Brandy said, already up and cooking. Before Regan could protest, Brandy took the flowers, read the attached notes, and put the flowers in a vase. "You don't look so happy. I thought from the way you've been moping for the last three days you'd be pleased to get some sign from him. Three roses with those notes attached would certainly perk me up."

"There are five roses," she said seriously. "One delivered at five, two at five-thirty, three at six."

"You aren't thinking—," Brandy began.

"I had forgotten about it, but Travis and I did have words over courting. I made some derogatory remarks about the inability of Americans to court a woman."

"Not a nice thing to have said," Brandy said, feeling very American. "Five roses before breakfast shows you what we Americans can do." With that she went back to cooking.

Feeling she'd offended her best friend, Regan went to the dining room to check that everything was ready. As she was leaving the room, the printer's boy delivered four yellow roses to her, each with Travis's note attached.

With an enormous sigh, Regan smiled at the roses, shaking her head. Did Travis never do anything on a small scale? She slipped the notes into her pocket and went to look for a vase.

By ten o'clock, her smile was gone. Every half-hour more roses were delivered, until by now she had a total of sixty-six. The quantity itself wouldn't be daunting except for the interest the deliveries were exciting within the town. The druggist and his wife came to eat breakfast at the inn, something they'd never done before, and as they were leaving, they stopped to ask Regan questions, namely, who is this Travis who'd hired their three children to deliver roses every half-hour? They were very mysterious about where the children picked up the flowers or who had contacted them, and they were discreet about the notes they'd read—but curiosity was eating them alive.

At noon, a bouquet of fifteen roses, each with a note on its stem, was handed to Regan, and that's when she began to try hiding. But the whole town seemed to be in conspiracy against her. At five minutes before the hour or half-hour, someone always found something important to say to her, something that would keep her in plain view of everyone when the next bouquet was delivered.

At four o'clock, she was presented with twenty-three roses.

"That makes two hundred and seventy-six," the owner of the mercantile store said, chalking the number on the wall beside the bar in the taproom.

"Don't you have any customers today?" Regan asked pointedly.

"Nary a one," he smiled. "They're all in here." He looked back at the jammed taproom. "Who'll give me money on when they're going to stop?"

Turning away, Regan left the room, thrusting the bundle of roses into Brandy's arms.

"Roses?" Brandy gasped. "What a wonderful surprise. Whoever sent them?"

Regan curled her lip and hissed before continuing down

248

the hall. She wouldn't put it past Travis to have instigated all the interest in the roses. Surely the townspeople had something better to do than sit around all day and watch her collect roses. Of course, the reason he'd hired every child in town for the deliveries was to create interest with the parents.

At seven o'clock, she received twenty-nine roses, and at eight, she got thirty-one. By nine she had received five hundred sixty-one roses, of every color a rose could create. Travis's notes, the same thing over and over, were in her pockets, in her desk drawers, in a box on her dressing table, in a copper pan in the kitchen. For all her complaining, she couldn't bring herself to discard even one of the notes.

By ten she was beginning to wonder if the flowers were ever going to stop. She was tired and wanted nothing more than to climb into bed and be still.

Just as she reached her door, a child thrust a bundle of thirty-five roses into her arms. Once inside, she carefully removed each note, read it, and then stored all of them in a drawer beside her underwear. "Travis," she whispered, no longer tired. At least alone in her room she could enjoy the roses.

Someone, Brandy no doubt, had put several water-filled vases in a corner, and Regan filled one now. As she did so, she remembered the last time he'd given her flowers, on their wedding night.

She was still chuckling when thirty-six roses were delivered at ten-thirty. Roses were also delivered at eleven and eleven-thirty. At midnight, yawning, Regan answered the knock at her door to admit Reverend Wentworth from the Scarlet Springs church.

"Won't you come in?" she asked politely.

"No, I must get home. It's far past my bedtime. I just came to bring you this."

He held out a long, narrow white box, and when Regan opened it, inside was a delicate rose of fine, thin, fragile, pink-tinted crystal. The stem and leaves were also glass, tinted a soft green. An engraved silver band hung gracefully down the side, reading, "Regan, will you marry me? Travis."

Regan was speechless, afraid to touch the elusive beauty of the glass rose.

"Travis was so hoping you'd like it," Reverend Wentworth said.

"Where did he find it? And how did he get it to Scarlet Springs?"

"That, my dear, is known only to Mr. Stanford. He merely asked if I'd deliver a gift to you at midnight tonight. Of course, when the box came and it was open, my wife and I, well . . . we couldn't resist a peek. Now I really must go. Goodnight."

She barely heard him, absently closing the door, leaning against it for a second, her eyes locked on the elegant, splendid crystal rose. Holding her breath, afraid she might break it, she put it in the little vase on her bedside table, next to the first live rose Travis had sent her. As she undressed, her eyes never left either rose, and when she went to bed the moonlight seemed to highlight each rose and she fell asleep smiling.

It was late when she awoke the next morning, already eight o'clock. After one quick look at her roses and sending all of them a radiant smile, she jumped out of bed and grabbed her dressing gown. One sleeve was twisted, and as she straightened it a blue piece of paper fell out. As it fell right-side up on the floor, she saw that it read, "Regan, will you marry me? Travis."

Hastily, she stuck it in her pocket, thinking that she hadn't noticed that any of the notes from yesterday were written on blue paper. She found Jennifer's room empty. The child was often up early and in the kitchen before her mother was even awake.

Still smiling, Regan returned to her room to dress. Today she was sure Travis would show up, would come to her on bended knee and beg her to marry him. She might, just might consent. She laughed out loud.

Her laugh stopped when she found another blue note inside the bodice of her dress. Hesitating for just a moment, looking suspiciously at the note, she whirled about and began to search her wardrobe.

The blue notes were everywhere—in her shoes, in her dresses, inside her drawers, wrapped in her petticoats and camisoles, even under her pillow!

How dare he! she thought, getting angrier with each note she found. How dare he invade her privacy in such a way! If not Travis personally, then he'd hired someone to go through all her things and place the notes there. And when? Surely some of them had been put there during the night, because even the dress she'd worn yesterday had three notes in it.

Angrily, she left her apartment and went straight to her office. As far as she could tell, nothing had been disturbed in this room. Thank heavens she locked it each night.

Sitting down at her desk, she didn't at first notice the thin bit of thread stretched across the leather blotter. Suspicious, her lips set firmly, she followed it down the front of her desk to the bottom, where it disappeared underneath. On her hands and knees, she slid down until she was flat on her back. Pinned to the bottom of her desk was a sign done in three-inch letters, "Regan, will you marry me? Travis."

Teeth gritted, she tore it away and was tearing it into tiny pieces when Brandy entered the room with a few dozen pieces of blue paper in her hands.

"I see he's been in here too," Brandy said cheerfully.

"He's really gone too far this time. This is my private office, and he has no right to come in here uninvited."

"I don't want to add to your anger, but have you checked your safe?"

"My—!" she began, but stopped. Only Regan had a set of the three keys it took to open the safe. The other set was locked in a bank vault a hundred miles to the south. Even Brandy never opened the inn's safe or knew how or in what order the keys must be used; she left all that up to Regan.

Quickly, Regan went to the big safe and started the long process of opening it. As she pulled the last door, a piece of wide blue ribbon fell out. Slowly pulling it, her jaw set, her eyes angry, she saw immediately what was written on it. She didn't bother to read it but reached in and grabbed a handful of ribbon and angrily threw it toward the trashcan.

"How did you guess?" she asked Brandy as she stood.

Brandy seemed a bit nervous and gave Regan a weak smile. "I hope you're ready for this. It seems that while everyone in town was here yesterday and their stores were closed, somebody, or maybe it was an army of somebodies, put these little blue proposals all over town. The doctor found one in his bag and four in his office. Will, at the mercantile store, found six in his place, and"—she paused to stifle a laugh—"the blacksmith picked up a horse's hoof and found one on blue ribbon wadded inside the horse's shoe."

Regan sat down. "Go on," she whispered.

"Some of the people are taking it well, but some are fairly angry. The lawyer found one in his safe, and he's talking about suing. But, in general, everyone is laughing, saying they want to meet this Travis."

"I never want to see him again in my life," Regan said with feeling.

"You don't mean that," Brandy smiled. "Maybe your notes are all alike, but most of the others are quite creative. There are bits of poetry, some things from Shakespeare, and Mrs. Ellison, who plays the piano, received an entire song which she says is very pretty. She's dying to play it for you."

Regan's head came up. "Is she out there?"

Brandy grimaced. "Everyone feels as if they're involved now, and . . . most of them are out there."

"Who is *not* there?" Regan asked bleakly.

"Mrs. Ellison's grandmother, who had the stroke last year, and Mr. Watts still had milking to do, and . . . ," she trailed off apologetically because she could think of no other missing townspeople.

"Mrs. Brown's sister is visiting, came in yesterday, and she's dying to meet you. Brought all six kids over, too."

Regan put her arms on the desk and buried her face. "Can a person die by will, just by wishing it? How can I face all those people?" She looked up at Brandy, her face horribly distressed. "How could Travis do this to me?"

Brandy knelt beside her friend and touched her hair. "Regan, can't you see that he just wants you so badly that he'll do *anything* to get you back? You don't know the hell he's been through since you left. Did you know that he lost forty-five pounds when you first left him? It was a friend of his named Clay who talked him out of giving up on life.''

"Travis told you all of this?"

"In a roundabout way. I did some prying, and it took a while to piece together all the facts, but I did. Right now the man is past any sense of pride. He doesn't care what he has to do to get you back. If he can enlist the whole town to help him, then he will. Maybe his tactics are a little . . . well, maybe he's not exactly subtle, but would you rather have one rose and a man like Farrell or, what was the final count, seven hundred and forty-two roses and Travis Stanford?''

"But does he have to do all this?" Regan pleaded, flipping the thread leading to the note that had been under her desk.

"You've told me repeatedly how Travis never asked you anything, but only told you what to do and how to do it. If I remember correctly, at the ceremony you said no to him just because he hadn't *asked* you to marry him. I don't believe you can accuse him of not having asked you now. And, too, you said you wanted to be courted." Brandy stood, smiling. "This courtship may go down in history."

Regan, in spite of herself, began to smile. "All I wanted was a little champagne and a few roses."

Eyes wide, Brandy put her fingers to her lips. "Please don't mention champagne. You may start a flood."

A giggle escaped Regan. "Will he ever do anything on a normal scale?"

"Don't you hope not?" Brandy said seriously. "I'd give a lot to be in your shoes."

"My shoes are all packed full of notes," Regan said, deadpan.

Laughing, Brandy started toward the door. "You'd better prepare yourself. They are waiting eagerly for you."

Brandy laughed at Regan's heartfelt groan before leaving the room.

Taking a moment to calm herself, Regan thought about Brandy's words. Everything about Travis was overscale, from his body to his house to his land, so why did she expect his courting to be any different?

Carefully, she retrieved the ribbon from the trash and tenderly folded it. Someday she'd show this to her grandchildren. With resolve, shoulders straight, she left her office and went toward the public rooms.

Nothing could have prepared her for what was awaiting her. The first person she saw was Mrs. Ellison's grandmother enthroned in a chair, smiling at her with one side of her face, the other side paralyzed by her stroke.

"I'm so glad you could make it," Regan said graciously, as if she'd issued invitations to this party.

"Seven hundred and forty-two!" a man was saying. "And the last one was made of glass, all the way from Europe."

"Wonder how he got it here and didn't break it?"

"And wonder how he got up to my loft? The ladder broke two days ago, and I ain't had time to fix it. But there it was, just as pretty as you please, a ribbon around a bale of hay and asking Regan to marry him."

There was a man painting a vine of roses on the wall behind the bar in her taproom, and beside it were numbers—5:00 A.M., 1 rose; 5:30 A.M., 2 roses, all the way down to 38 roses at 11:30 P.M. and one rose at midnight and the total at the bottom. She didn't bother to ask who the painter was or who had given him permission to paint on her wall. She was too busy fending off questions.

"Regan, is it true this man is Jennifer's father yet you're not married to him?"

"We were married at the time Jennifer was born," Regan tried to explain. "But I was underage and—."

Someone else's question interrupted her.

"I hear this man Travis owns half of Virginia."

"Not quite, only about a third." Sarcasm didn't dull their interest.

"Regan, I don't like this man leaving notes in my private safe. I have private documents in there, and a lawyer's word to his clients is sacred."

On and on they went, hour after hour, until Regan's smile was plastered on. Only a small voice at her side made her respond. "Mommie." She looked down to see her daughter's small face, obviously worried about something.

"Come on," she said, lifting her daughter and carrying her to the kitchen. "Let's see if Brandy can fix us lunch, and we'll go on a picnic."

An hour later, Regan and her daughter were alone together by a little stream north of Scarlet Springs. They'd demolished a basketful of fried chicken and little cherry tarts.

"Why doesn't Daddy come back home?" Jennifer asked. "And why doesn't he write me letters like everybody else?"

For the first time, Regan realized that her daughter had been excluded from the notes and roses. Thinking back, she knew Jennifer's room had been free of any marriage proposals.

She pulled her daughter to her lap. "I guess because Daddy is trying to get me to marry him, and he knows that wherever I go, you go too."

"Daddy doesn't want to marry me too?"

"He wants you to live with him; in fact, I think at least half of the roses are for you, to get you to come live with him too."

"I wish he'd send me roses. Timmie Watts says Daddy only wants you, and I'll have to stay here with Brandy when you go away."

"That was a dreadful thing for him to say! And totally untrue! Your Daddy loves you very much. Didn't he tell you of the pony he bought for you and the treehouse he built? And this was before he'd even met you. Just think what he's going to do now that he knows who you are."

"You think he'll ask me to marry him too?"

Regan had no idea how to reply to that. "When he asks me, it means he wants you too."

Sighing, Jennifer leaned against her mother. "I wish Daddy'd come home. I wish he'd never go away again, and I wish he'd send me roses and write me letters."

Rocking her daughter, stroking her hair, Regan felt Jennifer's sadness. How Travis would hate knowing he had hurt his daughter by excluding her. Perhaps tomorrow she could make up for Travis's oversight. Maybe she could find some roses, if there were any left within the state after Travis's harvesting of them, and give them to her daughter—from her father.

Tomorrow, she thought, and almost shuddered. What could he be planning for tomorrow?

Chapter 19

JENNIFER WOKE HER MOTHER THE NEXT MORNING, A
little bundle of roses clutched in her hand. "Do you think
they're from Daddy?" she asked her mother.

"Could be," Regan said, not really lying but giving the
child hope. She'd placed the little bouquet on her daughter's
pillow early this morning.

"They're not from Daddy," Jennifer said with great despair. "You put them there." With a fling, she tossed them
across the bed and ran to her own room.

It was some time before Regan could comfort her daughter, and she was close to tears herself before Jennifer quietened. If only there was some way she could get a message to
Travis and tell him of Jennifer's distress.

When they were finally dressed, both of them far from
cheerful, they held hands and together prepared for what the
day—and Travis—had planned for them.

The reception rooms were full of townspeople, but since

there was no new excitement, often only one family member was present. Stiffly, Regan fended off their questions and kept Jennifer near her as she checked the rooms of the inn and tried to keep up a normal routine. She was quite tired of being a spectacle for everyone to stare and gawk at.

By noon nothing new had happened, and the townspeople, deflated, began to go home. The dining room was filled but not packed, and Regan noticed Margo and Farrell dining together, their heads bent, almost touching as they talked. Frowning, she wondered what the two of them could have to say to each other.

But she had no more time to think about anything else, because the noise coming from the hall was rising in tone and pitch.

Eyes skyward, she felt like crying in despair. "Now what has he done?" she muttered.

Jennifer clutched her mother's hand. "Do you think Daddy's come home?"

"I'm sure he's done something," she said, and started for the front door.

Music began to fill the front of the inn as soon as they left the dining room. The sound of horses and wagons and other sounds she'd never heard before became louder and louder.

"What is it?" Jennifer asked, eyes widening by the second.

"I have no idea," Regan replied.

The front of the hotel was plastered with people, all frozen in their places at the six windows in front and the open door.

"Jennifer!" someone yelled, and all the people suddenly came alive."

"It's a circus!"

"And a menagerie! I saw one in Philadelphia once."

Jennifer's name was repeated several times before Regan could make a place for herself and her daughter on the front porch.

Just rounding the corner by the schoolhouse were three men, their faces painted, wearing satin clothes sewn with spots and stripes of outrageous colors, and they were doing flips, tumbling, jumping over each other.

Something on their chests seemed to be letters. It took Regan a while to make out the word because of the clowns' acrobatics.

"Jennifer," she said. "It says Jennifer."

Laughing, grabbing her daughter in her arms, she pointed excitedly. "It's for you! They're clowns, and they have Jennifer, your name, written on their suits."

"They're for me?"

"Yes, yes, yes! Your Daddy has sent you a whole circus, and if I know Travis, it's no little circus. Look! Here come some men doing tricks on horses."

More than a little stunned, Jennifer watched as three horses, beautiful, golden, long-maned horses, came galloping toward them, a man in each saddle, one standing up, another jumping in and out of the saddle, his feet barely touching the ground, and the last man's horse seemed to be dancing. As a body, they stopped in the midst of a storm of dust and saluted Jennifer. Grinning almost enough to tear her skin, she looked at her mother.

"The circus is for me," she said proudly, turning away to look at the other people beside her. "My Daddy sent a circus for me."

A stilt-walker followed the clowns and equestrians, and then came a man pulling a small black bear on a chain.

Everything had Jennifer's name written on it. The music was growing louder as the band came closer to the inn.

Suddenly a hush fell over all the townspeople as around the corner came the biggest, most bizarre creature anyone had ever seen. Lumbering slowly, its massive feet making the ground quake, the animal with its trainer leading it stopped before the inn. The man unfurled a sign down the animal's side: "Capt. John Crowinshield presents the first elephant to appear in these United States of America. And at a special request of Mr. Travis Stanford, this great beast will perform for—."

Regan read the sign to her daughter, who was clinging tightly to her mother.

"For Jennifer!" a second sign heralded.

"What do you think of that?" Regan asked. "Daddy sent the elephant to perform just for you."

For a moment Jennifer didn't answer, but after a long pause she leaned toward her mother's ear. "I don't have to keep him, do I?" she whispered.

Regan wanted to laugh, but the more she thought of her daughter's question and Travis's sense of humor. . . . "I sincerely, truly hope not," she said.

Thoughts of the elephant vanished as soon as it moved away, because behind the animal was a pretty little white pony covered with a blanket of white roses with "Jennifer" spelled out in red roses.

"What does it say, Mommie?" Jennifer asked with hope in her voice. "Is the pony for me?"

"It certainly is," said a pretty blonde woman in a revealing—scandalous actually—costume of stretchy cotton. "Your Daddy found you the sweetest, gentlest horse in this state, and if you like you can ride him in the parade."

"Could I? Please?"

"I'll take care of her," the woman said. "And Travis is on the grounds."

Reluctantly, Regan relinquished her daughter and watched as the woman lifted the child into the saddle. From the side of the pony, the woman took a vest completely covered in pink roses and slipped Jennifer's arms through it.

"Roses for me!" Jennifer yelled. "Daddy sent roses for me too."

Regan noticed she seemed to be looking for someone, and a quick glance showed Timmie Watts hiding behind his mother's skirts. Feeling rotten as she did it, Regan pulled the boy into Jennifer's sight, where the child promptly stuck her tongue out at him and pelted him with a rose. To clear her guilty conscience, Regan asked if Timmie would like to walk beside Jennifer's pony in the parade, which he accepted gladly.

Waving gaily and somewhat regally, Jennifer rode down the street toward the south end of Scarlet Springs. More men and women followed her, some walking, some on horses, all dressed outlandishly and garishly, followed by a seven-piece brass band. At the end of the parade, more clowns came, bearing signs announcing that a free performance of the circus, courtesy of Miss Jennifer Stanford, would be given in two hours.

As the last person disappeared around the curve of the road past the church, the townspeople stood silently for a few moments.

"I guess I better get on with my chores," said one man finally.

"I wonder what a person wears to a circus?" asked a woman.

"Regan," someone else began. "I'm sure this town's gonna lay down and die from boredom when you leave."

A hastily stifled giggle that could only be Brandy's made Regan turn.

"What do you think Travis is planning now?"

"To get to me through Jennifer," Regan replied. "At least I hope that's all he plans. Come in, we've got to get busy. We'll close the inn, put signs on the door, 'Gone to the circus,' and everyone can go."

"Great idea. I'll pack food for us and half the town, and we'll be ready in as little time as Travis has given us."

The two hours passed too quickly, and it seemed minutes before Regan was driving a wagon loaded with food to the circus grounds. A large enclosure had been made by stretching canvas walls around trees and posts. Long wooden benches had been set up, the ones in back taller than those in front, and already most of them were filled with townspeople. In one center section was a large space set apart by pink and orange ribbons blowing in the breeze.

"Wonder where you're to sit?" Brandy laughed at Regan's look of embarrassment. "Come on, it can't be as bad as you imagine."

The young woman in the pink tights directed both Regan and Brandy to the ribboned section and left them. Within minutes two horses, at full gallop, came tearing through the enclosure with one man on top, one leg on one horse, the other on the other horse. As he reached the end of the field, he jumped to one horse, turned both of them around, and, again at a gallop, leaped from one horse to the next.

"Oh my!" Brandy breathed.

After that, they had no time to think as the field filled with more and more horses. The horses did tricks; the men did tricks atop the horses. Two men stood on two horses, and a third man stood on the men's shoulders as the horses ran round and round the ring.

After the equestrians left, Jennifer rode into the ring, her pony led by the lady in pink, and Jennifer was wearing an identical costume of pink bits of gold glitter here and there. As Regan watched, her stomach in her throat, the woman took the little girl's hand and Jennifer stood in the saddle and slowly rode the pony once around the circle.

"Sit down!" Brandy commanded as Regan started after her daughter. "She can't fall very far, and the woman's holding her."

At that the circus woman let go of Jennifer's hand, and she cried, "Look at me, Mommie!" to which Regan nearly fainted, especially when Jennifer gave a jump and the lady caught her.

Jennifer took several bows as she'd obviously been taught, and all of Scarlet Springs applauded explosively. She ran to her mother, and Regan caught the child tightly.

"Was I good? Did I do it right?"

"You were splendid. You nearly scared me to death."

Jennifer seemed pleased at that. "Wait till you see Daddy."

It took Regan a while to calm her racing heart, and when she could speak again there was no time to ask after Travis as the elephant was once again paraded before them. The clowns did more tricks, making everyone laugh, and the little bear danced. But all the while Regan was looking for Travis.

The band had been playing constantly, and now it struck up some eerie music that made everyone quieten.

"And now, ladies and gentlemen," bellowed a good-looking man in a red coat and shiny black boots, "we bring you a death-defying act. Our next performer will walk a tightrope—without a net. If he falls . . . well, you can use your own imaginations."

"I don't think I like this part," Regan said, looking upward at the rope strung between two poles high above the ground. "Perhaps I should take Jennifer and leave."

The look on Brandy's face changed. "Maybe you should stay, Regan," she said in a funny voice.

Following Brandy's stare, Regan wasn't sure of what she saw.

Travis walked into the ring, one arm raised, as if he'd always worked in a circus. The costume he wore, of black cotton, fit him like a second skin, showing the big muscles in his thighs, his small tight buttocks, and his broad, hard chest. A black cape lined in scarlet satin hung from his shoulders. With a flourish, he tossed it to a beautiful woman wearing a tiny bit of green satin. "No wonder the man drives you crazy," Brandy said.

"What in the world is he doing out there?" Regan gasped. "Surely even Travis wouldn't do anything so foolish as. . . ."

She couldn't continue as the horns blared and Travis calmly began to climb the swaying rope ladder to the tiny platform high over their heads.

"That's my Daddy! That's my Daddy!" Jennifer yelled, bouncing up and down on the hard wooden seat.

Regan couldn't move. Her eyes didn't blink, her lungs didn't function, even her heart stopped beating as she stared at Travis on the platform above them.

At the top he again raised his arm to the crowd below, and everyone clapped loudly. There was complete silence as

Travis began his slow, careful journey across the taut rope, a long pole in his hand, and it seemed an eternity before he made it to the other side.

The applause made the benches rattle, and Regan buried her face in her hands, tears of relief coming quickly. "Tell me when he's on the ground again," she said to Brandy.

Brandy was unusually quiet.

"Brandy?" Regan said, peeking out through her fingers. Her friend's expression made her head swivel to look up at Travis again. He was standing on the platform, calmly looking down at her, seeming to be waiting for something. When she looked up at him, he hooked something onto the platform pole and another thing onto the wide black leather belt he wore.

"He's going to walk it again," Brandy whispered. "But at least he's using a safety cable this time."

Travis was several feet across the rope before everyone began to realize just what his "safety cable" really was. Slowly the banner began to unfold. "Regan" was the first word they saw, and after having seen the sentence hundreds of times in the last two days, they needed no one to read it for them.

"Regan!" they read as one. "Will" came next, then "You." Each word got louder and louder, and finally, when Travis stood at the opposite platform, they reread all of it together. If they'd worked for weeks they couldn't have orchestrated it better. "Regan, will you marry me?"

Regan's body turned red from her toes to her hair roots and possibly spread to the tips of her hair; it certainly felt as if it did.

"What does it say, Mommie?" Jennifer demanded as everyone around her began to laugh.

Regan was afraid to speak for fear of what she might say. She absolutely refused to look at Travis, who was climbing down the rope ladder amidst great cheering, clapping, and general hilarity.

"I'm going home," Regan finally whispered. "Please see to Jennifer," she said, and, her head held high, she left the ribboned seat and walked in front of the crowd and out of the canvas-wrapped enclosure. People were calling things to her, but she ignored them as she started the long walk back to the inn.

Using her key, she went inside her own apartment and thought perhaps she'd never leave it again, except maybe to sneak away one night so that she would never again look at a person from Scarlet Springs.

It came as no surprise to her that propped against her pillow was a note on heavy ivory paper. It was an engraved invitation, exquisite, costly, for her to join Travis Stanford for supper that night at nine o'clock. A handwritten message was at the bottom, saying he'd pick her up at the door to her apartment at eight-forty-five.

Feeling completely defeated, she knew there was nothing else she could do but meet him. If she refused, would he perhaps have his elephant knock her door down, or maybe he'd arrive riding it? She was ready for anything even Travis could imagine.

No one bothered her all the rest of the evening, and she was grateful to whoever had arranged such a phenomenon. She'd had more than enough of everyone's attentions.

At exactly eight-forty-five, a knock sounded on her door, and Travis stood there, dressed elegantly in a dark green coat and lighter green pants. He smiled at her and glanced at the pretty apricot silk dress she wore.

"You are prettier than ever," he said, offering her his arm.

The moment she touched him she forgave him. She wished she could have kicked herself for doing it, but all her anger and frustration, all her desire to shoot him, left her instantly.

Swaying, she leaned against him for just a second, and as she did so he took her chin in his hand and looked into her eyes. Searching her face, his eyes holding hers, he bent and kissed her gently, sweetly. "I've missed you," he whispered, before smiling and leading her toward a handsome two-seater buggy.

"Oh Travis," was all she could manage as he settled beside her, to which he laughed in a seductive way and clicked for the horse to move.

It was a clear, warm, moonlit night, heavenly fragrant and still. It was almost as if Travis ordered just such a night. After the last few days she had no idea what she'd been expecting from him, but what she saw when he halted the buggy was not it.

A quilt of patches of velvet tied with gold threads was spread on the grass beside the stream, and set on it were many cushions of midnight blue and gold. Crystal glassware, porcelain, and delicious-smelling food were laid out, all of it surrounded by candles whose sharp glare was shrouded by globes of pink frosted glass. It was a heavenly, unreal scene.

"Travis," she began as he lifted her from the wagon. "It's lovely."

He led her to the cushions and helped her into a comfortable reclining position before he opened a cold bottle of champagne. When she held a glass, he gingerly lowered himself to cushions opposite her.

"Travis, are you hurt?" she asked.

"Every damn bone in my body is hurt," he said with half a groan. "I've never worked so hard in my life as I have in the last few days. I hope you don't need any more courting."

She gasped as she started to speak but instead filled her mouth with champagne, working at not choking. "No, I think I've been courted enough," she said in all seriousness. "In fact, no one in town may ever need any more courting," she added.

"Don't press the issue," he said in warning, easing his back to a better position, grimacing at the ache. "Fix me something to eat, would you?"

Orders, Regan thought, but smiled as she heaped a plate full of hot chicken, cold roast beef, chutney, and a mixture of rice and carrots. "Was it difficult to learn to walk that rope?"

"In three days it was. Another couple of days, and I could have done it without the pole."

"You could have taken another day," she said sweetly.

"And give you time with that snob of an Englishman, Batsford? What's he been doing lately, anyway?"

"I'm afraid I've been a little too busy to notice, actually."

At that Travis smiled smugly and leaned back against the cushions, giving his attention to his food. "I'll be glad when you get home with me and I can get regular meals. Lately I've been eating with one hand, writing with the other."

"Writing? Oh yes, I wondered if the notes had been written by you. Personally, I mean."

"Who the hell else would ask you to marry him? Oh well," he smiled at her look. "I didn't mean that, and you know it. You think Jennifer liked the circus?"

"She adored it. Between the pony and the roses, I think you made her the happiest little girl alive."

The look on Travis's face was angelic. "I wasn't sure I was going to be able to get that damn elephant here on time or not. That's some animal! I'll wager it left enough manure behind for six acres of corn. I was thinking about taking a wagonload home with me to see how good it is. Chicken manure is, of course, the best, but you can't get much of that. Maybe this elephant—."

He stopped because of an explosion of laughter from Regan. Narrowing his eyes at her once, he looked away, ignoring her totally.

"Oh Travis, has there ever been anyone else like you on earth?"

With a wink, he grinned at her. "I did do well on that little rope, didn't I? Now give me some of that pie. You think Brandy'd like to come back and cook for us?"

Regan paused for a moment as she cut the pie. He'd asked her to marry him a few thousand times in the last few days, but never once face to face, and he'd never bothered to wait for an answer. And never had he said he loved her.

Handing him the pie, she spoke. "I think Brandy has other things she wants to do, but I am sure I can find a better cook than your Malvina."

Chuckling, Travis took a bite of the pie. "She gave you a hard time, didn't she? Our old family cook died six years ago, and Margo found Malvina for us. She never gave me any trouble, but she and Wes have had a few spats. You could have gotten rid of her, you know."

"I shall," she said, eyes glittering. "I look forward to doing it."

Travis was so quiet for so long that she glanced at him. In the moonlight, surely it was a trick, but his soft eyes looked almost wet. It couldn't be, because in essence she'd just said she was returning with him, could it?

"I am glad to hear that," he said quietly, then smiled to himself and returned to his pie. "Wes can help you with whatever you need while I'm in the fields."

"I think I'll be able to manage. What's Wes like? Does he spend most of his time in the house?"

"He's a good sort, sometimes a little headstrong, and I have to take him down a peg or two, but in general he helps me."

Regan tried not to smile. "You mean he voices his opinion and dares to differ with you, and you . . . do you come to fisticuffs?"

"See that?" Travis said defensively, pointing to a tiny scar on his chin. "My little brother gave me that, so there's no need for you to act like he's the injured party."

"And will you raise your fist to me when I dare to disagree with you?" she taunted.

"You've disagreed with me on every word I've ever said, and I've not hit you yet. You keep giving me children like Jennifer, and you'll always please me. Now let's go back. I need some sleep."

"Are you only interested in the children I give you?" she asked seriously.

Travis's groan, from her question or his sore muscles, was his only answer. "Leave it," he said as she started to clear away the food. "Someone will come later and pack it all." He propelled her toward the buggy.

"How many people have you hired in the last few days? And how did you get into my safe?"

Unceremoniously, he lifted and dropped her onto the buggy seat. "A man should always have some secrets. I'll tell you on our fiftieth wedding anniversary. We'll gather all twelve of our children and tell them the story of the world's most enterprising, creative, most romantic courtship ever."

Shall we mention the elephant manure? she thought, but didn't say anything as they drove back to town.

Chapter 20

AT HER DOOR, TRAVIS GAVE A BONE-POPPING YAWN, KISSED her hand as though it were an afterthought, walked through her bedroom and out the door leading into the interior of the inn, and started up the back stairs to, she assumed, his own room. Stunned, surprised, bewildered, Regan stood by her bed and stared at the closed door.

After all he'd put her through, after all the proposals of marriage, he takes her out to a moonlight picnic, never once mentions marriage but instead talks mostly about elephant manure, and afterward leaves her in her bedroom without so much as a goodnight kiss. All evening he hadn't touched her, hadn't even seemed to be aware that she was near him and so very hungry for him. Of course, she'd concealed her feelings quite well, she knew that, but surely he must have been feeling some passion or at least a longing himself. Maybe making love once in four years was enough for him.

After all, Travis was getting on in years; he was about thirty-eight years old now. Perhaps at that age a man. . . .

Her thoughts trailed off as she began to undress. When she'd put the dress on she'd unconsciously imagined Travis taking it off her. Maybe he didn't want a wanton for a wife, she thought. Yes! That must be it. He'd always thought they were married, and now that they weren't. . . . No, they weren't married all that time they were on board ship.

Sitting down on the bed, she pulled off her slippers and stockings. It could just be that Travis was tired, just as he'd said, and didn't have the energy for rolling around with her tonight.

She slipped into a plain white cotton nightgown, checked on her sleeping daughter, and climbed into her big, cold, empty bed. An hour later she was still wide awake and knew she'd never sleep tonight, not as long as she was in one bed and Travis in another.

"Damn his tiredness!" she said aloud, throwing back the light cover.

In her wardrobe was something she'd never worn, a gift from Brandy. It was a white silk negligee, soft, almost transparent, and so low-cut it left little to the imagination. There were only inches of bodice above a white satin ribbon, and those two inches were very tight, pushing Regan's breasts high above the fabric.

"He may be tired, but I doubt if he's dead," she smiled as she looked into a mirror. Flinging a cloak about herself, she went up the stairs toward Travis's room.

Travis was standing in the center of his room, smiling to himself, a glass of port in his hand, when Margo slammed into his room. His smile vanished immediately. "Get out," he said flatly. "I'm expecting Regan any minute."

"That trollop!" Margo hissed. "Travis, you make me sick! Do you know how you've looked the last few days? Everyone, this entire town, is laughing at you. They've never seen any man make such a complete ass of himself."

"You've had your say. Now get out," he said coldly.

"I haven't said half of what should be said. I've been asking a lot of questions in the last few days, and from what I gather you don't even know who this woman is. Why should she marry you, a big, dumb, crude American? You're so proud of that plantation of yours, but did you know your little Regan could buy it and not even miss the money?" She waited, watching to see how Travis was taking this news. He didn't pause or blink an eye, just looked at her with faint distaste.

"She's worth millions," Margo breathed. "And next week it comes to her. She can have any man she wants, so why would she want an American farmer?"

Still Travis didn't speak.

"Maybe you did know," Margo said. "Maybe you've known all along and that's why you're willing to make such a complete fool of yourself to get her. A man'll do a lot to possess that kind of money."

She didn't say another word as Travis's hand grabbed her hair, pulling her head backward. "Get out," he said, his voice low. "And may you hope I never see you again." With that he gave her a push that sent her slamming against the door.

She recovered almost instantly. "Travis," she said, throwing herself at him, her arms around his chest. "Don't you know how much I love you? I have always loved you, ever since we were children. You've always been mine. Every day I've died a little more since you brought her home and said she was your wife, and now this—all this idiocy over her, and I don't understand why. She's never loved you. She left you, but I've always been near, always close when you need me. I can't compete with her money, but I can give you love if you'll just let me. Open your eyes, Travis, and look at me. See how much I love you."

Peeling her arms away from him, Travis held her at arm's length. "You have never loved me. All you ever wanted was my plantation. I've known for years that you're in debt. I helped you often, but I'll not help you to the extent of marrying you." His voice was quiet, even gentle, and it was obvious he didn't like seeing her disintegrate like this.

When Regan quietly opened Travis's door, expecting him to be asleep and to slip into bed with him, she saw him holding Margo, his eyes looking down at her with gentleness, tenderness. Regan pivoted on one heel and began to run.

Travis discarded Margo onto the floor and took off after Regan.

Regan, knowing she'd never outdistance Travis to her own room, tried the door three down from Travis's, Farrell's room. Travis grabbed her cape just as she disappeared into the room, leaving him holding it as he heard the lock click in the door.

"Regan?" Farrell said, his eyes wide as he lit a candle, quickly pulled on his pants, and left the bed all in one motion. "You look terrified."

Eyes wide, Regan leaned against the door, her breasts heaving above the low gown. "Margo and Travis," she choked.

The next moment she sprang away from the door as something heavy hit it. At the next blow Travis's booted foot came through the wood, followed by his hand as he unlocked the door. Flinging it wide, he crossed the room in two long strides and grabbed Regan's arm.

"I've had enough games," he said. "This time you're going to obey me whether you want to or not."

"Now see here!" Farrell said, reaching for Travis's arm.

Travis looked him up and down, dismissed him, and turned to Regan. "You have twenty-four hours to pack, and then we're leaving. We'll be remarried at my house."

With a quick twist, Regan moved away from him. "And will Margo be at our wedding, or maybe you'd rather she spent our wedding night with you?"

"You can have all the jealous fits you want when we get home, but right now I am sick of walking ropes and trying to find all those goddamn roses you seem to need, and I am not going to put up with this anymore. If I have to I'll chain you to my bed, but you might as well know that you and my daughter are going to live with me."

He softened a bit. "Regan, I've done everything I know to prove to you that you love me. Haven't you realized it yet?"

"Me?" she gasped. "That I love you? I've never had any doubts. You're the one who's been unsure of himself. You've never loved me. You had to marry me the first time. You had to—." She stopped as she looked at Travis in amazement.

He staggered backward, his hands falling to his sides limply. Blindly, his face drained of color, he began to grope for some support. He seemed to age ten years in a few seconds as he fell heavily into a chair.

"Had to marry you?" he choked, his voice weak, hoarse. "Unsure of myself? Never loved you?"

For a moment he dropped his head in his hands, and when he looked back at her his eyes were red. "I've loved you since I first met you," he said quietly. "Why else would I have cared what happened to you? You were so young and frightened, and I was so scared of losing you."

His voice grew stronger. "Why the hell else would I have risked my life on board ship to save that puppy Wainwright you liked so much? Do you know how much I wanted to throw him overboard? But I didn't because you wanted him. And you say I never loved you."

He stood, his voice beginning to get angry. "And I'll have you know you aren't the first to have my baby. I did not *have* to marry you."

"But you said you always marry the mother of your children. I thought—," she said tearfully.

He tossed his hands in the air. "You were scared and angry, didn't even know you were going to have a baby. What was I supposed to say, that I have an illegitimate child at home, that his mother tried to sue me because I wouldn't marry her?"

"You . . . you could have said you loved me."

He quietened. "I swore before witnesses to love you for the rest of my life. What more could I have done?"

She looked down at her hands. "You've never asked me to marry you, not personally."

"Never asked you to marry me?" Travis bellowed. "Goddamn you, Regan, what more do you want from me? I've made a fool of myself in front of an entire state, and you say—."

He broke off as he fell to his knees before her, his hands

clasped. "Regan, will you marry me? Please. I love you more than I love my own life. Please marry me."

She put her hand on his shoulder, their faces level. "What about Margo?" she whispered.

Travis gritted his teeth, but answered, "I could have married her years ago but never wanted to."

"Why didn't you tell me that?"

"Why didn't you know without having to be told?" he shot back. "I love you," he whispered. "Marry me?"

"Yes!" she cried, and threw her arms around his neck. "I'll marry you forever."

Neither of them was aware of anyone or anything else on the earth, and they were shocked when the applause started.

Regan buried her face in Travis's neck. "Are there a lot of people out there?" she asked fearfully.

" 'Fraid so," he said. "I guess they heard the noise when you locked the door against me."

She didn't even bother to correct him, that the noise came from his foot smashing the door and not from her locking of it. "Will you take me away from here?" she whispered. "I don't think I can face them."

Triumphantly, Travis stood with Regan in his arms and started for the door. The townspeople and even the guests at the inn, several of whom had prolonged their stay from the first rose Travis sent, felt involved in this courtship and came running at the first sound of splintering wood.

The women, in heavy robes, curling rags in their hair, sighed heavily as Travis carried Regan away. "I knew it'd end happily," one woman said. "How could she have turned him down?"

"My wife's never gonna believe this story," a man said. "Maybe she'll forgive me for coming back three days late."

"You're a fool if you tell your wife this," snorted another man. "We ought to make a pact to keep it secret, or every woman in the country will expect the same kind of courting, and I for one am not walking any tightrope for any damn woman in the world. I'm telling my wife I spent these three days with another woman; it'll cause me less grief." With that he turned toward the male dormitory.

Eventually the people decided to go back to bed, jumping once as Farrell slammed what was left of his door in their faces.

For several minutes Farrell's cursing of America, Americans, and women in general did not stop. The two of them had ignored him, giving each other lovesick lies as if he weren't even in the same room. As he began to think of all the money he'd spent searching for Regan, courting her, he grew more and more amgry. Yet she fell for an animal that kicked down doors, a bumbling idiot who was considered a fool by everyone who met him. The woman was insane!

And she belonged to him, to Farrell Batsford. He'd been through hell to get her money, and he wasn't going to give it up now.

Quickly, he tossed a dressing gown on and went to find Margo. He knew she wasn't a woman to take this public humiliation easily; perhaps they could work out something.

"Mmm, Travis," Regan murmured, running her leg up Travis's. The early-morning sun made her skin golden.

"Don't start on me again," he said. "You nearly wore me out last night."

"You certainly don't feel as if *all* of you is exhausted," she laughed, kissing his neck, wiggling against him.

"Unless you want to put on a show for your daughter,

you'd better behave. Good morning, sweetheart," he called.

Regan turned away just in time to see her daughter, who took a flying leap at them and landed on Travis's stomach.

"You're home, Daddy!" she yelled. "Can I ride my pony today? Can we go to the circus again? Will you teach me to walk on a rope?"

"Instead of a circus, how about going home with me? I don't own an elephant, but I have lots of other animals and a little brother."

"Does Wesley know you talk about him like this?" Regan asked, but Travis ignored her.

"When can we go?" Jennifer asked her mother.

"Two days?" she asked, looking at Travis. "I have a lot to do before then."

"Now, sweet," Travis said. "Go to the kitchen and get some breakfast. We'll be along in a while. I want to talk to your mother."

"Talk?" Regan said when they were alone, rubbing against him. "I certainly like our 'conversations.' "

He held her at arm's length, and his eyes were serious. "I meant it when I said I wanted to talk. I want to know who you are and what you were doing in your nightgown on that Liverpool dock the night I found you."

"I'd really rather go into it some other time," she said, as lightly as she could manage. "I have an awful lot of work to do."

He pulled her close to him. "Listen to me. I know that what you've been through is painful. I've not pressed you since we left England, but I'm here now, and you're safe. I won't let anything harm you, and I want to know everything about you."

It was some minutes before she could speak. Against her will, she began to remember that night when she'd met Travis and her life before that. For years she'd been free, had come to know other people, to see how they lived, and she could see how much of a prison her childhood had been.

"I grew up totally without freedom," she began, at first without emotion, but as she thought of the way she'd been treated in her early life, she began to grow angry.

Travis never rushed her, only held her close to him, his arms and body keeping her safe, as she poured out her whole story. It was a long time before she got to that night when she'd overheard Farrell and her uncle conspiring together. He never said a word, but his arms tightened.

She continued her story, telling Travis how she felt about him, how he frightened her, but how she clung to him, wavering between her need to prove her own worth and wanting to hide behind his strength. She poured out all the terror she'd felt at his plantation, laughing somewhat at that scared little girl, afraid to give orders to her own servants.

She finished with the story of her leaving him, of the trail she'd left behind, of her tears when he didn't come after her.

"I could have helped you at home," he said when she'd stopped talking. "But I knew you would have resented me. The day Margo came, the day you burned your hand, I could have killed Malvina."

Twisting around, she looked at him. "I had no idea you knew about that."

"I know most of what happens on my own plantation,"

he said. "I just honestly didn't know how to help you. I knew you had to learn how to help yourself."

"Are you always right, my dear lovely husband?" she asked, caressing his face.

"Always. And I hope you remember it and obey me in all things from now on."

She gave him her sweetest smile. "I plan to fight you every inch of the way. Every time you give me an order I'll—."

She broke off when he kissed her soundly, just before he pushed her from the bed.

"Get up, get dressed, and go see that Brandy has enough food for my breakfast." A pillow landed on his face.

"Here I tell you I am massively wealthy and you don't even comment. Some men would like to get their hands on my money."

Eyeing her naked form, he smiled slowly. "I'm looking at what I like my hands on. As for your money, you can pay for that circus you wanted, and what's left you can give to our children."

"The circus *I* wanted," she sputtered. "All that was your idea."

"You wanted the courting."

"Courting! That was the most heavy-handed, awkward, gaudy, inept courting I've ever seen! Any Englishman could do better."

Lazily, Travis leaned back on a pillow. "I'm the one who had you coming to his room wearing a bit of transparent nothing, just begging me to make love to you, so maybe my courting wasn't so bad after all."

Regan sputtered for a few more minutes before beginning to laugh as she dressed. "You are insufferable. Shall I serve your breakfast in bed, or would you prefer a private dining room?''

''Now there's a good wench. Try and keep that attitude. I think I'll eat in the kitchen; just be sure there's lots of it.''

Regan left, still laughing, and Travis wondered how he was going to have to pay for his last remarks. But whatever she did, life with her was going to be a joy. She was certainly worth all the pain he'd been through in the last few years.

Slowly, contentedly, he began to dress.

Most of the townspeople stopped by that day to congratulate Regan on her forthcoming marriage and to say goodbye to her, as they knew she'd be leaving very soon. Contrary to what Margo seemed to think, no one thought Travis was a fool. The women thought he was wonderfully romantic, and the men liked the way he went after what he wanted.

At midmorning, Regan was up to her ears in work. A maid was complaining about some odd-colored ink on a set of sheets, and everyone else seemed to be complaining also. Or maybe it was Regan's imagination caused by her sadness at leaving the big inn she and Brandy had built.

''You're sad, aren't you?'' Travis asked, coming up behind her.

She still wasn't used to the keen perception of this man. She'd had no idea he was so aware of her needs and problems when she'd known him before, and now his sensitivity was startling.

''You'll feel better once you're at my house. What you need is a new challenge.''

"And what happens when I learn all there is to know about running a plantation?" she asked, turning toward him.

"Couldn't happen, because I come with the plantation and you'll never learn enough about me. Now, where's my daughter?"

"She's usually with Brandy at this time of day. I didn't check because I thought you were with her." After a moment's thought, she smiled. "Where is the pony you bought her? Wherever it is, that's where she is."

"I looked in the carriage house, but she isn't there, and Brandy hasn't seen her all morning."

"Not even for breakfast?" she asked, frowning. "Travis!" she said in alarm.

"Wait a minute," he soothed. "Don't get upset. She could have gone to a friend's house."

"But she always tells me where she's going—always! It's the only way I can keep up with her while I'm working."

"All right," Travis said quietly. "You look through the inn, and I'll walk around town. We'll find her in minutes. Now go!" he said laughingly.

Regan's immediate thought was that perhaps Jennifer had a stomachache from yesterday's excitement and she had gone back to her bed, forgetting to tell anyone where she was going. Quietly, Regan walked through her bedroom and slowly opened her daughter's door. Expecting to see her daughter asleep in her bed, she did not at first understand the turmoil of the room. Clothes were strewn everywhere, drawers open, the bedclothes half on and half off, shoes scattered on the bed and floor.

"She's been packing!" Regan said aloud, relieved at the sight.

It was as she knelt to pick up a shoe that she saw the note on the pillow. Jennifer would not be returned unless the sum of fifty thousand dollars was placed at the foot of the old well south of town two days from now.

Regan's scream of anguish could be heard throughout the inn.

Brandy, her hands and apron covered with flour, was the first to reach Jennifer's room. With an arm around Regan's heaving shoulders, she led her to sit on the bed, taking the note from her.

Brandy looked up at the people standing in the doorway. "Someone find Travis," she commanded. "And tell him to get here immediately."

As Regan stood, Brandy caught her arm. "Where are you going?"

"I have to see how much money I have in the safe," she said, dazed. "I know it's not enough. Do you think I can sell something in two days?"

"Regan, sit down and wait for Travis. He'll know how to get the money. Maybe he even has some with him."

Regan didn't seem to be aware of what she was doing as she sat back down, clutching the ransom note and one of Jennifer's shoes.

Travis burst into the room moments later, and at the sight of him she jumped up and ran to him.

"Someone has taken my daughter!" she cried. "Do you have some money? Can you get fifty thousand dollars? Surely you can get that much."

"Here, let me see the note," he said, one arm firmly

around her. He read it and reread it several times before looking up at the room.

"Travis," Regan said. "What do we have to do to get the money?"

"I don't like this," he said under his breath and turned to Brandy. "Have you been in the kitchen all morning?"

Brandy nodded.

"And you heard nothing? Did you see any strangers in the hall?" he asked, nodding toward the corridor that led to the kitchen and Regan's office.

"No one. Nothing unusual."

"Go find everyone on the staff and bring them here instantly," he commanded Brandy.

"Travis, please, we need to start getting the money."

Travis sat down on the bed and drew Regan between his knees. "Listen to me. There's something wrong here. There are only two ways to enter your apartment, past Brandy in the kitchen or through the back door. Brandy and her cooks are always in that hall going from the kitchen to the pantry, and no one could have walked out with Jennifer without being seen. So that leaves the back door, which I know you always keep locked. It hasn't been broken, so Jennifer must have opened it from the inside."

"But she wouldn't! She knows not to do that."

"That's my point. She'd only open it to someone she knew and trusted, someone she knew was a friend. And now my second point, who knows you can get fifty thousand dollars? No one in town knows me, and until yesterday I didn't know you had any money. Fifty thousand means someone knows a great deal more than the average Scarlet Springs resident."

"Farrell!" Regan gasped. "He knows better than I do how much money I have."

At that moment Brandy returned with the staff members, all of them quiet, wide-eyed—and behind them was Farrell Batsford.

"Regan," he said. "I just heard the awful news. Is there anything I can do?"

Travis brushed past him as he began to question the staff, asking if they'd seen anything at all unusual this morning, if they had seen Jennifer with anyone.

While they were thinking, remembering nothing, Travis grabbed a maid's hand.

"What is this on your fingers? Where did it come from?"

Stepping back, the girl looked frightened. "It's ink. It came off the sheets in number twelve."

Expectantly, he turned to Regan.

"Margo's room," she said heavily.

Without another word, he left the apartment through the back door and headed for the stables, Regan running after him. He was tossing a saddle onto a horse when she caught him.

"Where are you going?" she demanded. "Travis! We have to get the money!"

He paused long enough to touch her cheek. "Margo has Jennifer," he said as he continued saddling the horse. "She knew we'd find the ink, and she knows I'll come after her. That's what she really wants. I don't believe she'll harm Jennifer."

"Don't believe! Your whore has taken my daughter and—."

He put his finger to her lips. "She is my daughter too, and

if I have to give every acre I own to Margo, I'll get Jennifer back safely. Now I want you to stay here because I can handle this better alone.'' He swung onto the horse.

"I'm just supposed to stay here and wait? And how do you know for sure where Margo is?"

"She always goes home," he said grimly. "She always goes to where she can be near the memory of that damned father of hers.''

With that he reined away, applied a kick to the horse's side, and disappeared in a cloud of dust.

Chapter 21

IT WAS NIGHT, ALMOST DAWN THREE DAYS LATER, WHEN Travis jerked his horse to a halt before Margo's door. It had taken several horses to carry him all the way at the pace he'd demanded of them.

Jumping down, he slammed into her house, knowing exactly where she'd be—in the library, sitting under the portrait of her father.

"It took you a little longer than I expected," she said cheerfully as she greeted Travis. Her red hair was a mass of tangles about her shoulders, and there was a dark stain on her dressing gown.

"Where is she?"

"Oh, she's safe," Margo laughed, holding up an empty whiskey glass. "Go and see for yourself. I rarely harm children. Then come back and join me for a drink."

Travis took the stairs two at a time. At one point in his life he'd been a frequent visitor to the Jenkins house, and he knew his way around well. Now, searching for his daughter, he took no notice of the bare places on the walls where once a portrait had hung or an empty table where an ornament no longer stood.

He found Jennifer asleep in the bed he'd used when he was a boy. When he picked her up she opened her eyes, smiled, said "Daddy," and went back to sleep. She and Margo must have traveled all night, as the dust on her face and clothes showed.

Carefully, he put her back down in the bed, kissed her, and went downstairs. It was time he and Margo talked.

Margo didn't even look up as he crossed the room and poured himself a glass of port. "Why?" she whispered. "Why didn't you marry me? After all those years we spent together. We rode together, swam naked together, made love. I always thought, and Daddy always thought—."

Travis's explosion cut her off. "That's why!" he shouted. "That goddamned father of yours. There are only two people you ever loved: yourself and Ezra Jenkins."

He paused to raise his glass in salute to the portrait over the fireplace. "You never saw it, but your father was the meanest, cheapest liar ever created. He'd steal pennies from a slave child. I never cared much what he did, but every day I could see you becoming more like him. Remember when you started charging the weavers for their broken shuttles?"

Margo looked up, a desperate expression on her face. "He wasn't like that. He was good and kind. . . ."

Travis's snort stopped her. "He was good to you and no one else."

"And I would have been good to you," Margo said, pleading.

"No!" Travis snapped. "You would have hated me because I didn't cheat and steal from everybody around me. You would have seen that as weakness on my part."

Margo kept her eyes on her drink. "But why her? Why a skinny little, washed-out English gutter rat? She couldn't even make a cup of tea."

"You know she's no gutter rat, not when you demand fifty thousand dollars ransom of her." Travis's eyes began to glaze over as he thought back to that time in England. "You should have seen her when I first saw her—dirty, scared, wearing a torn and ragged nightgown. But talking like the highest-born English lady. Every word, every syllable was so precise. Even crying, she talks like that."

"You married her because of her damned uppity accent?" Margo spat angrily.

Travis smiled in a distant way. "I married her because of the way she looks at me. She makes me feel ten, no, twenty feet tall. I can do anything when she's around. And watching her grow has been a joy. She's changed herself from a frightened little girl into a woman." His smile broadened. "And she's all mine."

Margo's empty glass flew across the room, shattering on the wall behind Travis's head. "Do you think I'm going to sit here and listen to your ravings about another woman?"

Travis's face turned hard. "You don't have to listen to me at all. I'm going upstairs to get my daughter and take her home." At the foot of the stairs he turned back toward her. "I know you well. I know it's because of what your father taught you that you tried this treacherous way of getting what you wanted. Because Jennifer is unharmed, I'm not pressing charges this time. But if you ever again. . . ."

He stopped, his words trailing, and rubbed his eyes. Suddenly he was very sleepy, and as he mounted the stairs he looked like a drunken man.

Shortly after Travis left the inn, a bewildered Regan returned to her apartment. Farrell was waiting for her.

"Regan, please, you've got to tell me what's going on. Has someone harmed your daughter?"

"No," she whispered. "I don't know. I can't tell."

"Sit down," he said, his arm around her, "and tell me everything."

It didn't take but minutes before the story was out.

"And Travis left you here to suffer alone?" Farrell asked in astonishment. "You have no idea what is happening about your own daughter but trust him to get her from his ex-mistress?"

"Yes," she said helplessly. "Travis said—."

"And since when have you ever let another person run your life? Wouldn't you rather be with your daughter than here, knowing nothing?"

"Yes!" she said firmly, rising. "Of course I would."

"Then let's go. We'll leave immediately."

"We?"

"Yes," Farrell said, taking her hand. "We're friends, and friends help each other in time of need."

Only later, as they were in the buggy and headed south toward Travis's plantation, did Regan realize that she'd told no one where she was going. The thought left her quickly as she was too concerned for her daughter's safety.

They traveled for hours, the carriage much too slow for Regan's taste, and once she dozed, her head hitting the side of the buggy. She came awake abruptly when Farrell touched her arm. He was standing on the ground beside her; the carriage had stopped.

"Why are you stopping?" she demanded.

He pulled her from the seat to stand before him. "You need rest, and we need to talk."

"Talk!" she gasped. "We can talk later, and I don't need any rest." She tried to pull away from him, but he held her firmly.

"Regan, do you know how much I love you? Did you know that I was in love with you long ago in England? Your uncle offered me money and I took it, but I would have married you without the incentive of money. You were so sweet and innocent, so very lovely."

In her distress Regan lost sight of the fact that she was alone with this man in a remote piece of woods.

Astonished, she pulled back from him. "Oh, for heaven's sake, Farrell! What have I ever done to make you think I'm stupid? You never loved me, never have, never will. All you want is my money, which you're not going to get, so why don't you be a good sport, go home to your pretty, poor house in England, and leave me alone?"

One minute she was standing, the next she was slammed against the carriage, sliding down, as Farrell's hand knocked her backward.

"How dare you speak to me like that?" he seethed. "My family comes from kings, while yours are mere merchants. That I have to lower myself to marry a woman like you, who knows more of ledgers than laces, is—."

While he was speaking, Regan was regaining her wits. Much more important than her own problems with Farrell was her anxiety about her daughter. Still on her knees from the blow, she charged at him, using her head as a battering ram, and caught him directly between the legs.

Farrell doubled over in pain and gave Regan her chance to escape.

One glance at the buggy showed he'd unhitched the horses enough that it would take a long time to be able to use that means of escape. Pulling up her skirts, she started to run back toward the road, just in time to see a dilapidated old wagon disappearing around a curve. It took all her energy to catch the wagon.

An old man, his face bristled with gray whiskers, sat on the seat.

"There's a man chasing me," she called up, running with the wagon.

"Should he catch you?" the old man said, obviously amused by the situation.

"He's trying to force me to marry him—for my money—but I want to marry an American."

Patriotism won the man over. Without even slowing, he grabbed Regan's arm and hauled her into the wagon as if she weighed nothing. With another swift motion he pushed her to the back and covered her completely with grain sacks.

Seconds later Farrell appeared on horseback, and Regan held her breath as he shouted at the old man. After pretending he was deaf for some minutes, the old man refused to allow Farrell to search his wagon; he pulled a pistol when Farrell kept insisting. At last the old man reluctantly admitted having seen three men riding by, one with a pretty woman in the saddle in front of him. Farrell took off in a flurry of hoofs and dust.

"You can come out now," the old man said, grabbing Regan's arm and pulling her to the seat.

Rubbing her arm, she refrained from asking the man to stop tossing her about like one of his feed sacks. After several ferocious sneezes, she asked if he knew where the Stanford plantation in Virginia was.

"That's a long way. It'll take days."

"Not if we change horses and travel all night. I'll pay for the horses and any other expenses."

He seemed to study her for several minutes. "Maybe we could work something out. I'll get you there in record time if you'll tell me why that Englishman was chasing you and what you want with Travis, or is it Wesley you're after?"

"I'll tell you everything, and Travis is mine."

"Lady, you got your hands full," he said, chuckling as he yelled for the horses to start moving. Within seconds they were tearing down the road, and Regan was holding on with both hands, her teeth jarring together constantly. She couldn't speak or tell any story.

An hour later the man stopped the wagon, got down, and pulled her out after him.

"What are you doing?" she asked.

"We're going by boat," he said. "I'll sail you to Travis's front door." After a mile hike they came to a little cabin and a dock reaching into a narrow stream of water. The man disappeared into the cabin for a moment and soon returned with a canvas bag. "Let's go," he said, shoving her into a boat as worn-out as his wagon had been.

"Now talk," he said once they were under way.

Days later the man dropped Regan off at the dock of Travis's plantation, bidding her goodbye and good luck. It was early morning, and the plantation was silent as she ran all the way from the dock to the house.

The door was open, and as she tore up the stairs she

prayed Travis and Jennifer would be asleep in one of the rooms. She started throwing open door after door, cursing the house for being so large and causing her to take so much time.

She found him, just his hair showing above the sheet, in the fourth bedroom. "Travis!" she cried, flinging herself at him. "Where's Jennifer? Is she all right? How could you have left me not knowing and be here sleeping so calmly?" she asked, giving him a good cuff on the ear.

The man who sat up was not Travis. He was very much like him but a smaller version.

"Now what has my brother done?" he asked wearily, rubbing his ear, but as he looked at her he smiled. "You've got to be Regan. Let me introduce—."

"Where are Travis and my daughter?"

Wesley was instantly alert. "Tell me what's happened."

"Margo Jenkins kidnapped our daughter, and Travis went after her."

Before she could answer, Wes threw back the covers, not caring that he was nude, and began to dress.

"I always told Travis that Margo was no good, but he felt he owed her something so he always indulged her. She thinks she can have anything in the world, that it's hers by right. Come with me," he said, grabbing her hand and pulling her with him.

"You're very much like Travis," she said, gasping at the pain he was causing her wrist and trying to keep up with his long strides.

"There's no time for insults now," he said, leaving her at the library door while he loaded two pistols and stuck them in his belt. "Can you ride? No, Travis said you couldn't.

Come on, you can ride in front of me. The two of us together aren't as heavy as Travis."

If Regan had time or the inclination, she would have been disgusted with Travis's little brother. How could there be two men like Travis? And in another year or two Wes was going to be as large as Travis.

"I'm Wesley," he said as he dropped her into the saddle before mounting behind her.

"Somehow I assumed that," she said before they took off at a breathless gallop.

At the door to Margo's house, Wes let her down. "We'll go in separately. Remember, I'll be close by you."

With that he left her, and Regan walked through the front door. It took only moments to find Margo as she sat in the library.

"Just in time," Margo smiled graciously, but her eyes were red. "You're the third visitor I've had this morning."

"Where's my daughter, and where is Travis?" Regan demanded.

"Dear little rich Jennifer is asleep, and so is her beloved father. Of course, Jennifer will wake; Travis will not."

"What!" Regan yelled. "What have you done to my family?"

"No more than you've done to my life. Travis drank enough opium to kill two men. He's upstairs sleeping until death."

Regan had reached the doorway when a shot from outside made her stop. Paralyzed, she looked down the hall toward the door. Margo rushed past her and jerked the door open, and Farrell entered, half carrying, half dragging Wesley's bleeding body.

"I found him lurking around outside," Farrell said, pushing Wes into a chair, a pistol in his hand.

"What are you doing here?" Regan gasped, going toward Wesley.

"Leave him!" Farrell said, grabbing her shoulder. "Did you think I was going to give up so easily, after all the years I'd been searching for you? No, Margo and I planned all this long ago, while the rest of you were playing with that stupid circus. Wesley here will die of his wounds received in an unfortunate hunting accident. Travis's body will never be found, and his dear little daughter will inherit everything. I will, of course, marry the little heiress's mother, who will be so distraught over her husband's death that she'll commit suicide. I will then return to England, the sole beneficiary of your estate, and Margo will generously agree to be Jennifer's guardian and care for the Stanford plantation until she comes of age—if she lives that long. Now do you see why I'm here?"

"You are both mad," Regan said, backing away from him. "No one will believe so many deaths are accidental." She turned and started for the stairs at the end of the hall, but Farrell caught her.

"You're mine now," he said, advancing toward her, his body stained with Wesley's blood.

Regan's hand went out, and she turned over the candelabra on a low table. Immediately, the curtains over a nearby doorway went up in flames. Margo's scream filled the air as she grabbed a small rug and began beating at the flames.

"Release her," said a voice from the end of the hall.

"Travis!" Regan cried, fighting to free herself from Farrell. Travis looked horrible, as if he'd just been violently ill.

"I thought you put him out of the way," Farrell yelled at Margo as she fought the fire.

"It took me a while to get all the opium out of my system," he said, holding on to the stair banister.

"Stop talking," Margo screamed, "and help me put out the fire. It's spreading!"

Farrell tightened his grip on Regan and put the pistol to her head.

Wesley, nearly forgotten and slumped in a chair behind Farrell, used his draining strength to pull a knife from his boot, and with one lunge he plunged it between Farrell's shoulder blades. The pistol flew upward, fired into the ceiling, and Farrell fell forward.

Regan reacted instantly as she ran toward Travis and the stairs. "Get Wesley," she commanded. "I'll get Jennifer."

Regan found her sleeping daughter quickly, pulled her from the bed, and ran down the stairs in time to meet Travis working hard to get his brother out of the house. Neither man had much strength, and it seemed forever before they were in the fresh, sunlit morning air and out of the smoke-filled house.

Travis gently put Wesley on the grass. "I'll get horses and a wagon," he said.

"Travis!" Regan said, touching his arm, her eyes going to the house. A flame leaped out of the first-floor window. "We can't leave Margo in there to die. She has to come out."

Travis gave her cheek a quick caress and then ran back to the house. Minutes later he came out, Margo thrown over his shoulder as she kicked and clawed, cursing him vilely.

He dumped her on the ground. "That goddamn house

isn't worth anyone's life, not even yours," he said as she glared up at him.

Regan was bent over Wes, binding the gunshot wound in his side.

Travis had barely glanced away from Margo before she leaped up and ran toward the house. "My daddy is in there!" she was screaming.

Travis saw the first flames touch her skirt and knew he could not save her. Quickly, he grabbed his daughter, who was watching everything wide-eyed, and buried her little face in his shoulder.

Within seconds, Margo's whiskey-soaked dress burst into flame, and Regan turned away as Wes's arm went around her, pulling her to sob onto his shoulder.

It was a while before any of them could recover. Travis, touching his brother's forehead in affection, smiled at the man holding his wife. "Take care of my women while I go get a wagon," he said.

By the time he returned, they were surrounded by plantation workers who stood helplessly by as the house burned. It was too far gone to try to save it. Men were getting the horses out of the nearby stables, and two more men helped Travis put Wes in the back of the wagon. Jennifer sat by her uncle, too tired and dazed to speak.

When Travis and Regan were on the seat, he turned to her. "Shall we go home?"

"Home," she whispered. "Home is where you are, Travis, and that's where I want to be."

He kissed her. "I love you," he said, "and—."

"I'm bleeding to death, and you two are courting," Wesley bellowed from the back.

"Courting!" Travis snorted, clicking to the horses.

"Little brother, you don't even know what courting is. As soon as you're up to the excitement, I'm going to tell you about the world's best courtship. Maybe someday you can be half as creative—." He stopped and narrowed his eyes at Regan, who'd started laughing, and his look of injury made her laugh harder.

"I think I'd rather hear Regan's side of any of your stories, Travis," Wesley said, smiling, his eyes closed.

"Home," Regan said, wiping her eyes. "It's going to be very good to get home."

Travis began to smile also as he turned the horses toward the Stanford plantation.

JUDE DEVERAUX
ANSWERS QUESTIONS

I fell in love with every one of the Montgomery men. Will there be more books about them in the future?

When I finished *Velvet Angel*, I hadn't planned to write more books about the Montgomery family, but since then I have received hundreds of letters asking me for more of this family. Several of the letters contained long outlines of plots for stories about Montgomery children, American Montgomerys, outlaw Montgomerys, you name it.

It was a difficult decision (took about ten minutes), but I decided to write four more books dealing with the descendants of my lovely men. They are set in America and cover all four corners of the United States. I have no idea what the titles will be, and if you have any title suggestions, *please* send them to me.

In the back of *Velvet Angel* was a mention of a contemporary romance between the American Montgomerys and the English branch. When will this book be out?

You saw my attempt at contemporary fiction in *Casa Grande*, and you can still ask me for more?!

It seems that when God so kindly gave me the ability to write, He didn't extend it very far. All I want to do is write the very best historical romances that I possibly can—and historicals seem to be all I'm capable of. I don't want to write family sagas or occult books, and I have no intention of again trying to ruin the contemporary market.

In *The Black Lyon* you mentioned Dacre and Angharad, and it seemed to me that this would make a good sequel. Are you planning to write about them?

I had intended to write the story of Dacre and Angharad and had the plot ready. But when I turned in *The Velvet Promise*, which had many references to *The Black Lyon*, Rannulf being a major character in the book, I was told that thirteenth-century books didn't sell and that I had to change the book to the sixteenth century, which *did* sell, or my book would not be published. I spent a month changing the description and background and removing the Warbrooke family. The plot for Dacre and Angharad became *Highland Velvet*, changing Wales to Scotland.

In *Velvet Song* you mentioned the lion belt. When are you going to write about how the belt went from Lyonene to Alyx?

Every one of my medieval heroes and heroines has come from upperclass families, and I felt so much sympathy for Alyx because she was intimidated by her rich in-laws, that I let the reader know that she was actually upperclass too.

It was intended as a throwaway scene, and I wasn't sure my readers would even notice it, but I have received stacks of letters asking about the belt. Maybe someday I'll do more medievals, but for now I'd like to stay in America.

Are you a man or a woman?

I'm a woman. And my name is pronounced as in Saint Jude—the saint of hopeless causes.

Why are the Montgomery books all titled with *velvet*? What significance does the word have?

Velvet has no relation to anything. I can never come up with titles for my books, so I think I got the next one on the publisher's list. When I moved to Pocket Books, they had the task of coordinating the other three titles in the series with *The Velvet Promise*.